MY KIND OF
FOREVER

MY KIND OF FOREVER
THE BEAUMONT SERIES #5
© 2015 HEIDI MCLAUGHLIN

COVER DESIGN: Sarah Hansen at Okay Creations
EDITING: Traci Blackwood
EDITING: There For You

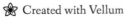 Created with Vellum

*To all the fans who have stuck with
Liam & Josie, Harrison & Katelyn and Jimmy & Jenna,
I thank you!*

# 1

## JOSIE

Liam's eyes go wide when the whoosh of the baby's heartbeat echoes throughout the room. He stares from the screen to me and back at the screen again. He missed this with Noah so it was important for him to be here when we found out the sex of the baby.

"That has got to be the coolest sound ever. No wonder JD listens to it all the time. I should record it, too."

He takes out his cell phone and holds it right next to the speaker on the monitor. Watching him take all of this in without reservation is such a relief. It's one thing to become an "insta-dad" to a then ten year old, but it's entirely different when you're part of the entire process from the beginning. Liam missed everything with Noah but hasn't missed a single step this time.

"Mr. and Mrs. Westbury, would you like to know the sex of the baby?"

I look at Liam who smiles so brightly it makes me love him even more. We need this—not because we're struggling, but because I know he feels incomplete when it comes to being a dad. When Eden is with us, he's the doting uncle that does everything for her, even rushing to change her diaper. She has Liam wrapped around her little finger and I don't think he'd want for it to be any different. Liam wants to experience the midnight and two a.m. feedings, the walks in the park, and the first babbling words. I want that for him as well.

Noah, on the other hand, doesn't want a sibling.

"Do you want to know, Jojo?"

There they are, the words I've been waiting for ... he wants to know but is leaving the decision up to me.

"Yes, I want to know."

"Perfect," the sonographer says. "If you look right here, you'll see his penis."

"It's a boy!"

"He has a penis!" Liam shouts, silencing the room.

We look at him and burst out laughing. Liam blushes when he realizes his outburst and turns his attention back to the sonogram on the monitor. He studies it as if there's a test at the end of the visit and I silently wish I had my camera or phone with me so I could take his picture. I want to believe this is how he would have been when I was pregnant with Noah, but my heart tells me otherwise.

It's hard to understand why he left, especially the way he did, but I accept it. We were young and naïve about what the future held for either of us. Life is rainbows and roses when you're eighteen and blinded by your first love. My life was planned around Liam's. I was going to be his wife, be his constant cheerleader as he played in the NFL. I was going to be the doting mother of two children in our big fancy house inside a gated community. I was going to be the wife who was in love with her husband no matter what.

Instead, I ended up being pregnant and alone. I ended up being a distant memory, an annoying mess of the person he once loved at the other end of a voice message, screaming how much I hated him but never blurting out the words that could've changed everything.

I often think back to those bleak days of being force-fed by Mason and Katelyn. Sleeping between my two best friends because they feared I would do something stupid. The only stupid thing I wanted to do was find Liam and tell him face-to-face that we were having a child.

When I went to his parents, desperate and scared, I knew it was a long shot. I knew if I could just talk to Bianca, she would reach out to Liam and tell him to call me. She'd tell him to come home, but it wasn't meant to be. Sterling refused to acknowledge that I was carrying his grandchild. To them, I was nothing but trash hell-bent on trapping their son. To them, Liam leaving me was the best thing he could've ever done.

They were right because had I told him, he would've come home and we would've gotten married. That much I'm sure about. Liam's a good man and he would've done the right thing. But I don't believe I'd still be with him today. Liam was right when he said we'd be divorced. I can see it play out in my mind. With a child and no college education, he'd be stuck in a dead end job. He'd sulk, sitting in front of the television drinking beer each night. His friends would have all achieved what they set out to do, leaving him behind. He was right to leave and follow his dreams. Even though it killed me to not have him by my side when Noah was born, I have him now.

The sonographer prints off a few pictures and hands them to Liam. He's mesmerized by them, staring at each one. Honestly, unless things are pointed out to me I don't know what I'm looking at. The first time I saw Noah, I cried. Not because I was overjoyed or scared out of my mind, but because I thought I was having a bean and that something was seriously wrong with me.

When Liam looks at me, he's beaming. The excitement in his eyes shows me that he wants this just as much as I do. Bringing another child into the world, into our lives, is the best thing that could've happened to us right now.

Outside of the doctor's office, Liam holds me in his arms. I can feel his heart pounding against my chest. He's excited, ready to burst.

"I'm going to stop by the nursery before I head home," I tell him.

Liam pulls back, keeping his hands clasped behind by back. "I want to celebrate tonight, have everyone over and share the news."

I run my fingers over his stubble. It's constant and I love it. He tried to go full-on beard with me, but I didn't like it. He looked like a chipmunk hoarding nuts in his cheeks. Since I complained, he's kept it trimmed and perfect.

Sometimes, when I look into his eyes, I see the same eighteen year old that I fell in love with. Even with our years apart, my love for him hasn't subsided. It will always be there because we share a son. It's there because he's my soul mate. Whether we're together or not, I'll always love him.

"Dinner sounds perfect. I'll stop by the store on the way home."

He kisses the tip of my nose before kissing my lips. I melt into him, not caring about the people around us. I'm happy and in love with this man and we're about to have a baby, another son. I want everyone to share in our joy.

"I love you, Jojo," he says with a wink as he walks away. My eyes fall to his backside as I watch the swagger in his hips. No wonder he's so good at his job—just staring at his ass makes me turn to goo.

"You're one lucky lady." I turn and smile at the white-haired older lady sitting near me. "I had that once in my life, but he's been gone for some time. Do you suppose you find that kind of love again?"

My eyes go from her to the door and back again. "Yes," I say truthfully. "I lost him once, a long time ago." Those are my parting words as I walk out of the doctor's office and head to the nursery.

My doctor's office is in a wing off of the hospital. It's super convenient when you're convinced that you're having Braxton Hicks contractions but are really in labor and your doctor needs to send you to Labor & Delivery. That was me with Noah. I didn't want to believe that the time had come, or that Liam wasn't going to be there. I thought for sure he'd call once I left him a message with his agent's office. I was wrong, but still held out hope.

The halls are busy as people come and go from different departments. I know a few of the nurses and we say hello as we pass each other. When I arrive at the nursery window, I'm elated to see the babies in their hospital bassinets. The mix of blue and pink reminds me of the last time I was here when Eden was born.

When I was with Nick, I never thought about having another child. Somewhere deep in my mind I felt it'd be wrong and that I'd be moving on. I was never fair to Nick and our relationship. He was easy and convenient. He gave me so many missing pieces from my life and would've completed me if I had allowed him to. As I look back at that time in my life, I realize how selfish I was by stringing him along. I wouldn't change the way he is with Noah, though, because Noah needed Nick more than I did.

I wave at Diane, the Labor & Delivery nurse working in the nursery room. She smiles and leaves the room, meeting me by the window.

"No flower deliveries today?" Diane was my nurse when I had Noah and we've maintained a friendship ever since. I give her a quick hug and turn back to the babies.

"I took the day off. Liam and I had the sonogram today." I beam, recalling his expression when he found out we're having a son.

"Is Liam excited?"

"He is. I know he hates himself for missing all of this with Noah. He's trying to make up for everything even though it wasn't his fault."

A baby starts to cry, and that's Diane's cue to go back to work. "Let's get coffee soon," she says as she walks away. Once she's back behind the glass, she picks up a little girl and holds her to her chest. I had hoped that this time around we'd have a girl, but a boy makes the numbers even. Peyton, Elle, and Eden will dote on him, likely putting ribbons in his hair which is something I can't wait to see.

"Baby stalking?"

I jump at the sound of Nick's voice, but am happy to see him. "What are you doing here?" I ask, even though I know he's working.

"Just checking on my littlest patients. You?"

"Sonogram day," I say excitedly.

"And?" His eyes are bright, awaiting my answer. I look around and see a few of the other nurses watching me. I didn't tell Diane what we're having, but I'll tell Nick. Just not here, not with how fast they'll put our news on social media.

"Do you have time for lunch?"

"I do. Shall we enjoy the fine dining of the hospital cafeteria?" Nick asks as he holds his arm out for me.

"We shall," I reply, taking his arm.

To people on the outside Nick and I shouldn't be talking, let alone touching. They'll gossip and start stupid rumors that Liam and I will ignore. For one, Nick is happily married to Aubrey whom I consider one of my best friends, and two, Liam and Nick are friends ... well, sort of. Best friends they'll never be, but Liam knows he owes Nick for the years he raised Noah. Nick and Aubrey are a part of our family.

The cafeteria is almost empty since we just missed the lunchtime rush. Nick hands me a tray and we go through the line. I'm not a fan of the food, but I am fan of their desserts. I grab a piece of pie and head to the ice cream machine, adding some vanilla ice cream to the top.

"I said lunch," Nick says as we meet at the register.

"I know, but I couldn't pass up the apple pie and ice cream."

Nick shakes his head as he pays for our lunches, greeting a few colleagues as we walk toward the window.

"So, how was your appointment?"

"It was amazing, and Liam was ... I don't know, Nick, I can't explain it. Like a kid in a candy store. His eyes were so expressive."

"That's great, Josie. Did you find out what you're having?"

"Yes!" I squeal. "A boy," I say low enough for only him to hear.

"Another football player?"

I shrug. "I don't know. Will you still be coaching in another six years or so?" We both laugh.

"I could be." He winks, and it takes a minute before I catch on.

"No way! Is Aubrey ..." Nick is nodding before I can finish my question. I stand and reach over the table, giving him a hug. "Oh, Nick, I'm so happy for you."

"Thank you. We're happy, too."

"This is such an amazing day, and I have Aubrey to thank for it. If she hadn't met Meredith, Liam and I wouldn't be adopting her little boy," I pause and think back to our appointment today. "She's so disinterested in everything. She wore headphones and played on her phone during the sonogram. You know I understand why she did that, but she won't even let me buy her clothes or anything."

Nick reaches across the table and holds my hand. "Meredith is lucky to have you and Liam."

I smile. "I don't have much time to get everything ready though. She's due in a couple of weeks."

Nick laughs and puts his napkin on the table, having finished his sandwich. I look down at my pie, which is now swimming in ice cream soup. "Sounds like the ladies will be shopping soon and the guys will be painting a nursery."

Beaming, I clap my hands. "I'll make sure Liam knows you'll help!"

"**H**ello?" I call out, *dropping my keys on the table by the door. Josie hates that I leave my keys here, but I can't seem to get it through my head that I need to walk down the hall and hang them on the board. I call out again, but there's no answer. Josie called me earlier, asking if I'd come home. I'd been down at Xander's gym, working out with him and just shooting the shit.*

*This isn't the first time she's called me and asked me to come home. We've been trying to conceive and her doctor has put us on a sex schedule. Aside from being with my girl, being told when I can have sex with her is getting annoying. It's all about her body temperature and ovulation chart. I should have that chart memorized by now considering it hangs in our bathroom. I can feel it mocking the fact that I haven't been able to knock her up yet every time I look in the mirror.*

*"Josie," I call out, as I start climbing the stairs. I pull*

my shirt off and throw it over my shoulder before moving my hand to my belt buckle. As much as I love my girl, the lack of emotion there is between us when we're together lately is really starting to bother me. I'll never pass up a chance to be with Jojo, but our lives have become more about calculations and less about feelings.

Our bedroom is dark and much to my surprise she's not laid out on the bed waiting. There's a light coming from under the bathroom door and I immediately feel like a shit for assuming she needed me to come home for sex, not because she's obviously sick. I knock on the door and twist the knob before she tells me to enter. We're long past bathroom pleasantries. I've held her hair many times when she's been throwing up.

This time, though, it's different and I drop to my knees to hold my sobbing wife in my arms. She clutches my chest, her nails digging into my skin. I hold her tightly to me and cradle her head as her tears wet my chest.

"What's wrong, Jojo?"

She doesn't answer, just shakes her head and sobs harder. I scan the bathroom floor, looking for any signs that she's sick or hurt, but all I see are the dozens of boxes and white sticks littering the floor of our master bath. I may be a guy, but I definitely know what a pregnancy test looks like, and from the sounds coming from my wife, I'm willing to bet she's not pregnant.

A string of profanities run rampant through my mind. I can't say them out loud because it'll make things worse. Her doctor said no stress, so my feelings really don't factor into this mess. I've been tested, had to perform for a cup while a crap ass porno played, only for them to tell us that *my sperm are strong. Josie went through her own battery of tests, all to come out normal. The diagnosis ... it'll happen. Apparently not today, judging by the way Josie is right now.*

*We stay on the bathroom floor for an hour or more. I can't look at my watch or even pull my phone out of my back pocket to answer it. I refuse to let her go. Nothing is more important than her right now. Seeing her like this kills me. I don't know what to do to fix this ... to fix us. Trying to conceive a baby has consumed us, both physically and mentally. We need a break from this entire baby making crap so we can get back to us. The problem is I'm not going to be the one to suggest it. If I do, I'll be accused of not wanting another child or not finding her attractive enough. Both couldn't be further from the truth. I just don't want to see her like this anymore.*

The day I found Josie like that was the day we decided to stop trying. That was three months ago. It was her decision, which she made after talking to her mom for hours. When she came to bed that night she asked me if I was willing to look into adoption. She had found so many different websites about adopting and within an hour we decided that adoption was for us, and we'd adopt toddlers and siblings if necessary. A newborn wasn't a requirement for us; we just wanted to open our home to children who needed to be loved.

And now, in a few short weeks, we're going to be parents to a newborn. I'll be waking up at midnight and two a.m. to change diapers and rock my son back to sleep. I'm doing it all because I have to make up for lost time. Josie should've never had to take care of Noah by herself, and even though the second time doesn't make up for everything I've missed, it's a start.

With the band's mail under my arm, I walk through my quiet house and down my back stairs. Harrison and JD are in the office working. 4225 *West* has hit a rough patch. Our sales on our recent album have dropped dramatically and our manager says it's because we aren't in Los Angeles networking with the rest of the music industry. JD is all for moving back, especially since Jenna doesn't have any ties other than us in Beaumont, but I can't uproot Noah. He's establishing himself here as an elite athlete. I also have a feeling that Harrison would forgo his position as our drummer if we decided to relocate. I know Katelyn has no desire to leave.

"'Sup?" I say as I sit down at my desk. I'm running out of space in my basement and had to convert Katelyn's old office to a space for the three of us. Our wives were all yelling us at respectively, with all the scrap pieces of paper we were leaving around the house. Or me yelling when I'd leave papers on the table that somehow ended up in the garbage. The last time it happened, I yelled and yelled and Josie stood there with her hands on her hips reminding me that my untouchable space was in the basement. When I started working down here, so did Harrison and JD. Now we have two long tables, one on each wall, a computer, and notes taped everywhere.

They don't answer me and I'm okay with that. We see each other every day and often at night. We're a family. Our wives are best friends and our kids play together ... well, Noah and Quinn do. Elle and Peyton entertain Eden when I'm not holding her.

I thought I'd be upset if we weren't having a girl, but I'm not. It's almost like I'm getting a second chance to raise a son—not that I'd change Noah, but sometimes I still question myself with him. And the fact that he's close with Nick still gives me an uneasy feeling. I feel like I toe the line when it comes to punishment because I'm afraid that Noah will blurt out that he's going to go live with Nick. I wouldn't let him, but I'm not sure I could stop him.

I rummage through the mail and rip open the large manila envelope. It's a series of images taken by some paparazzi; I shake my head as I flip through each one.

"How was L.A.?" I ask Harrison. He and Katelyn had taken the kids to his beach house for a week for spring break. I was jealous until now.

Harrison sighs, turning to face me. "Things are good. I saw Trixie and played a few sets for the house band." My mouth drops open and he shrugs as if it's no big deal that he went back to the bar that gave us our start. "What's that?" he asks, nodding to the pictures in my hand.

I swallow to push away the dryness in my throat. Laid out before me are images of Harrison and Katelyn. The headline is unfavorable, saying: *Harrison James of 4225 West wanders.* I know that's the furthest thing from the truth, but the pictures tell a different story. While Katelyn watches the game, Harrison is watching the cheerleader in front of him. His eyes are dead center on her ass. One of the images shows him shrugging as Katelyn stares him down.

"Nice spread," I say as I toss the images down onto

the table much to Harrison's displeasure. JD snickers behind him, causing Harrison to turn an ugly, embarrassing shade of red.

He shakes his head and covers the photos with a piece of paper. "Katelyn was so pissed, but I couldn't help but look when they're shaking their asses in my face."

"You look, but you don't get caught," JD adds because he's the master of looking without detection.

Harrison cuffs him upside his head and glares at him. "Anyway, we need to discuss *Metro*."

"Why?" I ask, sorting through the rest of our mail. Most of it is fan letters, in which one of us will respond. We take turns answering them, knowing how much it means to our fans when we reply personally. Each letter receives a signed photo from the three of us. Cheesy, I know, but it helps sales. At least that's what I keep telling myself.

"Trixie's closing *Metro*. With the surge of online videos and social media, playing gigs to get noticed isn't the thing anymore. Like I said, I played a couple sets, but most of the bands brought their laptops in and used electronic music as a backup. Trixie is losing money, the bar is run down, and I didn't see one agent while I was there."

*Metro* is the place where my grandfather was discovered, the place where Harrison and I developed as musicians, and the place where I met Sam. That place paved my way, and I almost gave up on music until Trixie called that fateful night and gave me the coveted "headline" spot. If she hadn't, I would've come home and begged for forgiveness. That's something I've never told Josie.

"When's she closing?"

"Two months. She's hoping to find a buyer before then, but no one wants to invest in a bar these days. It's old, not the 'hot spot' anymore, and in need of some serious repairs."

"We should do something for her," JD adds. I forget that he played there, too. We have ties to *Metro* and owe Trixie a lot, but we've never thanked her. Hell, once we signed with Moreno Entertainment we never went back.

"There's another thing you should know," Harrison says, but this time his expression is grim.

My insides turn, preparing for more bad news. "What's that?"

He clears his throat. "Some journalist named Calista Jones is writing a tell-all about you. Somehow she got a copy of Sam's diaries, and according to the word on the street, a few of your 'friends' added some colorful commentary."

"What?" My voice breaks and my heartbeat increases. This is the last thing that I need, and definitely the last thing that Josie needs. We're in a good place, and with the baby coming, the added drama will just be too much stress for her.

Harrison hands me his phone and I read through an excerpt of this novel. Everything that I don't want to remember about my past is about to come out and there won't be anything I can do about it. Sure, I can take to social media and ask people not to buy it, but I know that they will, even though they'll tell me they won't. It's in our nature to know all the juicy gossip of Hollywood.

"Well, this is fucking great," I mutter as I read what Harrison has shown me. She talks about the tattoo across my chest and the day Josie called the office and left me a message. But it's the words about the time that Sam and I hooked up in my tour bus that really jars me. The date is written there, and for the first time, I recognize it as our anniversary ... mine and Josie's. Dead doesn't even begin to describe how I feel inside right now.

The guys don't have anything to say. I don't blame them. I brought Sam into our lives, and aside from JD, she did everything she could to ruin us and we're pretty sure she set Alicia up to drug Harrison.

"We should get to work," I say without any conviction whatsoever. My mind should be on the joyous news I want to share, but thoughts of my past plague me. I'll have to tell Josie about this book and pray that she doesn't want to read it. Nothing good can come from a book written by a journalist ... one that I don't ever remember meeting.

"What are we working on?" JD asks as I shake my head.

"I have no idea," I reply, completely lost for yet another time in my life. I'm starting to think that my career is over because I'll be spending the rest of my days trying to make up for everything I did in the past to my wife. She's not going to understand. Hell, I don't even understand.

I'm fighting every urge I have to go baby shopping. Instead, I head home after stopping at the grocery store. Liam and I want to buy things for the baby together. He wants to be there when we pick out a crib, the bedding and, of course, he says that the baby needs rock star approved clothing. I think if he had his way, the baby would have his own motorcycle—and probably tattoos—right from birth.

It's hard to explain how I feel about adopting. I'm happy, elated and over the moon that in a few short weeks I'll be holding a baby boy in my arms who I get to call mine, but I'm missing the pregnancy part. I miss rubbing my hand over my stomach and feeling the fluttering and the kicking. I want Liam to touch my stomach and feel his child respond to him. Or have Noah read a story so the baby knows his voice when he gets here. We're missing these early bonding moments, but I still wouldn't trade what we have going on right now. The anxiety of being a new mother is there, even if I've done this before.

When I pull in I see a football flying through the air accompanied by the sound of voices. Liam is working with Noah and is teaching him everything he knows. As of late, there have been comparisons between the two of them. A reporter stopped us at the mall, asking us for an interview. He's twelve, almost thirteen, and not even in high school yet and they're matching him stat for stat with this dad. I could see it in Noah's eyes; the resentment is building. He was on his way to being a football star long before Liam showed up and I think it upsets Noah that people don't remember that. He's not Liam, and he's not trying to be.

I set the groceries on the counter and head out back to see my boys. I'm sorry ... *men.* Noah has informed me that he'll no longer be my little boy when he becomes a teenager so I need to make sure he's referred to properly. My response was to pull him into a hug. That lasted for about two seconds before he squirmed his way out of my arms. He's growing fast, too fast for my liking, but it was bound to happen.

"Looking good," I say just as Noah releases a pass back to Liam. He catches it with such ease, much like he did when he and Mason would throw the ball around in Mason's backyard. When I wanted to make out and do stupid, spontaneous teenage things, Liam wanted to work on his arm. It wasn't until senior year that he relaxed and now I know why. He was planning to quit football, even if he didn't know it at the time.

He changed our senior year. I can see that now. Back

then I was blinded by love, college, and freedom. I thought that Liam and I were invincible and nothing could bring us down or break us. Turns out, I was the one to break us because I couldn't see past the quarterback I fell in love with. I couldn't see the hurt and pain he was living with day in and day out. I only provided more stress by trying to do everything I could to keep my dreams alive. I was all set to just be his wife, but he gave me the opportunity to be someone better, someone extraordinary. He gave me the opportunity to grow up and find the *me* I needed to be without him guiding our path. It just sucks how it all happened.

"How was school, Noah?"

"Fine."

"Did you do your homework?"

"Yep."

He continues to throw the football back and forth with Liam, never taking his gaze off his dad. This is how our conversations have gone lately—I ask a question and get a one word answer in return. Sometimes I understand when he replies with "not fair" after some sort of punishment has been handed down. Lately, it's been because he hasn't turned in his homework. He earns great grades and does his homework, but forgets to hand it in. The only way Liam and I thought we could get the point across was to remove all of his electronic devices from his room. It hasn't really helped, but his forgetfulness is getting better. Funny how he never forgets anything when it comes to sports.

"Did you stop at the store?"

"I did," I answer Liam. "I picked up a variety ... chicken, steak, and hot dogs."

Liam tosses the ball back to Noah and tells him he has to start cooking dinner. He comes over to me, rests his hands on the chair that I'm sitting in, and kisses me. Noah makes gagging sounds in the background, causing both of us to smile. When he starts to pull away, I clutch his T-shirt, preventing him from leaving me. We're not into heavy displays of affection in front of Noah, but he knows that his parents love each other. Liam always has his hand on my back or on my hip or our fingers are locked together.

"Have you told him?" I whisper only for Liam to shake his head.

"I was waiting for you."

He kisses me again before he helps me stand. It's these small moments that make me wish I were pregnant because of how Liam is around me. Although, he'd likely want to put me in a bubble to prevent any injuries or potential dangers that could come my way.

Noah hasn't exactly been very welcoming of the fact that another human will be living with us. He wanted a dog, but Liam and I wanted a baby. We're the parents; we won the battle, but have paid dearly for it with pre-teen attitude.

Liam asks Noah to come into the house with us for a few minutes. The request is met with some type of boy grunt, followed by the kicking of grass. If Bianca and I were close I'd ask her if Liam was like this. Maybe Mason was and I can ask Mr. Powell how he dealt with the constant sighing, one-word answers, and eye rolling. I must be crazy to want to do this again. Right now I think crazy is a good thing.

As soon as the three of us sit down at the table I'm taken back to the time when Liam came over for dinner and we told Noah that Liam's his dad. Noah knew, of course, after he heard his teachers talking about Liam during a field trip to the sports museum. Mason and Liam had made such a name for themselves that the town wanted to remind everyone just how amazing they were.

Liam takes my hand in his and looks at our son who is looking anywhere but at us. I hate that he's so disinterested, but I get it. Liam takes a deep breath and squeezes my hand.

"Today, your mom and I got to see the baby. Would you like to know what we're having?"

"A monkey?"

"Noah," I say with a hint of displeasure in my voice. I know it's hard to make this adjustment, but sometimes changes are good for people, for families.

"What?" he says with a hint of laughter in his tone. "A monkey would be great! Then we could watch it pick its own butt."

Liam isn't taking Noah's bait and looks at him sternly. "It's a boy."

This time Noah rolls his eyes and pushes away from the table. "Great. Now you can start from the beginning and be there for everything that you missed with me. That's why you're doing this, right? So you can make up for what you missed? This baby isn't even going to look like us. You're taking some stranger's baby and the only reason she's giving you her kid is because you're famous."

I gasp and Noah looks at me. There are tears in his eyes. I shake my head, but he's already storming out of the room. Liam goes to stand, but I stop him.

"Are we making a mistake?" I can't believe the words that come out of mouth. My heart's breaking in two right now, half for my son who doesn't understand and half for the little boy who has yet to be born and is in need of parents who will care about him.

"Josie, we're not making a mistake. He's right though. I can't help but feel like this is my chance to make up for what I missed. Even now, there's so much that I don't know about having a pregnant wife. I can't feel your stomach or ask you how my baby is doing. I don't even get to go to the store and buy you pickles and ice cream only for you to tell me you don't want them anymore. I won't be able to hold your hand while you're in labor or be there to cut the cord."

I stand and force my way into his lap. Holding him to me, I stroke the back of his neck while I think of what needs to be said. I can't change the past and I know he's not asking me to. I don't want this baby to be a substitute, but if that's how Noah's looking at it, maybe we haven't considered everything.

"We want this baby, right?" he asks, pulling away slightly so he can see me. I nod and attempt to blink away my tears. "I have to find a way to help Noah understand that I'm not replacing him. The last thing I want is for him to run to Nick."

Threading my fingers through his hair, I look deeply into his blue eyes. "He won't run to Nick."

"Don't be so sure."

Sighing, I rest my forehead against his. Our lips meet briefly before I pull away and look at him. "Aubrey's pregnant. If Noah is acting like this with us, he'll do the same with Nick."

"I'm going to go talk to him," Liam says, tapping my hip to get me to stand.

"No, I will. I need the chance to still be his mommy."

There isn't a handbook on how to handle something like this and no one I can really ask. Harrison and Katelyn merged their families nicely, but there wasn't a baby involved. Even when Eden is here, Noah doesn't pay attention to her. I chalked it up to being a boy, but maybe it's something different. I don't want to think that Noah's jealous, but maybe he is—although most of us are jealous of the attention Eden receives. She has each of the guys wrapped around her finger.

I knock once before twisting the knob and pushing his door open enough to peek in. He's lying on his bed, tossing his football in the air. He looks so much like Liam at this age—even though he and I weren't friends back then, I still saw him around town. Katelyn and I used to watch him and Mason play football on Saturdays, riding our bikes over to the park. Then, high school changed everything for me.

Noah doesn't stop when I sit down on the edge of his bed so I do what any mom would do—I lie down next to him and catch the ball. I think it's funny, but he doesn't and lets out a huge, overdramatic sigh.

"Life sucks, doesn't it?" I hand him back his football, knowing he likes to feel the leather against his fingertips.

"No."

I pause, wondering if he's being truthful or sarcastic. At this age, it's hard to tell.

"Noah, I'd really like you to give me full answers. I came up here to talk to you. I know you're going through a lot of changes and if you don't want to talk to me, you can talk to your dad."

"I don't want to talk to him."

I roll onto my side and turn his face toward me. His blue eyes glisten with tears. "Why not?" I try to keep my voice stoic because he can't know that I'm falling apart on the inside.

"He wants to replace me."

"Oh, Noah," I cry out with my hand covering my mouth. "That isn't true. Your dad loves you so much. This baby isn't going to change that."

"Yes, it will. He'll want to be with the baby instead of throwing the football around or coming to my games."

I shake my head. "You're his best friend, Noah, and a baby isn't going to change that. It'll be years before he can do the things that you guys do together and when the baby is ready, you'll be off in college."

"Why do you want a dumb baby anyway?"

"Because this family has a lot of love to give to someone who needs it. His parents don't want him and I don't know about you, but I bet it feels really bad to not be wanted."

Noah looks at me for a minute or so. He has a few tears falling onto his pillow, but I don't bring attention to them. He's a big boy now, almost a man according to him.

"It's a boy?"

"Yeah. I'm stuck with another Westbury man. I'm never going to win any battles."

Noah laughs and wipes at his face angrily. "Can you promise me that nothing will change?"

"I promise, Noah."

# 4

## LIAM

It's moments like these that make me despise Sterling even more. If he had been a better father maybe I could handle the situation with Noah better. I'm flying by the seat of my pants with each problem that arises. That's not the way to raise a child. I could probably benefit from some classes or maybe even therapy to get over the issues I have with my parents. Either way, shit with Noah has to change. He has to know I'm here for him no matter what, even when I'm on tour or locked in the studio recording. He's my priority in life.

So is Josie, and that's why I need to tell her about this ridiculous book that is coming out. I understand that people have the freedom to say as they want, but you should never profit off ruining another person's image or potentially their life. Writing a book about me, my band, or anyone else for that matter, without their consent, should be against the law. I don't know what I'm more pissed about—the fact that this journalist was able to get her hands on Sam's diaries and Mr. Moreno allowed it, or the fact that shit happened in my life that I never intended to tell Josie about. The Sam shit I can deal with, but I'm not so sure that Josie will be very keen on finding out about the other stuff and how much of a douche I really was.

I start preparing dinner for everyone. Over the past year or so I've become a self-proclaimed master with the grill. No one tells me my skills make their food taste nasty, so the title stays. Josie is my dessert maker. She makes a mean chocolate cake. It tastes even better when she's not sharing it with my friends.

At least once a week we're eating at each other's houses. I believe there's some sort of secret agreement that we switch, but I can't confirm. I just do what I'm told and go where directed. It's best to not ask too many questions. The only time I need to be prepared is when we're going to Nick's or he's coming over here. I respect his relationship with my son, but that's as far as it's going for me. I can tolerate him, but I adore Aubrey. She's a fire-cracker for sure ... and a lifesaver.

Small, yet strong arms wrap around my waist, causing me to put the knife that I've been using down. After wiping my hands with the nearby towel, I turn and pull Josie closer to me. She's been crying, and as much as I want to cup her face and smooth out her frown lines, the last thing she needs from me are remnants of meat on her skin.

"Everything okay?"

"I think so," she says as she puckers up for a kiss for

which I'm all too happy to oblige. "Noah just needs a little reassurance that you're not replacing or making a substitute for him. He's concerned that you won't spend time with him. I reminded him that by the time the baby is old enough to do fun stuff with you, he'll be going off to college and he seemed okay with that."

I pull Josie into a hug so she won't see the hurt and confusion etched across my face. If I've done something to give Noah that idea, then I've failed him as a father. Maybe I need to take a step back and reevaluate how I am with him ... find ways to make him feel even more connected to me. Thing is, I'm not sure how. We share a common love for football and baseball, but aside from sports, Noah and I are two different people which isn't necessarily a bad thing.

I see a lot of me in Noah and it scares me. I was gung ho, balls to the wall, devoted to football. Camps, clinics, practice, and game films made me happy until I met Josie. She was the icing on my proverbial cake. I had her and football at the same time and was happier than a pig in shit. That was until the sport I loved started slowly eating away at my soul. What I loved doing soon felt like a chore. The desire to achieve greatness went away little-by-little every time I stepped out onto the field or had a game film to watch. I no longer cared if I broke records or held titles, but others cared and I had to go out and make sure their dreams were coming true.

My father was a whole other story—one that's hard to talk about. He's the reason I quit, the reason why I gave up on what could've been an amazing career. He's the reason I chose a school that I didn't want and the coach who didn't care if I was there or not. I gave my dad too much power over me and I won't do that to Noah. He needs to be the one to make decisions about his career. If he plays football, great! I'll be in the stands. If he decides to do something else, I've got his back one hundred percent. I won't be Sterling, but I also won't let him be a bum or walk all over his mother and me.

"Liam, are you okay?"

"What?" I pull back from her to find her eyes full of concern.

"Well, I'm not complaining about the marathon hug, but we have people due here any minute and your meat is getting warm."

Josie realizes her blunder the moment the words cross her lips. I cock my eyebrow and move my hips back and forth, earning an epic eye roll.

"You're horrible."

Laughing, I release her from my hold. "Hate to break it to you, but you said warm meat."

Josie slaps me on the ass before moving to the other side of the kitchen to prepare what looks like salad and hopefully a chocolate cake for later. I should probably run out and get some flowers for when I drop the bomb about the book coming out. Who am I kidding? Flowers won't even come close to making everything okay. I'm going to need a grand gesture, but I don't want it to look like I'm trying to buy her forgiveness. I'm not. I don't want it. I did what I had to do to at that time in my life. Had I known about Noah, I would've been back here in a heartbeat, but I didn't. I can't be faulted for my actions, at least I hope not.

"What are you looking at?"

Her question catches me off guard. I smile and shake my head slightly. "You. You're so fucking beautiful. I don't know how I got so lucky."

Josie shrugs. "Easy," she says as she walks over to me. "You asked, and I said yes."

---

The backyard fills quickly with the gang, better known as the band and their families. If I didn't know better, I'd think they all arrived together, but they're just punctual. I watch out the window, looking at my two best friends with their kids while the wives are in the corner giggling about something. Even my wife is with them saying who knows what.

JD is holding a squirming Eden, who's eager to get down and play. Once she was born, Josie, and I decided to put a swing set play structure in our backyard. The kids spend so much time over here we thought it'd be nice if they had a place to escape to and get out of our hair.

It's odd to think about how far we've come and how we ended up in Beaumont. Me being here is easy to figure out, but Harrison and JD didn't have to follow. They did and because of my decision to move back here, the band is struggling. We're not a guaranteed sold out show any more, and at best we're an opening act. We're not getting the calls we need, or the radio airplay. It's my job to fix this so the kids have futures. I'm just not sure I can fix it here.

As soon as I step outside, Harrison and JD give up on dad duties and come over to the grill. Last summer, Josie and I decided to spruce up the backyard and had a custom patio with an outside kitchen installed along with a fire pit and pool. The backyard became our oasis. A place where we can spend time as a family, or entertain our friends. I still prefer the tower on Friday nights, though, even if I can only go when it's the off-season.

I motion toward the refrigerator, and Harrison keeps up with his best man duties by grabbing us each a beer. There's a built in can opener right on my counter and the tops fall directly into a bucket. It's clear I'm amused by the simple things because that's one of my favorite pieces in this outdoor kitchen.

"I feel like I just saw ya," Harrison says as he hands me my beer. I take a long pull before setting it down so I can flip the meat on the grill.

"You work in my basement, of course you just saw me," I reply as I pull the lid down.

"Have you given any more thought to helping out Trixie?"

His question catches me off guard. I look at JD, who is magically off in la-la land with his bottle of beer. Clearly these two have been up to something.

"I wasn't aware of any options."

JD mutters something that I can't quite make out, and I look to Harrison for confirmation. He runs his hands over his beanie, his tell when something's on his mind.

"What's up?" I say to both of them.

"There's a benefit concert being organized. A few of the

musicians that have come through there are looking to save *Metro* from closing. They asked if we want to play. I told them I didn't know, but they asked me to come back and play in the house band," Harrison says straight to the point.

"Did you know this earlier?" Something tells me Harrison may have a hand in planning this benefit concert. It took a lot of convincing to get Harrison to leave *Metro* when Sam wanted to sign me, and eventually us. But he was worth it. I thought that then and I still think that now.

"I did, but wasn't sure how you'd react since I dropped the book bomb."

I nod. He's right. The book news is enough to ruin my day even though we should be celebrating. We will be celebrating. "Let's eat and discuss it later," I say as I take the meat off the grill.

JD whistles loudly and all the noise in the yard hushes. "Dinner," he says, much to the delighted screams of five kids.

As soon as everyone is situated and they're digging in, I tap my fork against my bottle of beer. I stand once I have everyone's attention. "I know we're together a lot and we're as close as any family, so tonight Josie, Noah, and I want to thank you for coming over and celebrating with us. Earlier this afternoon we found out that the baby we're adopting is a boy."

The cheers are loud and boisterous. I watch for any sign that Noah is going to have a meltdown or cause any drama and I see none. He's sitting between Quinn and Peyton, and the three of them are chatting away.

"Harrison and JD, I'll be requiring your assistance with getting the room painted."

"Wait, Dad?"

I turn my gaze to Noah, who is now standing. "I thought we could do it together."

Josie gasps and quickly covers her mouth, and I have to swallow hard to find my voice. "I wouldn't want it any other way, buddy," I tell him as I walk over to him and bring him into my arms.

Noah and I are both learning and adapting to the impending change. I have to learn what it's like to have a newborn around and he has to learn to share. Together, I think we can get it done.

# 5

## JOSIE

The way the mirror on my dressing table is angled gives me the perfect opportunity to watch Liam undress. This is my favorite ritual, morning and night. I'll take the chance anytime I can to watch him methodically peel off his clothes. He's a man who unties his shoes first, placing them back on the shoe rack. His socks are next, followed by his shirt. My peeping tom ways are often rewarded when he's wearing a dress shirt. Not only do I get to watch the muscles in his back flex as he pushes each button through the ridiculously small hole, but his undressing is prolonged. He takes his T-shirt off the same way every time, and when he pulls the collar from behind and the shirt slowly lifts inch by inch, my mouth waters. My lips become dry and my knuckles ache from my hand clutching my hairbrush. The clank of his belt buckle and the almost too silent pop of the fabric from his button down jeans have me staring intently into the mirror. My make-up is only half off, my mouth wide open, and I'm the picture of someone who needs serious help. And let's not get started on the way he gets dressed …

He knows I watch him. This is a game to him. He could sleep in or stay up late, but he doesn't. Liam gets up with me in the morning and goes to bed when I do at night and I'm starting to think it's because his intention is to have me committed. I may or may not have a drooling issue when it comes to staring at my husband. You'd think that after watching him grow up that I'd be used to his body, but the truth of the matter is, he didn't fully grow until he left Beaumont. I missed the transformation from teenage boy to man. Sometimes I think I'm happy that I did, but other times, I think about all the other women out there that have experienced his transformation. I hate them all. I'm jealous of them and I don't know why. I have him now. He chose me.

His jeans drop to the ground and he kicks them aside, depriving me of the chance to watch him bend over to pick them up. I find myself leaning into my vanity to get a better look as his thumbs dip into the waistband of his boxer briefs. Men find women's lingerie sexy and appealing. It turns them on. The look and feel teases them and they love it. I never thought about men in their underwear until I saw Liam in his. Over the years he's maintained his muscles, yet has a more defined physique. His boxers aren't sagging in places they shouldn't. My husband could be an underwear model with his form fitting briefs, although I don't know if I'd want the world to see what he only shares with me. The cotton fabric pools at his feet. He steps out of them and turns around, showing me his naked body ... a body only for my eyes, my hands, my lips, and any other part of me.

"How long are you going to stare at me?"

I swallow hard as my eyes flash to his and a wicked grin plays across my lips.

"Until my eyes no longer work," I tell him. "Or until you tell me to stop."

"Hmm, that'll be never," he says as he walks near me. It's when he's inches from my back that I can no longer see him; his presence is felt immensely in the energy we share. I've always known when he's near. It can be both a blessing and a curse. After my last round of pregnancy tests, when I asked him to come home, I knew he was at the door before he even said my name. I didn't want him to see me like that—a mess and crumbling on the floor because I failed again in giving him another child. I had hoped he'd respect the closed door, but he knew immediately and I can't fault him for being the caring man that he is. He wanted to fix me, take away my pain, just as I would do for him. However, knowing when he's about to touch me makes my skin tingle with anticipation. My body zings with electricity the moment before he touches me. He's like my own personal current that I need in order to keep functioning.

Liam's touch is light as a feather as he moves the strap of my nightgown down my shoulder. Lips that I'm eager for, ghost across my skin. I feel my skin pebble, the goose bumps rising with anticipation as my other strap falls, leaving my nightgown barely covering my breasts.

He looks at me, his eyes meeting mine through the mirror as he watches the tips of his fingers travel along my collarbone. It's been so long since we've been like this. There's no rushing, or lack of foreplay. I've missed my husband and I want to tell him as much, but I'm at a loss for words as he sweeps my hair to the side and presses his lips against my neck. Liam presses into my back as his fingers push my flimsy nightgown down.

"I really like this color on you," he says as he looks at me.

I glance at myself in the mirror. I can't see the midnight blue gown that I was wearing only moments ago. "I'm not wearing a color."

"You are, and it's flesh-toned. The most beautiful color I've ever seen." Liam quickly turns me on my stool and scoops me into his arms. His mouth captures the schoolgirl squeal I want to let out as his tongue meets mine. My arms wrap around his neck as he carries us the few steps to our bed where he gently sets me down.

"Seems we have a problem, Mrs. Westbury."

"What's that, Mr. Page?" I say Page purposefully, earning a deep grunt from him. He shakes his head slowly as he takes in every inch of my body.

"Is that what you want?"

Pulling my lower lip in, I nod almost hesitantly. It's a dangerous game, playing with Liam Page, but sometimes it's warranted. Sometimes it's needed. I've had the best of both worlds where he's concerned. At times I'll have the slow, sensual love making from my husband, while at others I'm rewarded with the rough and powerful fucking from my rocker.

I want the rocker tonight.

Sitting up, I push him away from the bed. His eyes

widen as I guide his hand into my hair. My nightgown bunches at my waist as I squat down, level with his erection.

"If you picked me up in a bar, what would you do?"

"Don't, Jojo," he says, not because he doesn't want to be with me, but because he fears I'm trying to be someone I'm not. He doesn't like to be reminded of who he used to be and I can understand that, but sometimes I want to be that bad girl who goes home with the rocker from the club.

Tonight I'm going to be her.

"I want this," I say as I take him deep into my mouth. I look up at him as my mouth starts to pull away. The grip he has on my hair tightens as I pull him in again. My hands are spread out on his legs. My nails are digging into his thighs. I look at him again, my eyes pleading for him to give me this little fantasy and he does.

Liam takes a tight hold of my head in both hands and moves me back and forth. I hold onto him for stability, fearing that I might fall forward if I'm not careful. Liam moans as his hips thrust into me. I take everything he gives me and watch as his face morphs into ecstasy.

In the blink of an eye, I'm on my back with my panties being torn away. "Yes," I whisper heavily as Liam buries himself deep within me. My leg is thrown over his shoulder as he pounds rapidly. Our bodies are slick with sweat, our thrusts matching our every breath. He holds my face, his hand spread out over my cheek while his thumb hovers over my mouth. My tongue darts out, licking the pad of his thumb as his eyes roll back. My hands grip the comforter as he moves in and out, increasing our tempo. When he grazes my clit, I scream out, begging for more.

"God, Josie, I'm going to fucking blow."

I want him to know I'm there with him, ready and waiting. I grab his ass and push him into me. He grunts, slamming harder until he stills, dropping my leg immediately. It aches, but I welcome the pain.

"Holy fuck," he says as his lips move over my skin until he's reached my lips. "We haven't done that in a long time."

My fingers run up and down his back as he lies on top of me. I don't want him to move, but we need to clean up. He pulls out, moving just off to the side, leaving our legs intertwined.

"Thank you for letting me have my fantasy."

He scoffs. "You know I'll do anything for you, but there are times when I worry. I don't want you to think I want that lifestyle back."

"I don't," I say as I kiss his forehead.

"Good," he sighs, "because there's something I need to tell you."

There have been many times in my life when my mouth has gotten the best of me. Case in point: I just made love to my wife and the first ridiculous thing I have to say is that I need to tell her something. This, of course, is after I tell her that I don't want my rocker lifestyle back, which isn't exactly true. The booze, women, and long nights isn't something I crave, but the scene is. I miss being surrounded by the music, the artists, and the vibe that Los Angeles has to offer. It's not something I can explain, or even delve into. It's an itch, a longing.

Resting on my hand, I brush the sweat-laden hair away from Josie's face. Everyone changes over the years ... except my wife. Realistically, I know she has, but in my eyes I still see the girl I fell in love with so many years ago. Her love for me has never wavered, even when I didn't deserve it. That's what I keep telling myself as I'm looking into her soulful blue eyes, preparing myself for the anger and hurt, but hoping for acceptance and encouragement.

"Let's take a bath," I tell her, losing the nerve I've been trying to build up. She doesn't balk nor does she agree as I jump out of the bed and walk into the bathroom. I turn on the water, letting the loud vibration of the tub filling drown out my thoughts.

Josie's fingers thread through the back of my hair. I'm in need of a cut, something I've been putting off because of our baby-making schedule. She comes to stand in front of me and images of taking her again run rampant through my mind. I kiss her softly and hold her face to mine. When I pull back, I see nothing but confusion and fear. Guiding her into the water, I maneuver my girl so she's between my legs. My fingers dip into the water and I let them dangle above her as the warm water drips onto her skin.

Taking a deep breath, I ready myself. "When my grandmother introduced me to Harrison, he was the drummer of a house band for a bar called *Metro*. He took me there, and that's where I got my start. It's where my grandfather got his start, too."

I pause, remembering the day I met Harrison at my grandmother's party. He had a beanie on his head even back then. "Trixie, the owner, she was this spitfire of a woman. Agents flocked to her bar to sign the next big act."

"Is that where you met Sam?"

I stiffen at the sound of Sam's name coming off Josie's lips. Sam has caused so much damage and continues to do so even though she's no longer here. "And JD," I say, avoiding the thought of Sam as long as I can. "Did I ever tell you that my grandmother was our groupie?"

Josie shakes her head. "You've never really discussed her."

"I should. I wish you could've met her."

She turns slightly in my arms. "Things could've been different." I kiss her again. I know the kind of different she would've wanted, and it doesn't match mine. "Why are you telling me this?"

Wrapping my arms around her, I rest my chin on her shoulder. It'll be easier to say what I have to without seeing her face. The question is, what comes first? The fact that I want to go to L.A. and help out *Metro* and possibly revive the career of *4225 West*, or do I tell her about the book? Both will, no doubt, cause an issue.

"I need to take the band back to L.A.," I say quickly. Once I start talking I can't stop. "We're struggling here and losing the fan base we've built. The money, the songs, and the exposure we need ... we aren't getting that recording in the basement and I can't do that to Harrison and JD. *Metro* is going under and Harrison and JD want us to go back for the benefit concert. I know it's bad timing with the baby coming, but ...

"There's something else," I say as I take a deep breath. "A journalist wrote a tell-all book about me. I don't know what's in it, but she somehow got a hold of Sam's diaries, or whatever, and used those."

I close my eyes tightly as I wait. Waiting for what, I don't know. The yelling. The punching. The look. I know there's some cracked ass saying about how everything happens for a reason, but I don't believe that shit.

Mason didn't have to die for me to come back. I would've ... eventually. *Metro* doesn't need to be closing for me to go back to Los Angeles—we have to or we need to hang it up. The band, as of right now, is not viable. We're not making money, and even though I've invested well that doesn't mean the money will always be there.

Josie pulls away from me. Her movements are slow and methodical. I know I've fucked up, and the timing is the worst possible. She steps out of the tub, leaving me cold and shivering, and exits the bathroom not even pausing to tie her robe. After pulling the plug on the tub and getting out, I wrap myself in a towel until I put on a pair of lounge pants.

My wife stands on our balcony which overlooks our backyard. I encase her with my arms, clutching the railing in front of us. I refuse to let her keep things bottled up. She becomes me when she does that and we don't need two of me in this house. Nothing good comes from holding in the anger.

"Talk to me."

"I don't know what to say," she whispers into the night air.

"Yell at me then."

She shakes her head. The last fight we had as a couple was the night of graduation. I wanted to quit it all right then and there, give up on everything and just disappear. Nothing, at the time, could compare to not having my parents at graduation. That was the lowest of the lows, and yet I remained in their house because I didn't have any other place to go. Sure, I could've gone to

Mason's, but I never wanted to intrude on anyone. I was my own problem to deal with.

"Why now, Liam?" she sniffles in between her words, stabbing me square in my heart.

"I know the timing sucks, Jojo, and I wish I could change it, but I owe it to Trixie to help save her club. I'm where I'm at in life because of the opportunities she gave me."

Turning, Josie faces me. Her eyes are red and her cheeks tear stained. "I don't owe her anything."

I frown. "Josie ..."

"No, don't. You got to say your peace and now I get to say mine. For ten years you were gone and you haven't been all that forthcoming about your life, which I get; you don't want to upset me, but I *am* upset because you're leaving and I can't stop you. You may be Liam Westbury in here," she points to my head, "but in your heart, you're Liam Page. I've accepted that, but right now I don't want to because we're about to have a baby and ..." She trails off, not needing to finish her thought because my mind is already finishing it for her.

"Jojo, I'm not leaving you. I'm going to work. You and Noah can come with me, or fly out on the weekends. I'm not hiding from you and our children."

"But you won't be here when the baby's born?"

I shake my head. It's going to take months to rebuild what we've lost, if not years. "As soon as he's here, I'm on the first plane out. Then we'll fly back to L.A. as a family. You'll love it out there, and with school almost out for Noah, you guys can spend your days at the beach. Linda can watch the baby and I'll work." I drop my voice and lean in, letting my breath tickle her neck. "At night, you can be the vixen up front, the one I take backstage."

She pushes me away. "Is that what you need? A vixen willing to screw you in the green room?"

"What?" I almost choke on my words. "You're crazy if that's what you think. I only want you. Yeah, it excites me knowing that you're in the audience listening to me sing about you and about us and that I get to go home with you."

I walk away from her and out of our room, taking the stairs as fast as I can, barreling through the house until I reach the basement steps leading to my studio. The fact that she even brought that shit up pisses me off. I gave up that lifestyle when I found out about Noah and did what I had to do to get her away from Nick. She's my life. Liam Page is my job.

He hustles through the crowded hallway moving no differently than when he's on the field, dodging the residents who are coming at him. I try desperately to call his name to no avail. My voice is gone, broken. The words I need to say to him are either caught in my throat, or nowhere to be found. Bearing down, I scream his name until people are looking at me. My new friends, classmates, and neighbors stare as make-up runs down my blotchy, tear-stained face. Liam ignores me and continues his pursuit away from me. Why? Why is he doing this?

Mason can catch him. That's what I tell myself as I dial his number. Again, I can only speak in wails and broken sentences. "Liam" and "gone" are the only recognizable words I know. The dial tone in my ear tells me to hang up, but I hold the phone to my ear, crying, begging for Liam to come back.

The pounding on my door causes me to drop the

phone. I run as fast as I can across my small room, only to find Mason standing there instead of Liam.

"What's going on?"

"He ... he's ... gone." I can hardly utter the words and fall to the floor. Mason is there to catch me before I hurt myself. The pain I'm feeling in my chest—it's unbearable. I sob in Mason's arms, barely able to catch my breath. He rubs my back, urging me to calm down, but I can't. The love of my life has cut me open with a jagged knife and ripped my heart out before slamming it back into the open wound.

"Are you hurt, Josie?"

Am I hurt? I'm not sure how to quantify the pain I'm feeling as hurt. Hurt to me is a paper cut, or a sliver. The suffering I'm experiencing goes far beyond that. What I'm feeling now is irreparable. I'm inevitably broken.

Mason carries me to my bed, setting me down softly. He picks up the phone, but my sobs are too loud for me to hear who he is calling. I can't stop crying, but I need to because I can't breathe. The pressure on my chest is suffocating. My body feels like I've been battered, tackled by a three-hundred pound lineman.

Gentle arms wrap around me, cocooning me into a bubble of warmth and love. Quiet words of reassurance are spoken, meant to guide me down a path of healing, but I'll never heal from this. Deep in my heart, I know he's not coming back. Katelyn barks orders at Mason, who leaves, slamming the door behind him.

I close my eyes and when I do I see Liam, standing at my doorway, refusing to come in. I should've known something was wrong. He shied away from my touch. The only *other time he did that was after our fight the night of grad-uation. Let me have a do over. Let me ask Liam what's wrong before he runs out on me.*

"Can you talk?" Katelyn asks

*My whole body shakes, refusing to acknowledge what just happened.*

"Did you lose the baby?"

*The baby. Our baby. My forearm shields my abdomen as if to protect the tiny bean growing inside of me.*

"No," *I mutter through tears.* "Liam."

"What?" *Katelyn sits up abruptly, almost knocking me into the wall.* "What's wrong with Liam?"

"Liam?" *Mason says his name as he comes back into our room with a bottle of water and two white pills. He hands them to me slowly.*

"What happened, Josie?" *He's in front of me, on his knees and pleading for answers. He thinks something awful has happened to his best friend.*

*Just contemplating saying his name again brings tears to my eyes. I can't control the sob that moves through my body. I try, but to no avail and I'm quickly hyperven-tilating.*

"What the fuck happened to Liam?"

"He ..." *I hiccup, trying to catch my breath,* "left me," *I finish with a shudder.*

*The room grows silent. They also know that Liam is gone and not coming back. If there was a chance I thought he was, I wouldn't be like this. The finality of his words, the way he said my name, has given me no hope.*

"Did you tell him?" *Katelyn asks, only for Mason to speak up.*

*"Tell him what?"*

*"I'm pregnant."*

*Mason grits his teeth and his hands turn into fists. He looks from me to Katelyn before storming out of our room again, slamming the door behind him. It's only a matter of seconds before the roar of his truck echoes back to our room. Katelyn sits down next to me, her fingers combing through my hair.*

*"Mason will find him, and when he does, he'll bring him to his senses."*

*I don't want to tell her she's wrong because deep down I'm holding out hope. Hope that Liam is outside, realizing the mistake he's made and wanting to fix it. Hope that I'm not going to raise this baby alone.*

That memory hurts to think about, but it's fresh in my mind almost daily and it shouldn't be. I forgave Liam a long time ago, and to hold on to the one memory that ruined us isn't fair to him. He would've stayed if I was able to blurt the words out, but I couldn't. I thought I was enough. I thought the love that we shared was enough to keep him grounded.

I wipe away a stray tear. I don't know if it's from that moment, or for thinking about Mason. It could be either. He was my rock from that day onward, never questioning or asking if I'd heard from Liam. He knew I would've told him if I had. I also know it was him who found out the number of Liam's agency.

The hall is dark and quiet which tells me Noah is still sleeping. I'm thankful that our outburst didn't wake him, or if it did, he's not letting me know. Liam and I don't fight and maybe that's the problem because right now I feel like I'm losing him. It's something I shouldn't have to experience again, however part of me is always wondering if he's just a figment of my imagination or a dream. Am I going to wake up and realize this life I've been living these past few years is nothing but a dream; a medically induced coma from an accident? Is Mason alive and well, coaching at the high school where he and Liam set records?

I don't want this life to be part of some accident or only in my imagination. The day he walked back into my life, I didn't think we'd end up together. I told myself that he was a drifter, unable to commit to anything. Protecting Noah was my priority, but the second he figured out Liam was his dad, I knew I had a battle on my hands. As much as I wanted Liam to go away and never come back, I didn't want him to leave. Not only for Noah's sake, but also for mine.

I love Liam and the paths we're forging together. Sometimes I wonder if I show him enough that I do. Telling him I love him is one thing. Showing him is something entirely different. I can't help wondering if I'm failing as a wife in that regard. Am I failing him as a partner?

There's a soft melody coming from his studio. I pause at the top of the stairs and listen, resting my head on the wall. The sound is familiar and one I haven't heard in a while. It makes me wonder if he's preparing his set lists for this event in L.A. or if he's just practicing. He's going to Los Angeles whether I like it or not ... that's something I have no choice but to accept.

The fear is there—the women, the drinking, and the

drugs. He's said drugs were never his thing, but booze definitely was. Habits are hard to break, and they're even easier to fall back into. I trust him, but not the women. The ring on his finger won't mean anything to them. He's Liam Page. I've witnessed that craziness firsthand.

My steps are slow as I reach the door. He's stopped playing and I use that as my sign to enter his sanctuary. I don't come down here often, choosing to let him have the space he needs and was accustomed to before he came back to Beaumont. We both have our own places to escape to with the flower shop being mine.

The studio is small, but useful. The guys spend a lot of time down here creating magic. Harrison's drums sit in the corner, while guitars and keyboards take up the rest of the space. Microphone stands clutter the center of the room. The once cream-colored walls are full of life with music sheets covering every square inch possible.

Liam's back is to the door, and if he's heard me enter, he doesn't acknowledge my presence. I know he's angry. I am, too. History does not favor us in this situation. We can either change it, or let something like this drive a wedge between us. Ideally, I'd go with him, however it's not possible. Noah's still in school and, with the baby coming, I can't just up and leave on a whim. My life isn't as flexible as his. And maybe his shouldn't be easily adjusted whenever he feels the need, but I married him knowing his career is very important.

My fingers trail over one of his newest tattoos. Noah's name is inked into his skin between his shoulder blades. It's bold and beautiful. He relaxes under my touch, hanging his head as I trace each letter, following the design.

"I imagine our new son's name will go here," I say, letting my finger glide over his back, right below Noah's name.

Liam clears his throat. "We need to pick out a name."

"We have time."

"Do we?" he asks as he turns on the stool to face me. His hands immediately find a home on my hips as if they're keeping me grounded.

An overwhelming sense of loss washes over me as I study his other tattoo. A football adorns his shoulder with Mason's number and stats. I asked him after he got it why his birthdate and the day he left us wasn't on there, and he said because he just needed to remember the way he lived.

"That night ..." I start, but hesitate so I can think about my words carefully. We've never spoken about the night he broke up with me. The night that ruined my life, albeit temporarily. "Mason—" I can't bring myself to say it without choking up. It's too hard to speak about him because he's missing so much.

Liam pulls me to him, resting his forehead against my chest. I hold him there, moving my fingers in and out of his hair. When he kisses my stomach I want to cry for the child we both desperately want, but are unable to conceive.

"I want to give you a child, Jojo. I'm so sorry I can't."

"You already gave me one," I remind him.

"I wasn't there, but Mason was."

When Liam looks up at me, tears overcome me and

are matched by his own. Using the pad of his thumbs, he wipes them away as fast as he can, leaving his own to fall onto his bare chest.

"I saw him go to your room. I waited in the parking lot, but you never came out. I told myself if you did, I'd stay or take you with me, but he showed up instead. Why didn't you come after me?"

"I knew it was over." The finality of my words, even years later, weighs heavily on my chest. I gasp for air and Liam's face shows concern as he holds my arms above my head until I can breathe.

"How'd you know when I didn't even know that myself?"

"You called me Josephine."

"**A**re you going to miss my baseball championship?" Noah asks, as I rummage through my side of the closet, pulling out enough clothes to last me a while. With Linda, our full-time housekeeper, staying here I'll be on my own to wash my clothes. It's a chore I'm not very good at, so I figure if I pack enough to last me, I should be okay.

"Are you going to make it to the championship?"

Noah scoffs, looking at me as if I've asked the dumbest question ever. Confidence is one trait he's gotten from me tenfold. If he tells me he's going to walk on water, I'll believe him. He's determined to succeed at everything.

"Of course we will. Nick says we're the strongest team in the state and have an excellent chance at making it to Williamsport."

I want to be a petulant child and roll my eyes at the mention of Nick, but I've made promises to my son and wife. I'm playing nice. I'm sharing, even when I don't want to. I pause and take a good hard look at Noah and conclude that he is light years ahead of where I was at his age in maturity. He has faith in his coach to lead them to the coveted prize of the Little League World Series. And if he does, if Nick comes through with these kids, you can bet your ass I'll be there.

"When playoffs start, I'll be home," I tell him, but he looks skeptical. He shouldn't look at me like that even though I know I've earned it. Here I am trying to build a life with him and Josie, only to leave when she's going to need me the most. Noah should remember that the second I found out about him, I wanted to be a part of his life. Has it been easy? No, it hasn't. He and I walk the line on who's the boss and how much authority I have. It's hard to be the mean guy when you're ten years removed from the situation.

Noah picks up his acoustic guitar and strums a few lines. When he asked me to teach him to play, I jumped at the opportunity. I also asked him if he wanted to learn the drums, piano, Karate, or take dance lessons. The latter earned me a dirty look. I refuse to be like Sterling and make him only play football. Noah's a damn good pitcher, as well, and it makes me proud that he's not specializing in only one sport. That's what Sterling wanted and achieved with me. I think his proudest moment was when the huge sign was perched in our front yard declaring the house as my residence. I hated the sign, but never said anything because it wasn't my place. I was just a pawn in Sterling's life, one that let him down completely.

Since I've been back in Beaumont, I have never seen my father. I'm not looking for him either. I'm sure I've passed him driving down the street or maybe even leaving the bank. Linda does all our shopping and he wouldn't dare step inside of Josie's shop. It's best we never speak. My mom is a different story. She's been over a few times to see Noah, but it takes her days to build up the courage to actually pull into our driveway. She's trying to get to know her grandson, even if she can't look Josie or me in the eyes. My mom also knows that Josie and I are waiting for an apology. It's not how she treated me growing up, but what she allowed Sterling to do to Josie when she came knocking on the door, pregnant and afraid, that is unforgiveable. She should've sought her out and gotten in touch with me, but she cowered in the corner, drinking herself into a stupor instead of doing the right thing. I can easily forgive her for her actions toward me but not Noah.

I shake my head to clear my thoughts about my parents and focus on Noah. He's tuned me out, getting lost in the simple chords of "She's Like the Wind". He didn't ask me to teach him this song but when I heard him practicing it, I couldn't stop myself from asking if he wanted to take up dancing. It was a low blow, I know. It turns out, Josie used to make him dance with her when she watched the movie, *Dirty Dancing*. He was learning the song for his mom and I had made a stupid joke about it. I quickly learned it so I could teach him and now he plays it better than I do.

"You're getting a lot better. You don't need to look at your finger placements on the fret board as often."

"I have a good teacher."

I shrug. I'm only as good as my student allows me to be, and he knows this. I could have him practicing every day, but I want him to be a kid. I want him to go outside and get dirty in the mud, race his bike down the street and come home when the street lights are on, exhausted and excited for the next day.

"Are you going to take care of your mom while I'm gone?"

Noah stops and sets his guitar down on my bed. From where I'm standing and he's seated, we have a perfect view of each other. Sometimes when I look at him I see me, other times it's Josie. It's hard to fathom that we created him and that I missed most of his life. When I glance at him now, I see worry and trepidation. I put those there in his mind.

I stop pulling clothes off my shelf and go sit by him. I remember so much at his age. How happy I was playing with Mason, how throwing a football around was fun and how we couldn't wait until high school. That all changed for me in middle school. For Noah, the change is there, just different. We've been performing locally for a while and he came with us on the one tour we've done since I've been in his life. This time it's different. This time he's going to experience what it's like to be the son of a musician. Most children grow into the role. He's being thrown in to it.

"Do you have to go?" he asks, picking at the hem of his frayed shorts. He bought them like that, much to Josie's chagrin. When I told her it's the style, she threw her hands up and left the store, muttering something about spending money on clothes with pre-made holes. But his shorts are identical to mine and I think that's why he wanted them.

"Yeah, I do. Trixie helped me a lot when I was a kid looking for a place to play. She'd let me play at her club and I slowly started to build a following. If it weren't for her and my grandmother, I don't know what I'd be doing right now."

Noah sighs, turning so he's facing me. One foot dangles off the bed, swinging back and forth, while his other is tucked under his leg.

"Why can't you wait until after school is out?"

Ideally, that's what we'd like to do but time is of the essence. Not that I expect my son to understand someone else's plight.

"The club that Trixie owns has been in her family for a long time and it's closing because she doesn't have the money to keep it open. There are a few of us going that started out there, and we're going back in hopes to help her stay open a little longer. I wish I could tell everyone that we need to wait but, if I do, I'll be too late. And Harrison and JD are going whether I go or not."

"Do you remember when you first came here?"

"Of course I do." I'm not likely to forget the two moments that changed my life.

"Nick was mad that you were at Uncle Mason's funeral and I heard him telling Mom that you're never going to stay and raise a family."

"Nick's wrong," I immediately tell him. "Mistakes were made when your mom and I were younger. So many things could've been different, but your mom and I can't change the past. I'm not leaving you guys behind. I'm going to work. I'm not any different from other dads."

This seems to spark a smile out of Noah. "Yes, you are."

I shake my head. "No, Noah, I'm really not. Every day I wake up, take you to school, and go to my studio to write or work on new music. My job is making me take a business trip, and that means I'll bring home all these cool presents or whatever it is that us dads do. It's really no different from when Nick went to Africa and came back with Aubrey."

The mention of Nick returning with Aubrey causes Noah's eyes to go wide. That scenario probably wasn't the best one to use since he left and came back with a wife.

"Bad example," I say, quickly diffusing the situation. "What I mean is parents sometimes have to go away for business, and that's all I'm doing. The band is going to play a few gigs, help out an old friend, and we'll be home before you know it."

"Do you think I could join the band?" Noah picks up his guitar and strums quickly and very out of tune while making a Gene Simmons face.

I set my hand over his to stop my ears from bleeding and try to fight back the laughter to no avail. My son is damn cute and funny, and he makes me believe in myself.

"You can be anything you want to be, Noah. I'm not going to stand in your way. I'll be standing next to you, guiding and offering you all the support that you'll need. When you succeed, I'll be the first one to congratulate you unless your mom beats me to it. And if you fail, I'll be there to pick up the pieces."

Dads aren't supposed to be sentimental, but I am. He's far too important for me to hold back and not tell him how I feel. My father did that. I won't. I won't have a troubled relationship with my son, or be that parent he can't come to whether it's good or bad.

I lightly punch his shoulder and get a grin in return. "Okay, enough heavy stuff. When are you going to play the song for your mom?"

Noah returns to playing, focusing on the song this time. He hums a few lines and makes it really obvious he really doesn't know the words.

"Can I help?" I ask, not wanting to step on his toes or get in his way.

"Sure."

"What if you play and I sing?"

A thousand watt smile beams on his face as he fist pumps the air. "Mom is going to freaking love this."

I quickly pull up the lyrics on my phone and read them over.

"Hey, Dad," he says, interrupting my studying.

"What's up?"

"Do you think we could go to the studio and pretend like we're actually laying down a track?"

Sometimes I just want to reach out, grab him and hold on, never letting go. This would be one of those moments. I've learned over the years, though, that too much affection is frowned upon when you're a teenage boy.

"I think that's a great idea. This way, once we

perform, your mom can listen to it over and over again and we won't have to treat her like a crazy fan girl."

"Oh, she's a fan girl all right."

I stop dead in my tracks and bust out laughing. There have been times when I'd serenade Josie, only for her to go completely crazy and chase me around the house. It's all in good fun. Noah doesn't have a clue about how crazy the fans can get, though, and that is something I'm trying to shield him from. The last thing I want is my son to witness women throwing their panties on stage, or cat fighting with security so they can get backstage. My favorite one is the one where they pretend they're sick and get to use the bathroom nearest the green room. It never fails that they sneak past security and end up waiting for us.

I'll take Josie's type of fan girl over that any day.

9

———

JOSIE

**J**immy tweeted.

That is the only viable explanation as to why *Whimsicality* has a line outside the door. I shouldn't complain, I'm grateful for the business. I'm just not prepared. Tonight was supposed to be about Liam and me. I was going to close the café before dinner and go home to my husband. With the band leaving tonight I need to spend every possible second with him. The last couple of days—actually, more like hours—have been crazy. The fight we had, followed by my revelation, has left us both hurting in ways we can't fix right now. Memories of the night he left still haunt me, and for me to throw it in his face was uncalled for. He's told me why he left, why things ended for us, and I need to accept it and move on. If I can't, I'm not in our marriage for the right reasons.

When Dana, one of my waitresses, called begging for help I knew something was up. While my business is successful, we're not over the top busy unless it's an open mic night or the guys are playing. Neither of which were supposed to happen tonight until Jimmy sent out his tweet: *4225 West impromptu gig at Whims before we head to L.A.!* It only took a swipe of my thumb to see what her panic was about.

And now that I'm here, I see the panic was well warranted. The band has treated the locals very well. If they're not playing for free, they're donating their time and money to different causes. Just last week, they were the hosts of a cancer walk that brought in the most money ever raised in Beaumont. When Liam moved back, and was subsequently followed by Harrison and Jimmy, I thought for sure that the paparazzi would be everywhere. At first they were, but Liam has made it a point not to hide. The only place he, Noah, and I are off limits is at home. Anywhere else he'll smile for the camera or give a quick interview if they ask him to. In turn, they leave Noah and me alone.

As of late, the photographers and journalists have been few and far between. I hadn't even noticed until Liam expressed a strong desire to return to Los Angeles to revive their careers. I had become so comfortable in my role as his wife that I hadn't realized that his career was suffering. His nights spent in the studio, long after Noah and I have gone to bed, haven't gone unnoticed. I just didn't know the band was losing its grip on the charts. I've been living blindly, or Liam has been sheltering me. Either way, it's not good for our marriage and it's definitely not good for his career.

When we married, I knew what I was getting into. I

never asked him to stop, and even if I did, I don't think he would've. Music is his outlet. It's his release. Liam loves me unconditionally, but his music is what grounds him. It's really no different from his football days. In front of a crowd, he's king. Their cheers fuel his body. He needs them as much as I need him.

I once read an article written by another musician's wife in which she explained it was only after their divorce that she realized the music was her competition. It wasn't the booze, drugs, or other women, but the music. Her words gave me pause. Her words reminded me that being married to someone like Liam, someone who is competitive, driven, stubborn, and compassionate about all things in life, is like being married to multiple people. Liam, himself, reminded me of that the other night. When he's on stage, he's Liam Page, a performer. When he's with me, with Noah, with our friends and away from the music, he's Liam Westbury. Accepting one without the other is not possible.

The shattering of ceramic grabs my attention. My eyes dart around the room, looking for the cause of the commotion. David gives me a sheepish look before he starts to clean up the broken mug. Having started last fall, along with Dana and Sarah, he's been working here for almost a year. I don't know what I'm going to do without them come summer. They'll go home once the college semester is done, and I'll be rallying Katelyn and Jenna to come in and work. Even if they agree, it'll only be temporary. Their lives have changed so much in the past few years, and neither of them have to work. Technically none of us do, but I can't give up the café or the flower shop. They were my dreams, and I followed them, just as Liam followed his.

A single tear falls from my eye, catching me off guard. I've been an emotional roller coaster since Liam said he was leaving. Last time we went with the band, but it's not possible now. I'm afraid to ask how long he's going to be gone. By the evidence left in our closet, he's planning for the long haul.

It's hard for me to understand why this woman means so much to him. I get that she gave him a shot, but I can't help thinking this is a bad case of keeping strings attached. His life is here, with me. I need him here, not gallivanting around Los Angeles playing gigs to raise money for a rundown bar. His big heart can stay here and help Ralph's, even if it's running better than ever because of the support the band gives it.

I have goose bumps on my arms before he even walks in the door. How, after all this time, can Liam affect me like this? He pauses and looks at me. His lower lip is tucked between his teeth and his head is angled just enough to cause the butterflies in my stomach to start fluttering. I take him in, all of him, with his torn up jeans hanging low on his hips, to his button down shirt showing just the beginning of the J of his tattoo. His sleeves are rolled up, adding definition to his arms, but it's his left hand that catches my attention. His freshly polished wedding band is the focal point. I put that there, and he wears it proudly. I hate that he didn't shave. I hate that I'm going to miss running my fingers through his stubble tonight and all I'll be able to do is imagine the feel of his skin against mine. My memory is going to have to be on point while he's gone and he knows that. He's standing there while Harrison and Jimmy filter around him, letting me drink him in, allowing me to burn him into my memory for later.

"God, your husband is hot."

"I know," I answer in kind to Dana. When I look at her, I swear I spot a bit of drool coming out of her mouth. I don't blame her. I go to bed with this man every night and here I am staring like a horny teenager wondering how I'm going to get that guy's number. If I weren't married to him, I'd be figuring out a way.

Behind him, Noah walks in dressed similarly to Liam. My mouth drops open, causing Liam to chuckle. I want to go over and ask the men in my life what's going on, but something tells me that I need to stay where I am. Liam says something to Noah, who looks at me and winks. I cover my mouth in shock and elation. Seeing them together like this is magical.

"I hope you have a shotgun," Dana says.

"Why?"

She shakes her head. "Liam Junior is going to have a flock of women coming after him."

"I'm not ready for those days."

"Yeah, well, they're coming soon." She leaves me standing at the counter, watching the men put their equipment together. I'm startled when a warm hand encases mine. I look down to find Peyton by my side. For all of my worries about Liam, I tend to forget about how much Harrison leaving is affecting Quinn and the girls. I thought Quinn would be used to it, but he always went on tour with the band, so this will be something new for him. It's a good thing he has Katelyn to help him through it. It's refreshing to see how well she and Quinn have adapted ... you'd think she's his biological mom. Peyton and Elle, on the other hand, are so attached to Harrison that it can't be easy for them to know he won't be there when they wake up in the morning. I'm expecting some serious meltdowns from Peyton.

"I don't like what he's wearing."

My eyes go from her to Harrison and back to her. She's dressed in her usual wear—gym shorts, a football shirt, and tennis shoes.

"You don't like what your dad is wearing?"

Peyton looks up at me with her baby blue eyes. Her long brown hair is in a messy ponytail, which I'm sure she did herself because she refuses to let Katelyn touch her hair.

"Noah. I don't like that he looks like that. Football players aren't supposed to dress funky."

I can only nod and keep my comments to myself. I've suspected a crush was developing, but thought it would pass. The five-year age difference, while it's an issue now, won't always be. Not that I expect them to end up together.

"I don't know why Noah is dressed like his dad tonight, maybe they got dressed together?" I'm grasping at straws here and she knows it. Since she and Harrison found a common bond, we've all been able to relax a little. Losing Mason, while extremely hard on all of us, shattered her world. For the longest time it was like we were walking on eggshells. That is, of course, unless your name is Liam or Noah. They can do no wrong when it comes to Peyton.

As soon as Noah pulls out his guitar, my heart starts to beat a little faster. Liam is encouraging Noah to do anything he wants, and when he asked to learn how to play, Liam happily taught him. Occasionally, I hear Noah practicing in his room, but he's never played for me.

"I think we should get a seat." I tug on Peyton's hand, and even though she sighs loudly, she follows. Katelyn, Elle, Jenna, and Eden have seats saved for us. Eden is yelling for Jimmy and getting angry that he's not coming for her. She has him wrapped around her finger. If ever there were a family that needed each other, it's them. Jimmy needed Jenna to change his ways, and she needed him to find herself again. Eden was just the icing on their proverbial cake. She makes them both better people.

"We want to thank everyone for coming tonight. I know there's a bunch of you still outside, and if you can hear me, please listen to Sarah at the door when she tells you to wait."

Liam pulls a stool closer to his mic stand and winks at me. "So, tonight, 4225 *West* is heading back to L.A."

The collective groan from the patrons reverberates through me. I can relate.

"In our careers, we all start somewhere and the place where we started is going under. We're going to try and save it. We don't know if we'll be successful, but we owe it to the owner to help her. So tonight, we're going to give you a little show before we have to catch the red-eye. But up first is my son who has something special to say."

My heart soars with pride as Noah steps up to the

microphone. He clears his throat, looks at Liam—who nods—and then looks at the audience.

"My dad helped me learn this song for my mom."

Katelyn squeezes my leg as once again, my mouth falls open. Noah and Liam sit down on their respective stools, both holding guitars. Noah strums the first chord, followed by Liam, who can't take his eyes off our son. A look of pride and encouragement is in the smile Liam holds as he watches Noah move his fingers up and down the fret board.

I know the song in an instant as the lyrics come pouring out of Liam's mouth. His eyes are focused on me as he sings. "She's Like the Wind" is one of my favorites and I used to make Noah dance to it with me over and over again. It has always reminded me of Liam and to hear him sing the words now brings tears to my eyes.

I don't know who to watch, Liam or Noah. My watery eyes are moving back and forth between the two loves of my life as they play this song for me. Harrison and Jimmy have chimed in and are playing the melody behind my guys, with Harrison even singing backup. The group effort isn't lost on me, even though I'm focused on the Westbury men.

Before I know it, the song is over and I'm bum rushing the stage, pulling both of them into my arms. Noah's arms are wrapped around my waist as I cry into Liam's shirt. So much for him looking dapper tonight, now he looks like a snot rag. Maybe that will deter any women from speaking to him on the plane.

"I don't know what to say. Is this why you wouldn't play in front of me?" I ask Noah.

He looks up, still holding on to my waist. "Yes. Dad tried to get me to sing, but that's his thing."

"It was beautiful, thank you so much." I let my fingers comb through his hair, which is just slightly longer than Liam's right now. He looks more like his dad with each passing day. I know deep in my heart if Liam hadn't come back when he did, I'd be looking for him.

When I glance at Liam, he's beaming with joy at Noah and his accomplishment.

"Thank you for this. I really needed it."

"Anything for the woman we love," Liam says, kissing me chastely on the lips.

The crowd behind us erupts in a cheer, much to my embarrassment. Noah takes my hand and leads me off stage so the guys can put on the show they promised their fans. Peyton slides one seat over to the left, instead of moving closer to her mom. She wants to sit by Noah who is all too eager to start talking to her. I know there's going to come a time when he won't have anything to do with her and that's going to be hard on Peyton. Not sure how Katelyn will prepare her for that day. I just pray it doesn't happen anytime soon.

# 10

## LIAM

The motorcycle speeds by, dangerously close to the limousine. Sam is yelling at the driver to step on it while the driver is cussing at her in some language I've never heard before. We're a wreck waiting to happen.

"The windows are tinted and we're over an hour early for our flight. What's the rush, Sam?" Harrison asks, as he pulls the strap on his seatbelt. His gesture reminds me to put mine on, and I kick JD in the shoe and motion for him to buckle up as well. I can feel Sam glaring at me, but I don't care. I'm not a free spirit like her.

"It's the rush, Harrison. You're rockers. Live on the edge, be free, and take a fucking risk every now again."

"I have a son, which means he needs me." Harrison pushes the button that drops the window between us and the driver. "Slow down, my friend. We're in no hurry. Don't listen to the crazy bitch."

"Ah fuck," I mumble as Sam's face turns red. If she

were a cartoon character, steam would be billowing out of her ears right now. Harrison doesn't give a shit, though, and neither should I, but I'm always the one that gets stuck with her.

As luck would have it, she doesn't say anything. For now, that's a good thing, but he'll likely pay later. Harrison has asked me repeatedly what I see in her. Truth is, I'm not sure. Most of the time she's a ragging bitch, but other times she's sweet and can be one of the nicest people I know. I don't know if she's suffering from a bad case of PMS or what, but she and Harrison do not get along.

The second we pull up to the terminal my seatbelt is off and I'm out of the door. I'm not waiting for the driver to come around to let me out. That's not who I am even if that's who Sam wants me to be. I can also carry my own bags and wheel my own suitcase, another habit that drives her batty.

At LAX the paps are everywhere. It's harder than hell to get through the terminal without getting your picture taken. And there's no point in fighting it. So while the car is being unloaded, Harrison, JD, and I stand here with our bags in our hands while our manager is barking orders at anyone who will listen. Why we're flying when the rest of our crew is on the tour bus, I have no idea, but I don't like it. I think treating them differently is wrong and the fact that they're leaving their families for months on end to live on the road, is a sacrifice they're willing to make and I should be making it, too.

Flash bulbs are going off like crazy. Our names are being called and told to look in their direction. We ignore them, but don't move from our spots, giving them ample opportunity to get their images. We're asked personal questions. Most of them invade our privacy. My favorites are about my mystery love child, mine and Sam's wedding (which will never happen) and if I'm sleeping with the newest 'it' girl.

When I first arrived on the scene, I'd answer anything. Unless it had to do with back home, those questions were dodged like a bullet. That was my old life, one I didn't want to bring into my new life ... or to even think about it, truth be told. The memories of home are painful and I'm still trying to get over them.

Walking through the terminal, we follow Sam, who manages to power walk in five-inch heels. She makes us follow behind her, forgetting that she works for us. A couple times we've talked about firing her, moving on to a different company, but when you look at the numbers and the tours and venues we're playing in, you can't help but give her some credit for getting us where we are. Yes, it's our music, but she's the one who is selling us to the promoters. No, firing her would be a bad idea, even if she drives us to drink.

A luxury of having money is that we fly first class, and we get to wait in the lounge until our names are called. It never fails that we'll run into a fan or two, but for the most part they just want to talk. They just want to get to know us and feel like we're all on the same level which is nice and relaxing until you meet the one crazy who was able to upgrade her flight. That's when Sam steps in. That's when she's very useful for us at the airport.

As soon as our plane touches down, the telltale clicking of seatbelts being slid out of their buckles echo throughout the cabin, breaking the standard rule of waiting until we're stopped at the gate. For the first time in years, we flew coach. Our last flight had been with Sam, giving each of us someone to share a seat with. I was always with her while Harrison and JD sat next to each other. This time we just took up a row, keeping our arm rests pushed back and our trays full of work.

Gone are the days where fans would greet us at the airport and paparazzi are here happily clicking the shutter button on their cameras for tomorrow's spread in Page Six. The lackluster fanfare for our arrival is disappointing, not that I expected anything different.

"Didn't you tweet that we were arriving?" I had asked JD to post what time we were arriving, hoping to stir up some attention. Apparently, tweeting your location only works in Beaumont because we're standing in the wide open at LAX and people are passing us right and left without a second glance. This is freaking Los Angeles, and no one cares that 4225 *West* is standing in the airport looking like idiots, begging for attention.

"Yeah, I did," he says, pulling out his phone. He rambles off the number of favorites and retweets he's received, but none of them matter. The lack of a welcoming crowd only proves what I've been saying all along. We need to be in Los Angeles if we want to be successful. This place is what makes or breaks you, and right now, we're definitely broken.

"Well, boys, we're back," Harrison says as he shoulders his bag.

"We should have a car waiting to take us to the Wilshire."

"Your home away from home," JD says, reminding me that I used to live there. My happiest memory is the day that Josie came to my place for dinner. I wanted to seduce her; remind her of the connection we had and could still have. I was on the cusp of doing something foolish, but pulled back. She was promised to another man and as much as I didn't care about him, I cared about her.

When we step outside, the black Town Car is there to take us to the hotel. I don't know why I chose the Wilshire. It was either familiarity, convenience, or just out of habit, but I'm currently second-guessing myself. There's too much history and bad memories mixed with only one good one. We pile in, with me being the last one inside the car. As soon as I shut the door, I want to beat the shit out of Harrison and JD for not bailing as soon as they saw Mr. Moreno across from them.

"What the fuck are you doing in my car?" I ask, not sugar coating the hostility rolling off my tongue.

He takes off his hat. He's aged tremendously since the last time we saw him. Our last encounter was in court when we filed a restraining order against Sam, and if I'm not mistaken that included Moreno Entertainment. Truth be told, the only thing the old man did wrong was protect his daughter. Any father would, but when you're running a business sometimes you need to forget your employees are family.

"I thought we could talk business."

"We're not interested," Harrison says. JD and I both nod in agreement.

Moreno cracks a smile. His bald head is shining

thanks to the oncoming headlights and I find myself trying not to laugh. If Noah were here, he'd be cracking jokes and this would be the one time I'd tell him not to mind his elders.

"It's no secret you guys are struggling." His voice is gruff, sounding like he's had one too many cigars. He probably has, although I've never seen him with one. I've spent ample time in his mansion, being catered to while I sat by the pool, and not once did I see this man smoke. Drink, yes. He can handle his liquor better than anyone I know.

I shake my head, biting the inside of my cheek. "We're fine."

He scoffs, knowing the truth. "Your manager is good, but he doesn't have the nuts to get you guys the deals you're used to. You guys are has-beens when you were destined to be on top. You packed up for your la la land life and look at where it's got you ... playing free gigs at your wife's café."

All three of us are silent and still, knowing he's right. But I did this. What I should've done was break up the band so they could pursue their careers. Instead, they followed me and started their lives, getting married and raising kids. I mean, that's what we are now—family men.

Moreno leans forward, pointing his hat at us. "You know I'm right and you know you miss it. You miss seeing your name in lights, flashing across the marquee. You want to hear your fans screaming your name, crawling over each other just so they can touch you. The bright lights of movie premieres, award shows and having that spotlight shine down on you, illuminating you from darkness it's why you became the group you are."

"We're fine," I say out of spite, but my voice lacks the conviction. I never want to admit a man like him is right, but fuck if he's not.

"Keep telling yourself that, Page. I can see it in your eyes. All of your eyes."

The car comes to a stop and Mr. Moreno starts to slide out. He doesn't look at me, only Harrison and JD. "Don't let this idiot ruin your careers. You know how to reach me."

Before any of us can rebuke his comment, the door is slammed shut and we're speeding down the road. The silence is so thick a chainsaw wouldn't be able to hack through it. I keep my eyes down, unable to face my friends, my family. I don't want to know what they're thinking and I'm in no mood to tell them what I am. They don't need to know that I've been considering moving back to L.A., that I've been trying to find a way to make it work before I give Josie the proposal. Each time I think about bringing it up, I remind myself of how selfish I am for even considering it. I came back to Beaumont for her and Noah. They didn't come for me.

I don't realize that we've stopped until the door is open and the driver is welcoming us to the Wilshire. I'm suddenly sick to my stomach with fear, thinking that as soon as I step out of this car and onto the streets of Los Angeles, I'm making yet another mistake. It seems fitting since the last time I made a life-altering mistake it had to do with this place. There's a power here that controls you, it guides and destroys if you're not careful. I need to be careful.

"Welcome home, Mr. Page. The Wilshire family has missed you," a short brunette greets me, and instantly wraps her arm in mine before she guides us into the lobby. Harrison and JD are left behind with the bags. I try to stop and wait with them, but her grip is firm and before I know it, we're in front of the elevator for the penthouses. Pulling my arm out, I put my hand up.

"I need to wait for my friends."

This doesn't seem to please her, evident by the frown on her face, but I don't care. For all I know she's an escort sent by Moreno. If he's testing my loyalty to Josie, he's a moron. There isn't a chick on this planet that can compete with my wife. And every other woman I've ever been with, including his daughter, I always compared to my Jojo. That should tell him something.

Harrison frowns when I reach him, and I just shake my head. I have no doubt we're thinking the same thing. As much as it would skyrocket our career, bring us to the forefront of mainstream, being with Moreno Entertainment is deadly. I hate to admit he's right, though, we need him, or someone like him. The only benefit of working with him is getting to stay in Beaumont. Everyone else will want us here or in New York.

As soon as we're checked in and keys are handed over, we're dragging our sorry asses into the elevator. Too many thoughts are filtering through my mind as we speed to the top floors and it takes a shoulder bump from JD to let me know we're about to get off.

We go opposite ways, each of us with our own places. We did this because Jenna and Eden are coming out in a few days to stay with JD. No one needs to be privy to what goes on behind their closed door. It makes me wonder if Katelyn will bring the kids out. I'm sure if she does, they'll stay at their beach house. And that leaves me. Josie won't fly to L.A. because of the café, and Noah's baseball schedule ... and the fact that the baby will be here any day now. I'll be left alone to contemplate and stress about the band and whether we're going to continue. We have two options: stay in Beaumont and do small shows every now and again, or return to the band we were when we were in high demand. I miss those days.

Opening the door to the penthouse, it's like déjà vu; even though this isn't the one I used to live in, it's just decorated the same. It's an eerie feeling, being back here, and realizing how easy ... and yet lonely, my life really was.

## 11

## JOSIE

L ast night I lay in bed and cried. I let my tears soak Liam's pillow as I hugged it to my chest. Every thought I had ended up the same ... my husband is gone. It's not the first time he's gone on tour. He's been to New York to see their somewhat manager, Gary. Each time I've been okay with his trips, until now. There's something about Los Angeles that scares me. I can't put my finger on it, aside from the fact that it's the place that ended us. If his grandmother hadn't lived there, he would've never gone. Liam could've easily played music while living in Texas for college or ... no, there isn't an "or" because L.A. was his calling and he probably would've ended up there with or without his grandma.

The house feels empty even though everything is still in its place. Everywhere I look, I see Liam. I just can't sense him. I flick the light illuminating our closet. Most of his clothes are gone, which is hard for me to fathom. If this trip is supposed to be short, why did he need to take everything? Wouldn't he just pack a few things, enough to get him by? His missing wardrobe feels like there's finality in this situation, that we're over, but he couldn't tell me. I know better than to think like that.

I pick up a few of his things that are scattered on the floor and put them in the hamper before making my way into the bathroom. Every woman dreams of having a master suite with a large walk-in closet and a bathroom big enough so that two people can share without feeling cramped. At one point, this was my dream. When I was younger, I knew what football players were making and how lavishly they lived. I selfishly wanted that. I wanted our house to be featured on television and written about in the press. It was my dream to live like Cinderella after I married my prince. And now that I have it, I'd give it all up just to have Liam walk through the door with a shit-eating grin on his face, announcing he's home.

*It's not going to happen.* That's what I tell myself as I look at my reflection in the mirror. The lack of sleep is evident by the puffy bags under my eyes. Coupled with my bloodshot, red-rimmed eyes, it looks like I've been on an all-night bender. He hasn't even been gone twenty-four hours and I already look like death. I'm not sure I have enough concealer or eye drops to hide the fact that I'm a wreck.

"The girls will look the same," I mutter to the mirror that sadly doesn't answer. It's ridiculous that I hope Katelyn and Jenna had the same shitty night I did.

After a long, hot shower, doing my hair and attempting to conceal the bags under my eyes, I'm stepping into a baby blue sundress. Today is my baby shower, or rather a shower for the baby boy we're about to adopt. I told the girls that I didn't need one, but they insisted.

As I smooth down the front of my dress, my hand rests over my stomach. The absence of a baby there while having a baby shower is not lost on me. I'm over the moon that we're able to adopt, that Aubrey was kind of enough to think of us, but having our own child is something I wanted Liam to experience with me. Now he's not even experiencing this moment and I find myself wondering if I were as pregnant as Meredith is now, would he have left … again? I try not to compare the first time to now. Had Liam known, he would've stayed.

When I get downstairs, Noah is sitting at the table with his hands folded. He looks up and smiles, reminding me of a young Liam, and dressed in his Sunday best. I can't get over how much he resembles his father, and as long as he doesn't act like him, I'll be okay. I know what Liam was like in high school because I was on the receiving end. I shudder at the thought of Noah taking girls to the dugouts, or having sex in this car. I have promised myself, though, that I'll be accepting of any girl he brings home. I'll never make her feel unwanted, whether I like her or not. No one should have to go through what I did.

"Are you ready?"

He rolls his eyes and stands reluctantly.

"Quinn will be there."

Noah shrugs. I know he and Quinn don't always get along. Noah loves his sports while Quinn is more artistic. They both enjoy music and video games, but Noah is more drawn to Peyton and I think it's because he's known her longer and they share a bond over Mason. I also think that Noah resents Quinn a little because he's grown up with Liam, something Noah didn't have a chance to do.

The drive over to Katelyn's is quiet. Noah stares out the window, only turning his head more when he sees some of his friends at the park.

"You can go later if you want," I tell him as we drive past.

"I'll call my ... Nick," he says, finishing his sentence. I pat his leg, only for him to move slightly away. The gesture isn't lost on me. He's getting older and having his mom touch him isn't cool.

"I know Nick will like that." Nick wants to tell Noah that Aubrey is pregnant. I just hope Noah takes it better than the adoption news. He doesn't realize this now, but I have a feeling he's going to be an amazing big brother.

The neighborhood where Harrison and Katelyn live is lined with cars. As I make my way to their house there's a spot in the driveway saying "Reserved for Expectant Mom".

"I think that's where you park," Noah says as I pull in.

"You think so?" I ask, hoping to engage him in a little bit of conversation.

"Yeah, they need you close so you can carry all that crap you're getting today."

I look at him questioningly and he shrugs. "What? I looked a baby shower up online and I bet tonight you'll be sitting in the baby's room going over everything, saying how I was once that tiny."

"You were," I remind him, earning an eye-roll.

He opens his door without saying anything. I hate that he's growing up. It won't be long until he's heading off to the same overnight camps that Liam went to and entering high school. He'll be walking the same halls that Liam commanded and at the pace he's going with football, he'll be making his own mark. Liam has already told him that there's no shadow looming over him and he's his own player. That is the one thing Liam fears—that Noah will be compared to him. Neither of us wants that for Noah.

Before I know what's happening, my son is opening my car door and holding his hand out for me to grab.

"Thank you," I tell him, my voice catching when he holds his arm out for me to hang onto.

"Dad said I needed to be the man of the house and he would do this, right?"

"He would." I nod, trying to hold back tears of happiness.

Noah guides me into Katelyn's house, which has been decorated in massive amounts of blue. Old classmates that I haven't seen in a long time greet me with congratulatory expressions. A few of them ask where Liam is and I want to say at home because men usually don't attend baby showers, but I tell them he's working. Always working.

My mom greets us at the door, offering me a quick hug before crouching down to talk to Noah. He's taller than her, but she likes looking up at him.

Eden comes running toward me and I scoop her up, relishing in her tiny baby hugs. She babbles non-stop as she and I have our own conversation until she wants down so she can chase the kids. Katelyn and Jenna both pull me into a hug; a hug that means something different to everyone else here. We're going through something a lot of women don't understand, and as long as we have each other, we should be okay. At least that's what I'm going to tell myself every day until my husband is back in my arms.

When we pull apart I see the same worry in their faces that I wear on mine. I want to reassure them that everything will be fine, but I can't even bring myself to think that. This trip means something different for me than it does them. I have a bad feeling that I can't shake.

"There's food, lots and lots of food," Katelyn says as she pulls me into the dining room. The twins are dressed identical in dresses, much to Peyton's chagrin. If ever there were a walking definition of a tomboy, she's it. Someday she'll want to wear dresses; she just doesn't know it yet. Quinn smiles and starts filling his plate full of food.

"Are you staying?" I ask him.

He shakes his head quickly as his cheeks turn a beautiful pink. "I'll be upstairs waiting for Noah so we can play video games."

"I'm sure he's looking forward to that, Quinn." He doesn't say anything else and quickly leaves the room after more women come in.

I make myself a plate of food and grab something to drink. Katelyn signals for me to follow her into the living room where I'm directed to sit in a large chair.

"We're going to help pass out presents, Aunt Josie," Elle says, as Peyton sits down next to me.

"You can sit here and help me open them if you want," I tell her, knowing she'll be up as soon as she sees her sister getting all the attention. Looking at Peyton, quiet and a bit withdrawn, I want to yell and shake Liam for taking Harrison away from her. She's just a little girl who wants to be with her dad but can't.

Everyone gathers around me; most are holding conversations amongst themselves and every now and again I hear Liam's name. The mumbled mention of him being gone again when another baby is on the way strikes a nerve. I want to stand up and yell, telling them to stop being jealous, catty bitches but I refrain.

Noah appears before me, proudly handing me a present. "Open this one first, Mom. It's from Dad and me." Once again I have to fight the tears from coming as I tear open the blue paper.

"It's a beautiful box," I tell him, winking. He shakes his head and smiles, knowing that I'm playing with him.

"Open it," he encourages.

And I do. I lift the lid of the blue box and pull out the velvet box inside. I open the creaking lid and it reveals two Tiffany baby rattles with blue ribbons.

"Dad says we'll have the baby's name put on it once you guys decide what to call him."

"And this one?" I hold up the second one that has Noah's named engraved. He shrugs and tries to hide his smile.

"I read that moms like these, so Dad had one made for me so the baby and I could match."

There's no hiding the tears this time as I pull him into my arms. "Thank you, Noah, I love it."

"You're welcome, Mom." I hate that he pulls away so quickly, but I get it. I dab at my eyes and pray that my make-up isn't running. I don't need any pictures depicting me as the Bride of Frankenstein today.

I slide my phone out of the pocket in my dress and type a text to Liam.

**Thank you. I love the rattles and I love you.**

I hold my phone for a second longer, waiting for the conversation bubble to pop up. When it doesn't, I try not to let that bother me. I know he's busy. That he's working. But I want to be a priority and want him answering every text I send as soon as I send it.

Now that the first present is out of the way, Elle has me flooded with more. Peyton has taken the job of moving the presents around to all the guests so they can "ooh" and "aah" at all of the cuteness. I'm opening every-thing from washcloths to clothes, including onesies that say, "I'm With the Band" and "My Dad Sings All the Lullabies". Images of Liam singing to our son flood my mind. I can't wait to see him sitting in the nursery, rocking his son to sleep.

All chatter stops when the doorbell rings. I look around and don't notice anyone missing, unless it's Harrison's sister and mom, but they wouldn't ring the bell.

"I don't think she wants you here," I hear Katelyn say, causing some concern.

"Excuse me for a minute," I tell everyone as I walk

toward the door. When I enter the foyer I see the cause of Katelyn's raised voice.

"What are you doing here?" I ask my very absent mother-in-law who is standing on the porch holding a gift. The usual defiance is gone as she stands there looking at me. Liam has only seen her a few times since he moved home, and never longer than five minutes or so. To say they don't have a relationship is an understatement. I know she's been making attempts to visit Noah, although she never makes it further than the driveway.

"Bianca," my mother says from behind me. I can feel her hand on the small of my back, and I can't tell if she's pushing me forward or trying to hold me back. "I'm so happy you could make it."

Katelyn and I turn to look at my mom, who is ignoring both of us. She steps forward and pushes the screen door open so Bianca can step in.

"I'm sorry I'm late. My nerves got the best of me."

"It's understandable, but there's plenty of party food left," my mom says as she ushers my mother-in-law into the other room. I can hear her make introductions as Katelyn and I stare at each other.

"Did you know?"

She shakes her head. Of course she didn't because she wouldn't allow it.

I bite my lip, trying to keep the anger away, but it's rolling in like a bad storm. "What am I going to do?"

Katelyn places both hands on my shoulders and looks me square in the eyes. "You're going to go in there and act like you own the place. Do not let that woman ruin your day."

I nod, but can't bring myself to think positively. I pull out my phone, hoping for a text from Liam, but there isn't one.

**Your mother just showed up at my shower!!!!! WTF??**

A bell slams against the glass door, making known to anyone in the bar that someone is walking in. I don't remember it being there before, but I really only used the front entrance a few times when I was playing here. Once I got my first gig, Trixie gave me the code for the backdoor.

"We're closed."

The voice is older, hoarser, but I'll never mistake it for anyone other than Trixie. Harrison, JD, and I linger in the bar while the stranger behind the counter finishes slamming bottles around. When a head of black and white hair pulled back in a high bun pops up, I know it can be none other than Trixie. None of us say anything as she mumbles to herself and it dawns on me that she was probably hoping that whoever was at the door left.

"I told you idiots that we're closed," she says with her back facing us. We give each other a look, all three of us with our brows furrowed.

Trixie slowly turns around and places her hand on her hip. A white towel is draped over her shoulder and she looks forty years older than when I last saw her. Time has not been good to Trixie. Gone is the flawless skin and ruby red lips that I remember from years ago.

"We're closed, morons. Or are you those stupid types that don't understand English. Did Sal send you down here to spy?"

I look at Harrison and JD who both shrug wondering who the hell Sal is.

"Don't you remember me? Or us?" She should remember Harrison. Not only did he work here for years, but he was just here performing drums with a band.

"Oh I remember you; you're Charlie Page's grandson."

Hearing the name of my grandfather, a man that I never knew, catches me off guard. I knew he played here —it's where he met my grandmother—but of all the times I've been here, Trixie has never mentioned him. I don't know anything about him other than he was a musician.

"My name's Liam ... I used—"

"Ack, I know who you are. Can't you take a joke? Liam the Virgin. I'm getting older, but I'm not stupid. I remember." She starts to laugh. I laugh, too, but it's forced. For a moment I thought she had forgotten about me. I hated the nickname she gave me. Not that I expect her to remember everyone that comes through here because, believe me, she's seen a lot of musicians, but it's not been that long since I used to frequent the stage.

"This one here," she points to Harrison, "came in a

few weeks back thinking he could just take over the drum set."

"And I did," Harrison says as he sidesteps in front of me to walk around the bar. He pulls Trixie into a hug, even though she resists and playfully tries to slap him away.

JD lines up behind him with a shit-eating grin on his face. "Remember me?"

"No, but you're hot so you can give me a hug, too." JD doesn't miss a beat when he pulls her into his arms.

"You just gonna stand over there or what?"

I shrug. "Aren't you closed?"

Trixie takes the towel from her shoulder and throws it at me. I catch it mid-air with ease, thanks to the hours of catch I've been playing with Noah. We both take steps toward each other and when we do, I pick her up into a giant bear hug.

"You've been missed," she mumbles into my shoulder.

"You too." I put her down and am taken aback when she places her hands on my cheeks.

"He said he'd bring you back, but I didn't believe him."

I glance quickly at Harrison who is ignoring us. He'd do anything for Trixie, and I would, too, but within reason. Coming here and performing is what I can do for her. Not only does it help out the bar, but I'm also hoping it will revive our status amongst our peers.

"We're here to help," I tell her. She steps back and looks at us with anxiety all over her face.

"I'm going to lose the club that my grandfather started. I didn't evolve, and no one wants to play here. I'm lucky to get one or two agents through the door on a good night. It's time to throw in the towel."

Harrison and JD move back around the bar and motion for us to sit down. "If there isn't enough money after the fundraiser, we'll be here to help you close the place down," Harrison says, as he holds her hand. "My mom will come up and help wait tables or wash dishes, whatever you need her to do. If that's not enough, I'll call my sister. She's always looking for an excuse to take a vacation."

"Coming to work at a rundown bar isn't a vacation," she reminds Harrison.

"It is if you're family. Seriously, Trix, we got this. You'll have so much music coming out of these windows that people are going to be lining up to get in."

Trixie looks toward the door, likely remembering the days when she had to turn people away. I could've been one of them if it weren't for Harrison and my grandmother. My grandma never actually told me that she was meddling in my career, but I sensed it. I never said anything because she had missed so much of my life and I wanted to give her a piece of something she could hang onto.

"Well, enough crap. Get to work. This place is filthy and I have some very important people coming."

"What, are we not important?" I ask, placing my hand over my heart and batting my eyelashes at her.

She looks at me, her eyes traveling up and down my body. "You're just a dime a dozen, Liam. I've seen hundreds of you coming in and out, most of them come crawling back when they fail or they run and hide. So no, you're not important."

Trixie stands up walks away, leaving me stunned. Gone is the firecracker that I met when I first came to California and in her place is a hardened, soulless woman who has been around the scene far too long. Maybe she's the warning we need to bear in mind: If you stay too long, it'll eat you alive.

"Mate, you need to check your phone. My wifey says your missus is losing her shit." JD is staring at me when he starts rambling. I pull out my phone and tap the home button, bringing it to life. I have several missed texts from both Josie and Katelyn.

"Fuck, this can't be good," I say, as I swipe the lock screen.

The first message is happy, which causes the dread to set in. The second, not so much:

Jojo: **Your mother just showed up at my shower!!!!! WTF??**

I don't even know what to think, or why Bianca would just show up at the baby shower. Hell, I didn't even tell her we're adopting a baby.

I don't know what to say. I didn't tell her about the baby or the shower.

As soon as I hit send, a conversation bubble pops up so I wait to see what Josie has to say. Whatever needs to be done around the club can wait a few more minutes. My wife—my family—comes first.

Jojo: **MY MOTHER invited her. My own**

**freaking mother!!!! Because why? Who knows??? It's not like she doesn't know how your mother has treated me all these years.**

I'm stuck between a rock and a hard place. If I had a relationship with my mother, I'd call her and ask her to leave, but I don't. At best, we're cordial if and when I bump into her at the bank or when she visits Noah. What baffles me is why my mother-in-law would invite Bianca to Josie's shower knowing their history. I really don't know what to say to my wife that can change the situation.

**I'm sorry, babe. Talk to your mom calmly & find how why she invited Bianca. I love you. I'll call you tonight.**

I feel good telling her that I'll call her tonight. The first time I was in this club I left with a chick who just musically rocked my world. Josie was the furthest thing from my mind, until later that night when she finally called and I listened to her tell me how much she hated me, how I ruined her life. If she had just said she was pregnant, my life would've been different. Her voicemail killed me, and if I kept hearing her voice I was going to cave and go back home. As much as I loved her, I needed to find myself. I needed to prove that I could be someone other than who my father groomed me to be.

I also remember my first night in Metro. The same night I earned the nickname Liam the Virgin. It has nothing to do with my sexuality, but the fact that I had never been in a green room before. I must've stared at the posters on the walls for hours, fanboying at all the acts that had come through these doors.

I used to stare at the door, opening and closing as the people came in in droves, racing to be at the front of the stage. I stood by, off to the side, watching in awe. That night I decided on a goal: One day, I would be up on this stage, with this crowd, singing to them. They would be chanting my name, singing my lyrics and begging me for more. That's what they did with ... Layla.

I turn and stare at the stage and picture Layla with her honey-colored eyes, red hair, and infectious smile staring back at me. That girl knew what she wanted and how to get it. As much as Layla was a mistake, she changed the game for me. She gave me what I needed even if I didn't know it at the time. She was my first after Josie and one I'll never forget, but undoubtedly should.

Pressing my home button again, the screen lights up with a picture of my wife. The girl turned woman who I have loved since I was fifteen. I never stopped loving her, not once did I ever tell another woman that I loved them because they could never compare to Josie. I think about her being at home and dealing with my mother and wonder what the fuck it is that I'm doing here. JD and Harrison could've easily done all the extras that need to be done for the fundraiser and I could've flown in right before the gig.

But no, I had to be here and knew Josie would understand. This is the business side of our lives and it's not something we can just fix in the studio. The band, as a whole, needs to pound the pavement, drum up some support, and make sure that Metro is back on top ... or that, at the very least, it goes out with a bang.

**I love you**

I send Josie those three words one more time before pocketing my phone. Taking a look around the club, I notice pictures need to be straightened, so that's where I start. We're not here to clean, but apparently that's what Trixie needs from us right now. JD is sweeping and Harrison is stocking the bar. We're all doing grunt work.

"Doesn't she have staff?" I yell out to anyone who wants to answer.

"You dumbass," Harrison says. "She's closed! Don't you remember she used to give her staff the day off and she'd come in and clean?"

I pause and look at Harrison, wondering why the hell he insisted on being here today.

"Did you tell her we'd clean the club?"

He smiles and continues to put away the clean glasses.

"Rat bastard," I mumble to myself as I straighten picture after picture. I'm starting to doubt that her normal staff actually cleans, unless the crowd just got rowdy last night. I'm about to give up and call someone to come and do this for us—I love my maid, Linda; she never makes me clean—when someone knocks on the door.

"I'll get it," I say, already bored with working. I push the door open and before I can say anything I'm holding an armful of Layla who is squealing in delight.

"Holy shit, it's you."

As I look over her shoulder, I see a photographer. I don't see a single one in LAX, but outside *Metro* with another woman in my arms, and sure as shit he's taking pictures.

"It's me all right," I say as I set her down. I move quickly to pull her into the club, away from prying eyes and whatever else may be out there.

13
———

## JOSIE

The nursery is a mess. Linda offered to unpack and wash everything, but I told her I would do it. Staying busy will keep my mind off the fact that Liam isn't here to experience this with me. The only baby item that is somewhat ready to go is the crib. Liam and Noah stayed up and put it together before Liam left. I'm thankful that they did. I think every dad should put together his child's crib. It's a rite of passage or whatever you want to call it.

Leaning against the doorjamb, I eye the packages and baskets that are piled high. The amount of clothes, toys, and necessities is overwhelming. I had a baby shower with Noah, but all my friends were college students and their money was better spent on laundry and pizza, not baby gifts. This time it's different, and I'm thankful even if the task before me is daunting.

I thought I'd be eager to come home and look at everything again, but I still can't shake the fact that

Bianca showed up. Her gift should've been given to Noah, and as much as I want to return Liam's baby blanket to her, I can't. My children should have a piece of their father—right now my son only knows of his father's younger years through home-made DVD's and photos from high school. We have no baby pictures whatsoever. Other than that, there is the random chance Noah flicks on MTV and catches one of his dad's music videos.

The blanket is draped over the crib now. For some reason I unpacked it the moment we came home, rushing upstairs to do so while Noah and Quinn took over the "man-of-the-house duties" and unloaded all of the gifts from our cars. If Katelyn saw it, she didn't say anything. And as I stand here and stare at it, it makes me long to have a mother-in-law who cares, one that would sit around a warm winter's fire and tell stories from when Liam was younger. I know he didn't have the same type of childhood I did. His was structured and focused. Anyone who knows Liam would never guess that his mother is withdrawn and emotionally unavailable. He's caring, nurturing, and attentive. He's everything his mother—and his father, for that matter—isn't.

The reds and blues of the quilt seem lonely, as if it needs someone to hold it. I remember holding Noah in his from the first day until it was nothing but a shell of its original self. I couldn't bear the thought of not seeing his blanket every day, so when it was worn and torn, I took what was left of it, along with some of the T-shirts he had outgrown, and made a new baby blanket. It's tucked away in my closet for when he has a child of his own.

As I stare at the quilt, I know I have to make a decision on whether this child will use it. Bianca should've stepped up long before now to make amends. She's been working on establishing a relationship with Noah, and maybe this is where the relationship building with us needs to start.

I pull the door shut, knowing that if I stand there any longer I'm going to drive myself to drink an entire bottle of wine. The outcome of doing so would not be good for me, or for Liam. The last thing he needs to hear about is my pity party for one when he's trying to work. Even if I call him, he'll reassure me that everything is going to be fine, that he loves me and he'll be home soon. I can't bear to unload all of my insecurities on him. He needs to believe that I'm strong enough to handle him being away on business because if he does what he wants to do with the band, a few weeks away can turn into months and months. Unfortunately, that's something I'm not quite ready to accept yet. But he doesn't need to know that right now.

What I don't understand is why this child is more important in her eyes than Noah. Even after he was born, and she'd pause in the grocery store and look at him, she knew ... she knew the baby in the seat was her blood and did nothing. There was so much she could've done for Noah, not for me. Noah deserved more.

I sit on a step, halfway between the first and second floor and hold my face in my hands. I'm letting years of pent-up anger get the best of me. I need to let it go, find the inner strength to raise above the level that Bianca keeps me at and show her that her son didn't make a mistake. Even if she thinks he did, Liam doesn't feel that way. My name is tattooed across his chest for Pete's sake. I'm not going anywhere.

I want to call Bianca and ask her what type of game she's playing, except I have a feeling Sterling doesn't know she came to the shower today. As much as I loathe the woman, I'm not going to make waves for her. As evil as she is, I firmly believe she's a product of her husband's brainwashing, because no decent mother would willingly treat her child the way she's treated Liam.

As angry as I am at Bianca, I'm equally pissed at my mother. I didn't even know they knew each other. The Prestons are from the wrong side of the tracks according to the Westburys. So why Bianca is even giving my mother the time of day is beyond me, but definitely something I need to look into.

The doorbell rings, causing me to sigh. I don't want to move from my pity step. It could be Nick coming to pick Noah up for practice, and while I'd be okay with him walking in, Liam would not.

"Noah's—" I pull the door open and start speaking before I realize that I don't know the person standing there. "Can I help you?"

"I have a delivery for Josephine Preston."

My insides turn at the sound of not only my maiden name, but also my full name. I hate to be called Josephine, and when I am, it's usually because something bad is about to happen. The man standing at my door is dressed in green. Not brown for UPS, dark purple for FedEX, or blue for the postal service, but gross puke green. He hands me a clipboard to sign, except I don't reach for it.

"Who is the package from?"

"I'm afraid I'm not at liberty to say, ma'am. Please sign here." He points to the X before handing me the pen. Everything in me is telling me to refuse the delivery and shut the door in his face, but there's a better part of me that's curious. I know I shouldn't be and I may regret this by the time my day is over. I hesitantly sign 'Josie Westbury' and press down as hard as I can so there's no mistaking my name. In one fell swoop the board is under his arm and he hands me a medium-sized cardboard box with no return name or address. Before I can ask him again who it's from, he's gone, passing through the gate and out into the street.

"What's that?"

I startle at the sound of Nick's voice and look up quickly to find him standing in front of me. My heart is pounding out of my chest right now.

"Shit, you scared me."

"Sorry. I called your name, but you look pretty focused on that box. Something for the baby?"

I shake my head and look at it one more time before tucking it under my arm. "No, I'm not sure what it is."

Before I can invite him in, Noah is barreling down the steps and toward the door dressed in his baseball gear. "Bye, Mom," he says, running past me to Nick's car.

"I think that's my cue." Nick smiles as he looks at Noah over his shoulder.

I nod, unable to find the words. I want to get inside and open this box, but I don't want to be rude to Nick.

"Hey, you sure you're okay? I can call Aubrey and have her come over."

Shaking my head, I cover my face with my hand to hide my embarrassment. "I'm fine, just spacey."

"I'll call you tomorrow before I bring him home, unless you want him back tonight?"

"No, you guys need some time together." Nick smiles and turns toward his car. "Hey, Nick, good luck tonight," I tell him as he throws his hand up in a wave. He knows Noah well enough to know that breaking the news that Aubrey is pregnant won't go over very well.

Once they're out of the driveway, I go inside and press the buttons on the keypad that turns my house into a fortress. Surprisingly, hearing the windows lock, the deadbolts slide into place, and the gate moving into position is calming. The security system is designed to keep people out, although even the most desperate person could find a way into the house if they wanted to. With Linda already off for the day, I'm all by myself.

Setting the box down onto the counter, I pull out the scissors and cut the tape on the box. It's filled with those annoying Styrofoam peanuts that stick to everything. The eagerness inside of me tells me to just dig in and search for the hidden treasure, but the way my name was written on the package tells me to proceed with caution. I scoop out a few handfuls, and soon enough, I uncover a book. As I pull it out, I wish I hadn't. My stomach drops when I read the title. It's the book he said was coming, but knew nothing about. It boggles my mind that people can pry into your life and write whatever they want as long as they include the word "source".

### Liam Page: The Untold Story

## An Unofficial Account by Calista Jones

The book in my hand feels like it weighs a hundred pounds or more. I flip it over and read the back matter.

---

**Stories told by his closest friends, lovers, and allies, journey through the life of Liam Page, as we follow his ascension from high school football star to main stream rock star.**

**Exclusive diary excerpts from his long-time companion, Samantha Moreno, share tales of their intimate relationship and take us through the darkest times in his life, her untimely death.**

---

I cover my mouth and rush to the bathroom, barely making it to the toilet as the contents of my lunch are forced out of my body. I choke and gag until nothing is left in my stomach and the only thing coming out of me is tears—hot, wet, and pouring down my face like a faucet.

Leaning back against the wall, I hold my head in my hands and sob. I don't even need to read it to know what it's about. This book is going to tell me everything I want to know, but have been afraid to ask. He's warned me time and time again that I wouldn't like Liam Page and I've disagreed. At times, I see hints of him. A glimmer every now and again, especially in bed, but he hides that persona from me.

Somehow the book is now in my bathroom, sitting on the floor, mocking me. Daring me to pick it up and turn the pages. Taunting me to find out that the man I love is nothing like I've known him to be. I can't do it. I can't put myself through the misery of hearing what his life was like without me, especially since he's in Los Angeles now.

I kick the book out of my way and move to the sink. Turning the cold water on, I rinse out my mouth and splash my face. The act is not refreshing, but needed. Two words are on repeat in my brain: Los Angeles. I should ignore them and this book. It should become bonfire material.

Resting against the sink, I stare at the book. As if there is an imaginary force pulling me toward it, I can't stop myself from bending forward to pick it up. The cover is black and red, the same as the 4225 *West* logo. I inspect it before I crack the binding. There are pictures—pictures that I'm sure I don't want to see and will need to skip through when I get there.

I open the book and find that it's been personalized to me.

> *Dear Josephine,*
> *To all the ones before, during, and after.*
> *Calista Jones*

Who the hell is Calista Jones? Is she trying to tell me in not so many words that my husband is cheating on me? That thought alone sends me back to praying to the porcelain gods, but nothing is coming out except sobs. I cry out from the pain destroying my stomach and the sharp knife being jabbed into my heart. Everything in me is yelling that Sam did this, but she's gone. The only way she could've done this is if she wrote it before she died. Unless the crazy bitch isn't dead and everyone has been lying.

I sit back on my legs, realizing I never let go of the book when I was trying to throw up. As much as I don't want to read it, I have to. I have lingering questions and this may provide me with the answers.

It may also destroy my marriage, my life, and everything that I hold close to my heart. He didn't tell me not to read it.

My brain is saying burn it but my heart is telling me to turn the page ...

So I do.

## 14

## LIAM

Layla Richards looks around the club, probably recalling similar memories as I had when we played here. I follow her to one of the high top tables and sit down across from her. She is nothing like I remember with her red hair, wild make-up, and questionable clothing all gone. In their place is chin-length hair, which is now dark, and considerably toned down make-up. The barely there clothes she used to wear have been replaced with what I consider normal attire. The one thing that hasn't changed is the color of her eyes, which are in complete contrast to her hair. Looking at her now, you wouldn't believe she was the lead singer of a rock group.

"It's so good to see you," she says as she grabs for my hands. I let her because it's harmless and Layla is just a friend.

"You too. I hate that we didn't keep in touch. What have you been up to?"

"Oh gosh," she says as she falls back into her chair. "When was the last time I saw you?"

The last time I saw Layla is a night I wish I could forget. I'd love to go back and make sure it never happened, make it so I never crossed the line with Sam. I was lonely and for a brief moment thought that Layla and I could revisit things, and even though Harrison had warned me, I still liked Layla.

I rub my chin and drag my thumb over my lip. "The last time I saw you some fucker popped me in the face."

Layla's eyes go wide as she covers her mouth in shock. "Oh my God," she says, but it sounds more like ohmygob because her hand is covering her mouth. "Holy shit, I remember that."

"Your husband, if I remember correctly?"

She waves her hands as if to dismiss what I'm saying.

"What a nightmare he was."

"Was?" I ask, inviting more conversation. I'll take her whole damn story if it gets me out of cleaning the club. I'm sure Layla isn't here to clean either.

"Let's get something to drink first," she says as she heads toward the bar. I watch as she moves around with ease, making herself a drink. "Do you want something?"

"Sure, why not?" The why not should be because it's before noon, and I shouldn't be drinking. The sure is because I'm here and what else am I going to do? It's pretty much all a lame excuse on my part.

After a few minutes she returns with two glasses of some orange and pink looking drink. I'm either a hard liquor or beer type of guy. Fruity shit and I do not get along. When she places it down in front of me, I try not to roll my eyes. I hesitantly pick it up and take a sip and surprisingly don't gag, but am wondering what the hell it is that I'm drinking.

"I think you forgot the Vodka."

She shakes her head and takes a long drink of her concoction. "I don't drink, smoke, or do any of the stupid shit I used to do."

It takes me a moment realize she's talking about drugs. The first night we met, she offered me something, and I took it, no questions asked. I had just been told via voicemail that I had ruined Josie's life and I needed to feel numb. I needed to forget about the lives that I had ruined when I left mine behind and Layla was the answer to that—in more ways than one.

"Good for you. What made you change?"

"Took some ecstasy, had a one-night stand, and ended up pregnant."

I swallow hard, knowing that's what we did minus the pregnancy part ... I hope.

"So you have a kid?"

"Yep, she's almost twelve."

Layla finishes her drink as if nothing is amiss. I've barely touched mine and have suddenly found that I'm not very thirsty, though my mouth is parched and my tongue feels numb. I can't even begin to describe what I'm thinking or feeling. I do the math quickly, using Noah's age when I found out about him. They're about a year apart and as I mentally tick off the months in my mind all I can see is Josie's face as she hears the words that I may have another child. This will kill her and end us. We have been unable to conceive another child and to hear that a fling—one that I went to days after breaking up with her—could have possibly had my baby because I was stupid will kill her. She'll leave me and I'll deserve to be alone.

Maybe if I don't ask if I'm the father, she'll never bring it up and I'll never have to tell Josie. Of course, that will never work because the guilt will eat away at me and I'll end up caving. My life, as I know it, may be over. She will maim me, stringing me up by my toes in the basement.

No that would be too easy. I can see my wife looking me in the eyes and telling me to get to the fuck out. She won't even bat an eyelash. It won't even matter that this happened while we were broken up.

"Liam?" Fingers are snapped in my face, breaking me from my train of thought.

"I'm sorry, what were you saying?" I adjust myself in the chair, seeking some sort of comfort, but finding none.

"My husband ... he didn't want to be the father to another man's child and the night he punched you in the club, he said he was done with my 'ways'." She waves her hands dismissively in the air as if it's no big deal. My life is falling apart, tearing away at the seams and she's acting like this is just another day for her.

"Do you have a picture of your daughter?"

"Yeah, sure," she says, as she digs through her purse, pulling out her phone. My palms are sweating as she swipes through her photos looking for the one that is going to seal my fate. Fuck, I need a shot ... or fifty to get me through this.

Layla slides her phone over for me to look. I wish I

was the observant type and could tell if this child is mine or not, but I can't. She has brown hair, hazel eyes, and could look like Noah ... maybe. I'm not sure. Hell, I stood next to my son in the bathroom and saw him in the mirror, but never fully looked at him until he told me he'd seen me kissing his mom on TV. Staring at the girl now, she looks like Layla, and that's probably because she's standing next to her. She takes her phone back and locks the screen, ending my viewing session. Part of me doesn't want to know if this is my child and would rather go back to Beaumont in the dark, but the other part of me needs to find out. As much as it would hurt Noah, he'd have a right to know that he has a sister.

"What's her name?" My voice is low, broken, and barely above a whisper. My life is fucked. There's no fixing this unless I lie, and I'm not about to do that. Layla doesn't answer, nor seem to even acknowledge that I asked a question. I want her phone back. I want to look again, to study the photo or maybe multiple ones so I can compare. Put her daughter and Noah side-by-side and see if they match.

At this rate I'm dad of the fucking year. I've missed both my children growing up, coming in after most of the hard stuff is done, but being there for the ever so lovely teenage years.

"Are you feeling okay? You look like you've seen a ghost."

"I'm f-fine," I stammer. "Why didn't you ... keep in touch?" I wanted to ask her why she didn't tell me, but changed my mind at the last second. This answer will be easier to hear rather than a meaningless excuse.

I hate to think of where I'd be in life right now had she told me. I know I would've gone home for Mason's funeral and developed a relationship with Noah, but it's unlikely Josie would've given me the time of day. She'd be married to Nick now and probably pregnant with their child because he has no problem getting his wife pregnant. I, on the other hand, can only conceive children when I'm eighteen fucking years old. Sterling is going to be so proud of me when he hears I fathered another child.

"This business makes it hard, and you didn't exactly have a likeable manager. What happened to her anyway? Better yet, where the hell have you been? I heard you went all rogue and moved out of L.A."

Right now I want a strong, stiff drink that's going to knock me on my ass and make me forget about how screwed up my life is. I need to numb my brain and keep it from over thinking.

"My best friend died, and I went home for the funeral. Going home changed a lot of things for me. As for Sam ..." Running my hand over my hair, I sigh. There was a time in my life when I liked Sam. It wasn't anything like what I felt for Josie, but the feelings were still there. What I couldn't deal with were the lies and how controlling she was. She just couldn't let things happen organically between us. My biggest mistake was leading her on and telling her that we'd try right before Mason died.

"When you go home after being gone for ten years without keeping in contact with anyone, you learn a lot about yourself and the people you left behind. I had a high school sweetheart who I had broken up with days before I met you." Layla's eyes go wide with understanding at what I'm telling her. "Anyway, I was home and shit started falling into place. We have a son that Sam knew about but hid from me. Once I found out, I terminated my contract with Moreno Entertainment and put down permanent roots back home ... bought a house and all that grown-up shit we're supposed to do." I sigh, thinking about how everything changed after that. "Sam, she grew desperate and sabotaged our tour. We lost a lot of money, sued Moreno Entertainment, and are still waiting for payment. Two years ago, I married my girl and a couple days after, Sam killed herself."

Layla covers her mouth in shock. I would, too, if I were hearing this for the first time, but the shock of hearing about it doesn't even come close what it was like actually living it. Sam harassing Josie was a nightmare—telling her that I was going to take Noah away from her, showing up at our house with nothing but lingerie on. Her destruction of our tour was the last straw. Something had to be done.

"Anyway, shit's crazy right now. The band isn't making any money. We all have families to support. We're out here to help Trixie, but I'm hoping I can work a few deals and get us some headliners or something."

"Do you guys still want to tour?"

Nodding, I finally take a drink of whatever it is that Layla made. "I miss it. I miss being on the road and performing. Right now we do a few sets at the local bar and my wife's café, but it's not the same."

"I know what you mean. After I had Naomi, shit got

hard. Touring with a baby was stressful, but I didn't want to leave her. I also didn't want to quit partying, but something had to give. So now I write music. My songs are selling to artists bigger than I ever would've gotten, so I still feel successful."

All thoughts have turned back to her daughter when she says her name. It's fitting that her name is similar to Noah's. It's showing me how much of a fuck up I am and makes me wonder what the fuck Josie is even doing with me. I put the glass down and take a deep breath.

"When I can meet her, Layla?"

"Who?" she asks. I hate that she's playing dumb. It's the most annoying thing when women do this. She knows exactly what I'm referring to and still won't come out and say what I don't want to hear.

"Naomi."

"Why would you want to meet her?"

I put my drink down and fold my hands together. "I've lost enough time with one child; I don't want to lose anymore. I can understand if you don't want me to be a part of her life but I'd at least like to meet her. She has a brother just a bit older than her. They should at least know each other."

Layla's eyes go wide, and she starts shaking her head. "Naomi isn't your daughter, Liam."

I take her words in, repeating them over and over again in my head. Relief washes over me, yet I'm still confused. "But you said—"

"What I said was that I got pregnant after a one-night stand, which yes, you and I had and yes, we had done ecstasy, but it wasn't you who knocked me up."

"Are you sure?"

Layla smiles. "Positive. Naomi's dad is actually in her life. They have a good relationship. You have nothing to worry about. No need to start writing me checks."

"It wasn't the checks I was worried about."

"What was it then?"

I pull out my phone and bring up a picture of Josie and Noah. "It's them. That's my wife, Josie, and our son, Noah. I left her, eighteen and pregnant. I found out about him when I went home for my buddy's funeral."

"She's gorgeous. How come she never called you?"

"She did." I lock my screen and put my phone away. "Sam hid the messages from me. Anyway, we're about to adopt and once again, I've up and left before the baby is due to arrive. I've been sitting here thinking about how she's going to kill me. So don't take this the wrong way, but I'm really happy your daughter isn't mine."

"But Liam you'd make such a great baby daddy."

Before I can respond, she's off the stool and behind the bar, making more of her juice. "I'll take mine with some rum!" I yell out to her, earning a loud chuckle. One crisis averted for the day ... and right now, I think that's about all I can handle.

# 15

## JOSIE

---

I'm in Beaumont—Liam's hometown.
I can see why he left. There's
absolutely nothing here. I'd be so
bored and am thankful that he'd never
invited me back before. I saw her
today, the one he mumbles about. I
know the baby she carries is his, but
Liam doesn't need to know. He's a
rising star and this would derail
everything I've worked so hard for.
Daddy was right. We're his
family now.

---

Nothing, and I mean absolutely nothing, could've prepared me for this. Each page is getting harder and harder to read. The questions I once had have been answered, and not in a good way, and I find myself questioning everything that is written in black and white before my eyes. I know Liam. I know him better than the person writing this book, and for the life of me I can't see him like this.

I am not naïve. I know he changed when he went to college. Noah having to grow up without him is evident by that, albeit not by Liam's choice. But to read that my son was purposely hidden from his life is heartbreaking. These people didn't do anything for my husband except create a puppet that they wanted to control. I hate ... hate to think about where we'd be today if it hadn't been for Mason.

---

**I loathe typing B-E-A-U-M-O-N-T into my computer, but Liam is insistent. Why he's going to the funeral for a guy that he hasn't seen in ten years is baffling. These people mean nothing to him, and yet he's leaving me again. I wonder if I should tell him that his friend came looking for him all those years ago. That he pounded his fists on the desk in reception demanding that he see him. He even waited in the**

**lobby for two days for Liam to come in, but I made sure to keep him away. NOTHING was going to take my Liam from me, and yet here is the same man, taking him back to that wretched place.**

---

Tears rush from my eyes, wetting the pages of this garbage. I remember when Mason disappeared for a few days, never telling me where he went. I'm not sure if he ever told Katelyn. When he came back, though, you could tell he wasn't the same person. Katelyn thought he had cheated on her, but he didn't. She knew that in her heart, but couldn't help and second-guess why he was being so secretive. Now we know.

I throw the book to the ground and let the tears fall freely, hoping to expel the negative energy from my mind and body. Reading this was a mistake, and when they say curiosity killed the cat, they weren't joking. I feel dead inside. My heart feels as if it weighs a hundred pounds or more and is barely beating. I need Liam to hold me, reassure me that Sam is dead and will never come back to interfere in our lives. And if she isn't dead, she'll wish she were after I'm finished with her.

Glancing around, I realize I'm still in the bathroom, having never moved once I turned the first page. My stomach growls, but the thought of food is nauseating. I'm not sure I could eat anything and if I did I'm not sure it'd stay down.

My legs are stiff as I start to stand, using the wall for guidance and leverage. Never, have I been so consumed with something that I've let so much time pass. Even after Liam left I had to function. The baby growing inside of me needed me to survive.

Darkness filters through the blinds in my kitchen. Glancing at the illuminated clock on the microwave tells me that I've been in the bathroom for about six hours. That's far too many hours wasted on something that means so little to my life. It's the journal excerpts that gave me pause. Reading and re-reading them over and over to let the tales of Sam and the other women soak in is what took me so long to process the garbage that has been written in that stupid book. It's like a car crash on the highway. You know you shouldn't look because it's disrespectful to stare, but you turn your head anyway as you drive at a snail's pace, only to mutter an, "Oh God!" and say a silent prayer of thanks that it wasn't you in that accident.

When I saw the mangled truck that Mason drove the night he was killed, the sentiment of "Oh God!" had an entirely different meaning. The officers were slow to release the wreckage to the towing company and something deep inside made me drive by the scene the next morning. His truck, one that I had been in so many times, was a shell of what it used to be. It was easy to see how he didn't survive even as his words echoed through my mind, "Nothing can break this baby." He was wrong. An eighteen-wheeler with failing brakes coming down a hill did. That semi didn't just destroy Mason's truck, but all of our lives as well. However, with that destruction came hope and something new. Because of Mason, I was given another chance with Liam and I'm a fool to let some unauthorized biography based mostly on his psycho manager mess that up for me.

Do the words hurt? Yes, but they can't matter to me. I won't let them. I don't know who this Calista Jones person is, but the story she tells paints the picture of a much different person than the man I love. I'm smart enough to accept that the Liam I fell in love with isn't the same man I married and I know he would say the same thing about me. We grew up, each of us in our own ways, but I don't care what people say, your first love is never forgotten no matter how many years pass.

My phone sits on the counter, mocking me. If I had to bet, I'd say Liam is on his way home because we've never gone this long without talking. I know him well enough to know he's pacing, pulling at his hair and pounding his fists against the windows overlooking the town he loves so much. When he booked his suite at the Wilshire, the night that I met him there came rushing back. I was teetering that night, willing to give myself to him so I could remember what it felt like to be under his control. To have him hovering over me, willing my body to be at his command.

He wouldn't let me. Instead he paced, often moving out of my grasp just as I had him in it. It pained him not to touch me, and each time I'd look into his eyes, his resolve was breaking mine down. When I reminded him that I was engaged, it was for my benefit not his. I had to say the words out loud to remind myself that I already gave myself to another man.

When it comes down to it, Liam isn't any different. He willingly gave himself away to his painkillers, as he called them. I can't hold that against him.

I push the home button on my phone and look at the notifications. Liam has called and texted, along with Katelyn and Jenna. Swiping my finger across Liam's missed call, I enter my passcode, listening to his voice sing out into my ear. In the first message he's telling me that he's checking in and would like me to text him when I'm free. In the second he wants to know what I'm doing and why I haven't texted him. It's in his third message that I detect panic in his voice when he tells me that he loves me and really needs to hear my voice. The fourth message he leaves is mostly cussing and asking where I'm at. The rest of the messages are from Katelyn and Jenna, following the same pattern as Liam's: What am I doing, why am I not answering the phone?

I don't bother reading his texts messages before replying.

**I'm sorry. I'm home and have been sleeping. Just tired**.

The lie—or, technically, omission of the truth—comes easier than it should, but telling him that I've been reading the book that he doesn't want me to read won't sit well with him and fighting over the phone is not something I want to happen while he's in L.A.

**Can you come over?**

I send that to Katelyn, knowing she'll be here the second she wakes. After starting a pot of coffee, I return to the bathroom and pick up the trash ... also known as the novel. It's sad to think that people will spend their hard earned money on something like this, but the gossip-mongers will be out in full-force and taking this as gospel, especially the part that tells the world that the only reason Liam and I are married is because of Noah and how I blackmailed him, threatening to take everything away from him. It's funny to think that it was me begging Liam not to take Noah away from me. Alone, he could offer Noah such a better life and could easily have had his high-powered attorneys destroy me. Sam tried, though, on his behalf. It was that night that I knew Liam and I would be okay. When I showed him the papers that Sam had dropped off, he was livid, promising me he would never do anything of the sort. Sadly, somehow that part didn't make it into the novel. I guess Calista Jones failed fact checking in school.

The sound of the buzzer blasts through the house notifying me that someone is at the gate. The video monitor by the door shows me Katelyn, sitting in her car. Turning off the alarm and pressing the button that opens the gate, I return to the kitchen and pull out two mugs and pour the freshly brewed coffee into them. It's going to be a long day for me and knowing she's come here in the middle of the night means she's been waiting for my text.

"What the hell, Josie?" she says as she comes through the door. Katelyn puts her bag down on the counter and pulls me into a hug. "Liam called and said you weren't answering. I called you and when you didn't answer I called Nick to see if he had Noah and to find out if you were going anywhere. What's going on?"

"This," I tell her as I hand her the book. "It was delivered earlier, and I decided to read it."

Her face and shoulders drop as she looks at me. Tears form around the rims of my eyes, but they stay at bay. She knows what I'm going through, as she went through something similar with Harrison, all thanks to Sam.

"Did you read it?"

I nod. "Most of it."

She sets it on the counter and brings the mug closer to her, adding some of the cream that I had pulled out before she walked into the kitchen.

"You know, you told me not to believe everything I read or see in the press about Harrison, right?"

"That's what the guys tell us to do. We have to trust them."

Katelyn holds her mug in her hands, warming them even though it isn't cold out. "When Harrison and I were in L.A. a few weeks back, we went to a basketball game. It was more for Peyton than any of us, but we do things as a family so we all went. I was minding my own business, when I happened to glance up at the jumbo Tron and find my husband gawking at one of the cheerleaders in front of us. I was so angry and embarrassed that I never stopped to look at the bigger picture. Aside from showing complete disinterest, he had nowhere else to look. The girl was right in front of him, shaking her ass. But that didn't excuse him from looking.

"I spent the next few days angry with him. I would stay inside when he took the kids out to surf and I made sure to keep my ass covered. Those girls were in their twenties and here I am over thirty and shit is starting to sag. Harrison finally had enough and told me so that night. He reminded me that we made promises to each other and nothing should ever come between us. He also said that there are people out there that will make us second guess the people we love and if we allow that, we're going to be living our lives always looking over our shoulders."

She pauses to take a drink. "Now tell me, why did you read it?"

"Because I was curious and because I'm jealous."

"Jealous of what?"

I set my cup down and cover my face, ready to admit for the first time that everything he's done with his life was better than what we had planned. "I'm hurt that those people got his time when Noah didn't get shit and he deserved it more than any of them. I'm jealous that I wasn't enough for Liam to be a part of it. I'm jealous that other women know him the way I do and that they think they have the right to talk about him. I'm jealous that I missed ten years and will never get them back."

Katelyn steps toward me, placing her hands on my shoulders. "You do realize that not many marriages work in this situation. I think you should count your lucky stars that he grew up before he came back to you or you'd be on the front page of those rags with the headlines that make your blood boil. Believe me when I tell you it's not easy to see people calling me a gold-digger and not worth a marriage proposal. Harrison has said time and time again that we'll get married, but it's not what he wants. I'm happy with the way things are and I don't question his loyalty to me and the girls, but the outside world doesn't get that."

"The outside world is going to think that I black-mailed Liam into marriage. I think I'd much rather have the title of gold-digger."

Leaning against the wall, I stare out the large window at the active nightlife below me. All night I've been trying to get ahold of Josie. Each time my text messages have gone unanswered and my phone calls end up going to voicemail. Logic would say to call our house phone, but that would require us to buy a landline phone and we haven't done that yet. The phone line is used strictly for our alarm system.

Calling Katelyn was out of desperation. I didn't know what else do to, except call Nick, and I wasn't going to do that. I would've flown home before I dialed his number and asked him to go check on my wife. Call me stubborn or stupid, either way it wasn't going to happen.

Now I stand here, worrying and wondering what the hell happened to my wife. A million thoughts run through my mind from a kidnapping, stranded on the side of the road without cell service, to a car accident.

The latter is unlikely because someone would've called me, but I can't stop the thoughts from being there.

I've stopped wondering if she was one of the bodies walking down the street, stopped imagining her face on every brunette I saw. I stopped thinking that she was miserable in her life because the truth is, she wasn't until I came back. If I hadn't, she'd be married to Nick. It pains me to think that she could've been his wife, but sometimes I wonder if he was the better choice.

Horns honk and police car lights create a swirling wonderment on the streets of Wilshire Blvd. The exclusive clubs are packed with today's best—best actors, actresses, musicians, and Hollywood royalty. That was my forced crowd, the one Sam insisted that I fit into. Being on my arm during a premiere was her glory, even though I hated taking her. I much preferred my fake girlfriends because I knew when the night was over I could do what I wanted. With Sam, I had to play by her rules for the night.

As I look around the living area of my penthouse, it's like déjà vu. Everything is as I remember it, even if this wasn't my apartment. What I remember the most is having Josie here, eating dinner across from me and introducing her to Liam Page. I knew the looks I was giving her affected her, and that she enjoyed it. She's my best memory of this hotel, and the only one I want to think about.

The ding of my cell phone has me fishing it out of my pocket. Her name is backlit, causing me to sigh heavily in relief. Opening her message, I read it quickly, trying to comprehend that she's been home this whole time and is just tired. I haven't spoken to her in over twelve hours and that is all she has to say to me?

I type out a quick "Let's talk" and send it. I have an uneasy feeling about all of this and need to hear her voice.

Jojo: **In a bit. I'm with Katelyn**.

I stare at my phone in disbelief. A small wave of relief washes over me knowing she's with Katelyn, but why the hell is she blowing me off? I pocket my phone and continue to stare out the window, letting the anger build. I don't expect her to be at my beck and call, but I do have a certain expectation that she wants to talk to me. I know we've been apart before and maybe she's already accustomed to the distance. If so, I'm not doing my job as her husband, not that I really know what I'm supposed to do other than love her. She has to know that she's my world and that I'd do anything for her—the immensity of that scares me. I fear the day she asks me to quit being Liam Page because I'm not sure if I'll be able to do as she asks. But I won't lose her either, not to the music side of my life.

The sun starts to rise, peeking over the horizon. It catches me off guard, causing me to squint and move away from the window. Where did the time go? It's felt like only minutes have gone by while I've waited for Josie to call me, not what many people consider a full day. My steps are slow and deliberate as I walk into my bedroom. The king size bed holds no appeal to me, but sleep beckons. Spending hours waiting for a phone call while staring out a window can be draining. Not only is my body tired, but my mind is about to shut down. Long gone are the days of me pulling all-nighters that can last up to three days.

Falling onto the bed, I pull the pillow under me and hug it to my chest. It's a void filler for the body that I wish I were holding instead. Hell, just to hear her voice right now would help my mind unwind and allow me to fall asleep. I wrangle my phone out of my pocket and hit the voice recorder. I say, "Jojo, I love you" and send her the file, hoping it will get her to call me. I need to hear that she loves me because right now I'm afraid I'm just fucking up right and left.

I startle awake at the sound of pounding. My eyes are shut tight and fighting to stay that way. Rolling over, I cringe when something hard hits me in the face. I search blindly for the object and the size alone tells me it's my phone. Sitting up slowly, I swing my legs over to the edge and hold my pounding head in my hands. I open my eyes slowly and rub the sleep away. I can't believe I fell asleep last night—or early this morning, whatever time it was. Reaching for my phone, I press the home screen but nothing happens.

"Fuck," I yell, realizing that my phone is dead. I plug it into the charger sitting next to my bed and make my way to the door with the intent of maiming the person on the other side. I don't bother to look in the peephole before opening it.

Big mistake.

Mr. Moreno doesn't wait to be invited in; he pushes past me as if he owns the place. Knowing my luck, he probably does, which would explain the over eager escort waiting for me at the door when we arrived. For some reason I peer out into the hallway. I'm not sure if I'm looking for Sam, even though I know she's gone, or trying to mentally prepare myself to flee my room.

I contemplate leaving the door open so I can make a run for it, but know Mr. Moreno can't physically hurt me. Career-wise, he can destroy me, and right now that's not something I need to happen. Letting go of the door, it slams shut, but doesn't even faze him. He's looking at the faux art hanging on the walls. It's the same on each floor, varying from room to room. I know this because JD had to come in and take a picture to show Jenna.

"I love what you've done with the place." His sarcastic tone causes my heart to race. I hate that he has any power over me at all. When we settled in court, I thought that was the last I'd see of him and I am pretty sure our restraining order included him. It's something I need to look into, especially since he's making repeat appearances on our behalf.

"I seem to remember different art when you and Sam lived together."

"We never lived together," I bite back. "She stayed with me ... briefly."

He smirks and dismisses my statement with a wave of his hand. Mr. Moreno is a smart businessman, but personality-wise he's always scared the shit out of me. Sam hinted once about having ties to the mob, which is common in old town Hollywood. Frank Sinatra did, so why wouldn't someone like Moreno?

Glass is clanked together, catching me off guard. I shake my head and chide myself for losing focus while he's here. Mr. Moreno has poured himself a drink, effectively charging up my wet bar. I'll be sure to send him the bill for the incidentals when I get it. He wasn't invited, and I'm definitely not willingly entertaining him.

"What do you want?" I ask, needing to get him out of here and out of my life for good. I sit on the edge of the cream-colored chair, unwilling to get comfortable. He sits across from me. His left leg rests on his knee and his fedora is perched on the edge of the armrest. The amber-colored scotch swirls as he drinks, prolonging his impromptu visit.

I refrain from getting angry because I think that's what he wants. He knows anger fuels emotions, and he wants me to say something that is going to bind me to him. It's not going to happen even if it's the smartest thing for the band. If the band decides we want to re-sign with Moreno Entertainment, then we will make that decision together.

"You need me," he says bluntly. He's right; I do need him, or someone like him. He's a pit bull, a shark. People are afraid of him, including his clients. But he gets the job done, and that's what the band needs, someone who is going to lead the path that we want to carve out for ourselves.

"Maybe it's you who needs me." I'm not sure where the confidence came from, but it's there and flashing like a beacon in my eyes. Why is he so eager to have us back? We sued his company and won, wouldn't that put a bad taste in his mouth? Unless, of course, he's trying to screw us, and that is definitely something I wouldn't put past him.

He scoffs at my suggestion. I knew he would, but now that I've said it out loud, it's the angle I'm taking.

"You're pissing away your career. If you don't want to be someone, let the kid go. He has potential."

"Kid?" I question.

"The Davis boy. It's in his genes to be on stage in front of sold out crowds. He knows this and is just biding his time with you."

"I think you're wrong."

Once again he dismisses me with his hand and a smirk. "Let me tell you this, Liam, I am not anything like Sam. I don't give a shit about whom you fuck behind your wife's back or who you knock up. What I care about is making money and so do you. You know damn well that you were at the top of the charts until you decided to go back to Sleepy Hollow."

He stands and places his half-full glass on the side table next to the chair. In one quick movement, his hat is on his head and he's standing before me.

"You know I can take you to the top. Sam is gone, and no longer an issue. If you think I need you, you're sadly mistaken, but I'm willing to right the wrongs that my daughter committed against you. Think about it, Page." He leans closer and I can smell the scotch on his breath. "Millions of screaming women throwing their panties on stage for you, posting about you on social media and saying how they'd leave their husbands for you. Sold out tours across the country and dollars in your pocket. You can bring your little wife, or leave her at home and take a mistress. I don't give a fuck. What I do care about is money and 4225 *West* has the potential to make all of us very rich."

Mr. Moreno walks away, pulling the door open quickly. He turns and looks at me. "Before you make a decision, talk it over with the guys. Make sure they're okay with you pussy footing around in your basement while their bank accounts are dwindling."

The door slams on his way out, causing me to jump. I'm antsy and slightly freaking out. I don't know how or why I'm so tongue-tied when he's near—probably because he's a wolf in sheep's clothing and right now I'm looking like his lunch.

The simple fact that he thinks it's okay to cheat should be enough for me to tell him to take a flying leap off a cliff, but I know he's right about one thing: this decision, any decision, needs to be made as a band. I fear Harrison and JD will want to sign, leaving me the lone man out.

I walk into my bedroom and grab my phone, pressing the home button and dialing Josie. In the past I'd turn to booze or women, but I don't need that shit anymore.

I just need her.

## 17

## JOSIE

I look down at my ringing phone to see Liam's face light up my screen. My finger hovers over the talk button, but I can't bring myself to press it. I'm not actually angry with him as much as I am with the whole situation. I knew we weren't together and hadn't been, but seeing our anniversary date as a happy occasion for Sam is painful. It's as if he did everything he could to erase me from his life and, for the most part, he was successful. I know not to believe everything that I've read, but the excerpts from Sam's diary hit a little harder for me because I'm sure, deep down, that most are true.

Katelyn's been gone an hour, leaving me to get lost in my own mind. I wouldn't let her peruse the novel because I didn't know how she'd react to the part about Mason. Thinking back to Sam's thoughts makes my stomach turn. I can't imagine what it would do to Katelyn.

My phone dings with a voicemail from Liam. I know

I'm not being fair, but I need time to decompress and absorb what I've read. If I tell Liam, he'll either have excuses, or become angry with me because I've read this book. I'm sure he has no clue that it was delivered and is probably banking on the fact that I would never buy something like this. I don't even look at the gossip sites or magazines because they're out to make money off other people's misery, which isn't far from what this book is doing. I'm letting it affect me when I shouldn't.

One of the passages that stood out the most was about his grandmother's house. Picking up the book, I fan the pages, stopping and skimming until I come to a diary excerpt from Sam. The pages are full of them and they're really the focal point of the story.

---

**Liam's grandmother has died. Her death has allowed him to lean on me more than he has been. I've been able to assert myself more and more since her passing, and I think he appreciates it. He asked me to sell her house, or donate it. It's his grief talking, and even though he's my client and I'm supposed to do what he says, I'm not. We can live there once he realizes we're meant to be together.**

---

"Meant to be together," I say those words out loud,

hoping they sound differently than what I'm hearing in my head. They don't. In fact, they anger me. The fact that this woman thought Liam was meant for her pains me, rips my heart out, because it has me wondering if he's meant for me. I have spent far too many nights in my life second-guessing Liam Westbury and I don't want to do it now. He came back to me ...

Or did he just come back for Noah?

Pushing away from the table, I storm upstairs and into my closet. My arm reaches for the pull cord to the attic, but I hesitate. I know he has boxes up there from his time in L.A., and maybe they yield something about me, about us. Did he keep journals? Did he write about me in side notes of songs he wrote while he was away?

I close my eyes and pull, fearful of what might fall down; the dust, spiders, and who knows what else lives up there. The attic is Liam's job. He stores our holiday decorations up there and brings them down when needed, along with other household items we want to save. It's the catch all for anything we don't want seen. I've only been up here a few times, and as I climb the rickety ladder now I'm second-guessing myself. But I have to know if he ever felt anything for Sam, or if he ever thought about me while he was gone. He's says he thought about me all of the time, but the nagging suspicion reading this book has caused me won't go away and I need it to.

The string to the light dangles in front of me as I climb the steps. It's out of reach until I'm two or three steps from the top. I pull gently, afraid that if I pull too hard the frayed string will break, and with Liam not home to fix it, my quest for answers will only continue.

Boxes line the walls—each one of them marked with what's inside. I trail my fingers along the lettering: Noah's school work, baby clothes, sheet music, and records. This attic doubles as his storage space since the basement studio isn't big enough. I start with the box labeled sheet music. Removing the lid, I find that the papers are nice and orderly and blank. I pull that box down and look at the one behind it, continuing this unless I see something that makes sense to me.

After what seems like an hour, I look around and see that I've destroyed the clean attic. Boxes are everywhere, some missing their lids, and I'm no closer to finding something that will help me feel like Liam is where he wants to be. I don't care if he didn't say the words in that book. They were said and I have to know if they're true.

A box titled "Grandma" catches my eye and I move quickly toward it. I hesitate before lifting the lid because I'm about to search through the belongings of a woman I didn't know, a woman who took Liam away from me and is someone he loves dearly. He hardly speaks of her, and when he does, he doesn't divulge much. All I really know is she died, that's it. I don't know how or when. Maybe it's her death that truly brought him home to me, not Mason's funeral. I run my hand over the top of the box and grab it with both hands, setting it on the floor.

As I stare at the box, I notice that the cursive handwriting on it isn't Liam's and because of what I've recently read, I'm pretty sure it's Sam's. She was there when she died. She was the one to comfort him. She was the one to help him through the loss of someone he cared about deeply. I wasn't given that chance. I know I seem bitter but I'm not, I'm just really angry.

The way I see it I can be angry with two dead people who can't defend their actions now, or open this box and see what Grandma Betty can tell me. Hopefully, she's the key to figuring everything out.

Removing the lid unveils a pile of papers and a few smaller boxes. Picking up the first stack of papers, I blow the dust off and unfold them. This is the deed to her house, and it's in Liam's name. Sam said in her diary that she didn't sell the house like he had asked and it makes me wonder if it's still there. Has it sat empty all of this time?

The next section of papers reveals a death certificate. Its dated only months after he left me. My heart drops, beating a bit faster knowing I wasn't enough to bring him back after his grandmother passed away. These are two things I now know from my investigation: Liam possibly still owns his grandmother's house, and he lost her early on in his new career path.

Setting the certificate aside, I dig in and pull out a wooden box. The name "Betty" is engraved on the outside. Opening it reveals jewelry; diamonds and rubies. Sizes of rings I've only seen in stores are sitting there and in need of some serious attention.

The next box holds pictures. I immediately recognize Bianca. My finger trails down the image, mesmerized by her beauty. Her dark hair is pulled up high, and she's wearing a light-colored dress with the most vibrant smile. I've never seen her smile like this, but would like to. I think Noah and Liam deserve to see the sparkle she has in her eyes in this picture shine for them.

I look inside the box and see that I have another wooden box and a folder left to look through. I wish I could say I'm satisfied with what I'm finding, but I'm not. Liam should have this stuff out on display, or locked away for safekeeping.

The other wooden box is engraved with "Charlie" and I'm guessing that belongs to his grandfather. I run my fingers over the letters and think that Charlie would make a great name for our newest addition. I had thought Liam would suggest Mason, but he hasn't said anything yet and I may offer up Charlie as an option.

Opening the box reveals an old folded piece of paper. I carefully unfold and read the words meant for someone else.

---

*My Dearest Betty,*

*Death knocks on my door, and yet you stay by my side. I should've never left you and Bianca. I was stupid, selfish, and thought the grass would be greener on the other side. I was wrong. Being away from you was a mistake and one I'll never be able to change. The only thing I can do, is make sure you'll always be taken care of. Someday I hope that you forgive me for wronging you the way I did.*

*Love, Charlie*

---

Wiping away the tears before they hit the paper, I find myself needing to scream at love lost, yet again, because of foolish mistakes and death. Liam never knew his grandfather and his grandmother weren't allowed to see him. Life shouldn't be this way. At the end of the letter is a bank and routing number. It's all Charlie wanted, to take care of his one true love. I fold the letter up and press it to my heart. Charlie's wedding ring, watch, and pocketknife are the only things left in the box aside from a few pictures of Betty and Bianca.

The folder is heavy when I pick it up and I can easily deduce that it's full of paper. I close my eyes and pray this will have what I'm looking for. I undo the clasp which falls apart in my hand. It's not old, just overused. I pull out the stack of papers. My heart catches in my throat as I gulp for air. I flip through the pages and pages of notes, all in Liam's handwriting. I don't understand why they're in this box. Why would they be in a box for his grandparents and not for him? The pages are dated, and in order, starting with the day he left.

**All she had to do was hold me.**
**Tell me everything would be okay.**
**Her words ... they broke me and yet she cries.**

I remember that day vividly. I don't need a reminder.

**She hates me, but I love her.**
**I want to tell her.**
**Call her.**

**Beg her.**
**Her voice will break me.**
**Shatter me.**
**I said the one thing to end it.**
**Josephine.**

The sob escapes before I can control it. My lips tremble as tears rush down my face, my breathing labored. Each inhale is painful, and it feels as though I can't exhale because I can barely catch my breath. I let it all out, screaming loudly until my throat is dry and scratchy. The tears won't stop, and I don't expect them to as long as I'm reading his words.

**She wants to get married, but I don't love her.**
**When I look at her, she's not the one I see in my dreams.**
**She's blonde and my fantasy is a brunette.**
**She's pregnant, and I want nothing to do with her.**
**I DON'T WANT HER**
**Never have.**
**I'm weak. I'm weak. I'm weak.**

I flip to the end, unable to read anything about Sam and her fake baby. She tried to trap Liam, and it almost worked. It would've if he hadn't left.

**A piece of me has died.**
**My best friend, gone.**

**He never knew how sorry I am.**
**I'm going home.**
**She'll be there.**
**Will I be able to tell her?**
**That I still love her?**
**With every breath – the love I have grows**
**stronger.**
**Fuck distance.**
**Fuck life.**

Holding the papers to my chest, I let everything pour out of me at once. I'm an idiot for doubting him, for thinking that he wasn't being honest with me. We have a good life and I almost let the pain I feel from not having him here with me ruin us.

"No more," I say to a room full of memories. "Sam can't hurt me anymore."

I won't allow it.

I start picking everything up, leaving his grandparents' box for last. I want to talk to him about it, bring their stuff into our lives. We should be celebrating their lives, even if she's the one who pulled him away from me.

No, that's not true. Liam would've left regardless. Betty just guided him on his journey.

## 18

LIAM

Finally, her name and beautiful face appear on my screen. I excuse myself from the conversation between Harrison, JD, Layla, and Burke —*Metro*'s long-standing bass player and doorman—and walk to the greenroom.

"Hello?" My voice is a breathy sigh, full of relief. Knowing she's on the other line calms me.

"I'm sorry I disappeared on you. I have no excuse other than I miss you."

"I miss you, too, Jojo." Her words give me pause. I know she's stressing about the baby coming while I'm gone and the best that I can do is promise her I'll be home. Or maybe once he's arrived, she can come out here. Noah won't be done with school yet, but Nick would watch him while Josie visits with the baby.

"So anyway, how are things there?"

"Are you okay?" I ask instead of answering her question. There's something off in her voice and I'd be lying if

I said I wasn't concerned. Without a doubt she's my number one priority, even if I'm not showing it right now.

"I'm good. I'm just really tired."

I laugh, hoping to diffuse the tension I'm feeling over the phone. "Have you been out partying already? You girls shutting down Ralph's at night?" I pray she says yes because the alternative in my mind is that she's been crying her eyes out since I left. I don't know what I'll do if she says that. My options are limited unless she wants to come out here. Logically, I could quit the band, but I won't do that to Harrison and JD. And I think she knows that.

"No, nothing like that. Sleepless nights. No one to cuddle next to and your pillow no longer smells like you. I've taken to wearing a few of your shirts that were left."

The thought of her curled up in my shirt brings a smile to my face. "Would you like me to send you one tomorrow?"

"Yes," she says without hesitation. The only thing missing is her laugh. I really need to hear her giggle because then I'll know everything's okay.

"I love you, Jojo."

"I love you, Liam. Tell me about L.A. Do you remember the time that I was there?"

My groin stirs at the recollection of her in a red dress. The valley of her breasts was exposed, begging for me to mark her as mine. I had to do everything in my power not to cross the line and by line I mean taking her to bed to make her scream my name.

"I'll never forget that night. I wanted you so badly and not just in my bed, but in my life. I wanted to see how you fit here. There were so many times when I'd stand at the window and imagine you down on the street. I'd look for you in the crowds at a concert. I always said that if I saw you, I'd never let you go until you told me to."

"Why are you telling me this now?"

I shrug, even though she can't see it. Taking a deep breath, I prepare to start spilling my guts. "I bottle shit up, you know this. I wish I didn't, but sometimes it's easier. Right now, I'm second-guessing myself as a husband, a father, and a musician. I want to be home with you and Noah, but I want to be here as well. I'm trying to find a happy medium, but I don't know what that is. When I was here before, you were on my mind every single day. Songs have been written about you, repeatedly, and that was never enough. It's like I'm torn in two, Josie. The Page/Westbury parts are fighting for dominance and I honestly don't know which side is going to win."

"You're a wonderful father and an amazing husband. You're the husband I thought you'd be, the only difference is there's no football, and that's okay because that means no injuries, no free agency, no one talking about how old you are. You're successful and have worked hard to gain what you have, what you give Noah and I. I don't want you to change, Liam."

She pauses, catching her breath. I can tell from her voice she's been crying and even though she's assured me nothing's wrong, I know she's not being honest with me.

"I want you to be who you want to be. Noah and I will support you no matter what."

Her words trigger a wave of relief within me. Suddenly, I feel ten pounds lighter. "You're too good for me, you know that, right?"

Josie sighs and giggles. She finally fucking giggles and now I'm smiling like a damn fool. "I'm not but I like that you think I am. We're good for each other."

Before we can get into how things are going, Noah's home and chatting my ear off about baseball practice and spending the night at Nick's. He tells me that Aubrey made him a tent for over his bed, and while he's too big for it, he slept in it anyway so he wouldn't hurt her feelings. He hangs up before I can ask him to put his mom back on the phone.

*I'll call after Noah's in bed.*

I shoot her a quick text. I'd rather let her spend some time with Noah, instead of sitting on the phone with me. Besides, with him in the room, we can't really talk, so I'll call her tonight. As I walk down the hall back to the club, I stop at the picture of my grandfather. I wish I had met him, had been a part of his life or he mine. My grandmother loved him, even though he left her. It takes a strong woman to hold on that long. Josie is strong like my grandma, while my mother isn't. I don't know what would possess anyone to give up their life for someone else. Not in the sense that you're committed to each other, but to forget who you were. Because of what my mother did, likely at the request of my father, I didn't get to know my grandmother and neither did my son. I'm not sure I'll ever be able to forgive her or Sterling for that.

I t feels amazing to be back on a stage. We need to make a few adjustments for this venue, but we still have a few days before the first show. Tickets went on sale this morning and are selling like crazy. Even if Trixie closes *Metro*, she'll have enough money to pay off debtors and get some repairs done. The club is really in need of a makeover.

As soon as the equipment is put away, I tell the guys that I need to speak with them. They both give me the "we don't want to talk business" look. I don't really blame them. Right now, business is at a standstill but we're going to fix that one way or the other. Being in L.A. is an opportunity that we need to seize, grab the bull by the horns so to speak.

"Let's get dinner," I suggest. Food is always a great way to break the ice. Dropping the bomb that Moreno came to my place won't go over smoothly. Harrison and JD agree, and I follow them out the back door. The car service we're using is waiting and as soon as the driver sees us come out, he puts his magazine down to open our door.

"It's nice to see back in the magazines, Mr. Page. The camera sure does love you."

I pause, resting my hand on top of the door. "What are you talking about?"

"You and Ms. Richards are on the front of every magazine and website out there."

My blood turns cold as I take in his words. This is not

good. I had forgotten about the paparazzi being outside the club when I let her in yesterday.

"Mate, your headline is the shit," JD says as he holds his phone out for me.

On his screen is a picture of Layla and me. It's fuzzy and meant to give off that stealth look and I can see why. Without the image being crisp, you can't see us hugging. Instead, you see me trying to kiss her and it looks as though my hands may be in inappropriate places. As if the picture wasn't bad enough, the headline reads: "Former lovers reunite as Page steps out on his wife" in bold letters going across the screen, really driving the point home. The only consolation out of this is that Josie doesn't look at this shit, but I still have to tell her. I can't hide this from her.

The former lovers part gives me pause. No one, aside from Harrison, Sam, Layla, and her ex knew that we had slept together so I'm curious where the photographer picked up his information. It's definitely not common knowledge.

Harrison pulls me into the car, still clutching JD's phone. He takes it back, clearing the screen and leaving me with my own thoughts as the car takes off. Nothing is going right with this trip. First Josie goes radio silent, then Moreno shows up, and now this photo. The next bomb to drop will be the book ...

"Motherfucker," I blurt out, earning stares from both Harrison and JD.

"Care to share?" Harrison asks. The answer should be no, but he's my best friend, and he knows I'll tell him everything.

I shake my head and ask myself how I could be so stupid. I should've pressed Josie harder on the phone about why she wouldn't call me. I've been gone on tour before and we talked all the time. She's never blown me off like that.

"JD, can you look and see when that book about me is coming out?"

He nods and starts moving around on his phone. I could look, but he knows his way about the web much easier. I swear it's an age thing.

"Looks like it was three days ago, mate."

"Fuck, fuck, fuck!" I growl as I pound my fist into the door of the car. Everyone else is silent as I throw my temper tantrum. "The headline ... whoever wrote the article read the book. No one knew about Layla and me, at least anyone that would tell. And the other day, Josie wouldn't talk to me. I have a feeling she's read the book."

"She wouldn't," Harrison says, and I want to agree with him, but the way things were left I'm not so sure. Josie didn't want me to come out here, and if she saw the book in the store, she'd buy it. Hell, if our roles were reversed, I'd buy it and read it in the car. My past is just that, my past. If I wanted people to know shit about me, I'd write my own fucking book.

All too soon we're in front of the hotel. I follow JD out of the car with Harrison behind me. There are a few paparazzi standing on the street and the minute they see us, their cameras are raised. Normally, I wouldn't mind, but not today. I keep my head down as I walk into the hotel which will now be my sanctuary. That and the bar next door. No media are allowed in either place and that makes it perfect for me.

Harrison and I follow JD into the restaurant. He uses his British charm to snag us a private table away from unsuspecting eyes and prying ears. Technically, we should take this to one of our rooms, but we're hungry and want to spread out.

The waitress quickly takes our food and drink orders, shutting the door behind her.

"Aside from this book shit, what's up?" Harrison doesn't waste any time cutting to the chase.

"Moreno came by earlier. He wants us back and is making a strong case. We have to ask ourselves where we want the band to go. Are we happy staying in Beaumont and doing a gig here or there? Or do we want stadiums and the shit we had before?"

Our waitress returns and makes quick work of leaving our drinks. I down mine before she has a chance to leave and set the empty back on her tray. "Another one, please," I ask, receiving a nod.

Harrison leans back in his chair and plays with his glass. "The kids have lives in Beaumont."

"I know."

"But we have a place here." He shrugs. "They like the beach house, but it's not a place to raise a family of five."

"I'd have to talk to the missus, but little one is small enough that she won't know the difference."

"I don't know if I could take the girls away from Mason." Harrison drives it home with that statement. It's been a month or so since I've visited his gravesite. Sometimes it's too hard to go there, and then when I do end up going, Mr. Powell is there and I have to wait for him to leave. I always feel better after talking to Mason and wish I had reached out to him years ago.

Taking a deep breath, I lean forward and face my band mates. My best friends. My family. "I'm going to be honest and tell you I'm split. The musician in me wants this ... maybe not with Moreno, but with another successful manager. Gary's great, but he's not cutting it. The other side of me knows Josie will not go for this and asking her will mean the end of us ... and I refuse to go down that path. I left her once for music, I won't do it again."

I let the words sink in. I can see it on their faces; they know I'll choose her over the band. Harrison and JD can decide to sign with Moreno or shop for someone new. I left her once for music. I won't do it again.

I may have just sealed my fate as a musician. If that's the case, so be it. I'll teach music at the school and watch my kids play sports. Come to think of it, right now retirement has a nice ring to it.

## 19

## JOSIE

"We are down two and Noah's up to bat. We have runners on second and third," I tell Liam. He's been on and off the phone with me during the game, which I know has to be boring for him. But our team is trying to get to the district finals and we need to win. If Noah had been pitching today, I would be biting my nails off.

"How many outs?" he asks. I can hear a guitar in the background and I know he's interrupting their rehearsal to be on the phone with me.

"One." If Noah gets out, we have one more at bat to try and tie this game.

"What's the count?"

"Two and two. Stupid calls," I mutter because behind me is the home plate umpire's wife and the last thing I want is for her to say something to her husband and him to find a way to hurt Noah's game.

The pitch is delivered and I can tell Noah's going to

swing; it must look good to him. The loud clink from the bat connecting with the ball has me on my feet. My heart is racing as the ball flies through the air and the center-fielder back peddles, which is a mistake. Even I know you're supposed to turn and run. His glove is extended, missing the ball by about a mile.

"Run!" I stand and start screaming at the top of my lungs, and because my son knows what he's doing, he's currently rounding second base while none of the outfielders have even picked up the ball. Nick is on third base windmilling his arm so Noah knows to continue. The other parents are standing, yelling for Noah to run faster. If he scores, we're in the lead.

The ball is thrown toward home. Nick is yelling. Noah drops his leg and slides into home just as the ball lands in the catcher's glove. I look at the umpire and wait for his call.

"Safe," he yells as his arms go wide.

"What's going—"

"Oh God, baby, I'm sorry for yelling. Noah just hit a home-run. We're up by one." I'm so excited that I can barely keep still; even as I sit down my legs are shaking. I'm given a few pats on the back by other parents as well.

"Woohoo," Liam yells and repeats what I just told him to the guys. "That's my boy."

The next batter strikes out, ending our inning. "Liam, Noah's going in to finish the game. Oh, sweet mama, I don't know if I can take this."

"He'll be fine. Nick knows what he's doing. He wants Noah to close out the game."

"Yeah, yeah, I know. Its just, you're not here and I need something to squeeze."

Liam laughs. "Thanks, Jojo. I'm glad you only need me next to you so you have something to dig your nails into."

"Har har. Okay, batter up."

Liam stops talking and knows I'll give him Noah's pitch count. It's easier if he doesn't ask me questions so I can focus and be nervous for our son who looks cool as a cucumber out on the mound. Our catcher, Junior Appleton, looks to Nick for the call and gives Noah the signal before setting up the location he wants the ball.

"Swing and miss."

"Ball ... shitty call."

"Be nice, Josie."

"I am," I mumble into the phone. I can't help it if the umpire is blind. "Hit, thrown out at first."

"How does he look?"

"Perfect. God, Liam, he reminds me so much of you, only younger. He's just standing there waiting for the next batter. Even Junior looks good. Pitch is on the way. Strike!"

"He's got this."

"Strike. I'm so nervous."

"He's doing fine, Josie. Where's Aubrey, why aren't you sitting with her?"

"Strike out. Um, I don't know."

"Katelyn?"

"She's here, but refuses to sit with me right now."

Liam laughs, but I don't find it funny at all. My best

friend should accept me no matter how crazy I get during my son's sporting events.

"Two outs, Liam. He has one more and we're on to districts."

"I'll be sure to be back for those games."

"He'll like that. I know he misses you." Noah doesn't say much about Liam being gone. It's been a week and our lives have been pretty normal. I think it's easier knowing Liam's just a plane ride away, not that he can't hop on a plane when he's on tour but it's different. If I call him now and ask him to come home, he will. He doesn't have any scheduled obligations in L.A. right now.

"Ball."

"Strike."

"Foul ball."

"One and two with two outs. I think I'm going to have a panic attack."

"Don't worry, Katelyn is on her way over."

I look up and sure enough she and Peyton are walking toward me.

"I had Harrison text her, asking her to fill in for me."

"You do love me," I say as Katelyn and Peyton sit down. Katelyn wraps her arm in mine and gives me a side hug. I know why she doesn't sit with me; I'm bat shit crazy and Nick often has to tell me to zip it. I can't help it. That's my boy out there.

"I love you more than words, Jojo."

Before I can respond, I'm standing and screaming in his ear again. Everyone is rushing Noah on the mound with Junior being the first one there. The kids are jumping up and down, cheering loudly.

"We won!"

"I figured, baby. Tell Noah I'm proud of him and I'll call him later. I love you."

"Love you, too, bye." I hang up and make my way to the field. Peyton is hot on my heels as we walk out to congratulate Noah and the rest of the boys. I'm not the only parent out here; Candy Appleton and her current beau of the month, plus some others are also on the field.

Candy offers me a smug smile and a stupid finger wave. I mentally flip her off. I'll never get over finding her and Liam sitting next to each other, smoking, at her party. Of course, every chance she gets, she twists the knife a little deeper on how she spent graduation with him while I was too busy with my family.

Noah runs to Nick first and I try not to let that bother me, but it does a little. I'm his mom. He should be looking for me first. Nick picks him up and swings him around. I know he's proud of Noah. They both worked so hard to get here.

I'm lost in thought when Noah starts yelling my name. "Mom, did you see my home-run?"

"I did!"

He stalls and looks at the stands. "I wish Dad saw it."

"Well, he heard it. He's been on the phone with me for most of the game. I was giving him the play-by-play."

"That's cool."

"Yeah, it is." Sadly, it's the best he's going to get right now, but Liam did say he'd be home for Districts and that's more important.

"Hey, Peyton, do you want to come over and shoot hoops or something?"

I watch the exchange between them and the way Noah looks at her. He's so patient and caring. I know they're going to grow up and will likely part ways the older he gets, but seeing him with her now shows me how much he's like Liam.

---

The late afternoon sun shines through the windows of Whimsicality adding sparkle to the flowers that are on display. Standing across the street, it's easy to see the patrons move in and out of both the florist on one side of the shop and the café on the other. As I watch them, I realize that my dreams are coming true, even with the minor detour for construction; I'm living a life that couldn't be any better. Except for Liam being away. But even if he were playing football, he'd be gone a lot. I think I was destined to have a traveling husband. At least we're not always moving, or he's not always being sent from team to team. Having his office in our house is the perfect set-up.

"Hello, Josie."

I turn at the sound of my name and find Bianca standing behind me. Everything about her seems off. She's dressed in a 1950's skirt suit with matching hat, white gloves, and is clutching her purse with both hands in front of her stomach. If I didn't know better I'd say she's hiding a scandalous pregnancy, but we all know that's not the case.

She tries to smile, but it's forced and looks almost painful. "Do you think we could sit for a minute and talk?" Bianca walks toward one of the open benches in the park and sits down. Looking at her, I can't help wondering if she's even the person Sterling married anymore, or if her robotic ways were all his doing to create the perfect wife and family. From the outside that's what he had and was almost able to pull it off until Liam ditched out on Sterling's idea of life and bailed.

I sit down next to her but keep a safe distance. Everyone knows how the Westburys feel about me, they've not kept it a secret, and the last thing I need right now is town gossip. She can stay on her end and I'll stay on mine.

"You had a very lovely shower." She speaks without looking at me or taking her hands off her purse. If I didn't know better, I'd think today was Sunday by the way she's dressed.

"Thanks."

"It's too bad that Liam wasn't there."

"He's working. Besides, baby showers aren't really for guys. If he had been here for it, I'm sure he, Harrison, and Jimmy would've been doing band stuff."

"I shouldn't have come. I upset you on your day."

I let out a sigh and think about the answers I could give. "You're right, you shouldn't have. But my mom invited you and you came. What's done is done."

Bianca stares straight ahead, showing no emotion, just holding her purse like it carries her life inside.

"I'm not a very good person."

I scoff without intending to. She drops her head and continues to speak. "Sterling had this fantasy for Liam as soon as he started carrying on about football. He molded him into a copy of himself, but what he thought was a better version. What he didn't bank on was Liam having a heart and following it, whether it was you or his music career.

"I had a dream once, too, but then I met Sterling. I was destined for stardom. My mother was a beautiful actress and my father a well renowned musician. We lived an amazing life, and even after they divorced, my father was still in love with my mother. I started acting at a young age. As soon as I hit my teens, the movie roles started coming in fast and furious. I had my whole world in the palm of my hand until I met Sterling.

"He was this strapping young man who was visiting Los Angeles one summer, working for his uncle who was the president of the bank that we used. He was older, out of college and well on his way to owning his own branch. His uncle convinced my mother that his nephew would make a great escort to a birthday party I had to attend. My mother thought it wouldn't hurt to give the boys around town a little run for their money.

"And boy did he ever. Sterling romanced me with the best of them. Operas, parties, trips on his uncle's yacht. He was good looking and all of my friends had eyes for him. Plus, he was rich. When the summer ended, we parted ways. But I was pregnant and my parents were livid."

I cover my mouth to hold in a gasp, but Bianca doesn't stop talking.

"I was barely sixteen and pregnant. In my era, you didn't have unwed or single mothers. Pregnancies and children were hidden away. And in Hollywood they just didn't happen. My father was so angry he withdrew all of our money from that bank and went to a competitor. Back then, it was a status thing for banks to hold celebrities' money and my father did the worst thing he could to the bank.

"Sterling, of course, wanted me to move with him to New York. He was starting a job there and would be able to provide for me and the baby. Still, being underage, my parents were adamant that I did not speak to him.

"I was given two options: have an abortion or go to a home for unwed mothers and give my child up for adoption. I wanted neither, but I also didn't want to have a child or live in New York. I wanted to make movies and win Oscars. I wanted everything to just go away.

"And one day, it did. I woke up in pain and bleeding. My mother said that it was the best thing to happen to me. I thought she had been right until Sterling came back the next summer. I saw him from across the street and knew right there and then that he was the man I was going to marry. My father had passed not months before and there I was, waiting for my knight in shining armor.

"We had a grand romance and he filled the void of my father passing. That summer, Sterling was the best man ever. He loved me and showered me with affection. We went to party after party, even though he hated them. They were beneath him with the drinking, drugs, and sex, and he threatened to leave me if I didn't stop going. I was in love, so I stopped accepting invitations. My friends, who had once loved him, couldn't wait for him to leave. I thought they just misunderstood him. He thought Hollywood was going to corrupt me and ruin his image.

"My mother thought he was ruining my career and we'd argue. She found him naked in my bed once and asked if we were being careful. He told her it was my responsibility to make sure a child wasn't conceived. She was livid and forbade me from seeing him, but I didn't stop.

"When the summer was ending and he was about to leave, he asked me to go to New York with him and I said yes. I was foolish, angry with my mother, and hurt that my father had died. Sterling was my savior.

"I remember that night so clearly. It was pouring rain when he showed up at my house. My mother called the cops, and I made the decision right there and then. I was barely seventeen and being torn between my mother and this man that I was so in love with. I looked my mother in the face, told her I hated her, and walked out."

Bianca opens her purse and takes out a tissue and dabs her eyes. Everything is silent around us, as if people have stopped to hear the story of Sterling and Bianca Westbury. Honestly, I'm shocked her story hasn't been made into a movie yet.

She clears her throat and continues. "Sterling knew I had money and was counting on us using that money. My father had left me everything when he died. Unfortunately, we had two problems: I wasn't eighteen so I couldn't get access to my trust, and because my money was no longer in the bank he worked for, we couldn't get it that way either. I came up with this grand plan that I would forge my mother's name on a withdrawal slip and no one would be the wiser. Except she was because by the time we got to the bank the next morning, she had moved the trust to an undisclosed location. There was a note that the bank manager gave me letting me know I could have the funds when I turned eighteen and I presented myself, along with my mother, for withdrawal.

"Sterling was beside himself with anger and told me that I was to never see my mother again. We got in the car and drove off, stopping in Vegas for a shotgun wedding, as the minister called it, even though I wasn't pregnant. My face was plastered all over the entertainment section of the newspaper, and by my eighteenth birthday I was nothing but a memory ... a has-been. I'd never have a career in Hollywood again."

Bianca turns and looks at me with tears in her eyes.

"After a few years of marriage, I realized I didn't love Sterling like I should and wanted out. He wouldn't allow it. He wanted a family, but I was faithful to my contraceptive at the time. One night, he caught me off guard and it would have been inappropriate for me to ask my husband to stop what he was doing so I could make sure a baby wasn't created. When I told Sterling that I was pregnant and wanted to go home to tell my mother, to fix things with her before it was too late, he took away my independence. I had a nurse with me at all times because he was afraid I'd miscarry like I had before. I never had any privacy to do what I wanted.

"I make no excuses for Sterling, only for myself. When Liam brought you home, I saw me in you. I saw a young girl with goals and dreams and her friends around her getting pregnant. I didn't want that for my son. I was blinded by my own hatred for the things I've done in my life that I couldn't see what was right in front of me.

When you came to the house, pregnant and alone, I should've sought you out behind Sterling's back, but I didn't because I'm a coward. I've done you wrong, Josie, and I apologize."

Before I can get a word out, she's walking away from me. I think about going after her, but my feet are cemented to the ground. I wipe away my own tears and let her words sink in. I have a feeling I'm the only one who knows her life story, and I think I need to know more.

As soon as I hang up with Josie, I know I need to get away from everyone here. Being at *Metro* is pointless. We're just sitting around shooting the shit about where we've been and wondering when we'll be the next hour-long segment on VH1 profiling our failing careers.

Listening to Josie provide the play-by-play of Noah's game really struck a chord with me. I should be there, and the fact that Josie didn't hound me about it tells me two things: I either have the best fucking wife in the world or she's accepted the fact that this is our life. I know it's a combination of the two and right now I'm feeling like I don't deserve to be her husband.

I walk the streets, not worrying whether anyone will see me. Aside from the images of Layla, nothing else has been in the press. I stop dead in my tracks when I think about those images. I'm a selfish prick for not telling Josie about them. She's got too much on her plate right now ...

that's the ridiculous excuse I'm going to use to justify my actions until I can grow a set and tell her. My hesitation is because I'm not prepared for her response. Telling her that the images don't mean anything won't be enough to keep her thoughts at bay. I know she trusts me, but she doesn't trust Los Angeles. Not that I can blame her. This town is already trying to ruin our relationship.

As soon as I turn the corner, I'm facing the Ducati dealership—the same one I bought from long before I left Los Angeles. Now, my motorcycle sits in my garage, coming out only occasionally. Standing here, I realize how much I miss riding my bike.

"She's a beauty, isn't she?"

A salesman appears to the side of me. He's dressed in a suit and is eyeing my distressed jeans and designer shirt with strategic holes in it.

"She is." The thought occurs to me that I need an escape while I'm here and this just might be it. "Do you have rentals?"

The salesman puts his hands in his pockets and pretends to ponder my question. I know they do, but he's looking at me, wondering if I can afford to rent one of their bikes. He can't tell that my shirt cost over a hundred bucks and my jeans twice that. He looks behind me, noticing that there isn't a car parked in front of his store and is likely wondering how I got here.

"So ... about that rental?"

"Yeah, I mean if we have the loaners in stock, we can." This is his way of brushing me off. We'll go inside and he'll sit behind his computer and type, likely sending a message to his manager, telling him that some bum wants to rent a Ducati. The manager will come out, pretending he doesn't have an idea of why I'm here. It's a game and I've played it before.

He doesn't say anything as we walk into the dealership. The smell of new rubber permeates through the air. These bikes have very few, if any, miles at all. It's been so long since I've paid attention to what new bikes are coming out and I'm surprised by the difference in the new Scrambler. It's all Ducati, but with a motor cross feel. The back roads of Beaumont would be like heaven on this bike.

"She's new, just came out. If you're into just cruising along or know of any dirt roads, that's the bike you want. However, she's slow with only seventy-five horsepower."

The all black bike with yellow accents is easy on the eyes. I could definitely see teaching Noah how to ride something like this.

"What's the price?"

"Oh, huh ..." He scratches his head. "She's just under ten thousand."

Ten thousand is nothing, but I didn't plan on spending money on something so frivolous. I'm already worried about making sure the money I do have continues to grow even when the music stops. I could be faced with paying two college bills if either boy doesn't receive a scholarship. I'm fully expecting Noah to receive one, but he could change his mind about sports and chose a different path.

"I'll take it," I tell him without second-guessing myself. I know I don't need it and I know that I'm contradicting every reasonable thought flooding my mind, but

I'll just have to add it to the list of things I need to tell Josie about. Fuck, if that list isn't getting long.

The salesman looks at me like I have two heads. I probably do. I pull out my wallet and hand him my credit card. He takes it, looking at the name and back at me.

"I'll just ..." He points his thumb over his shoulder. He's nervous and probably hoping that I don't say anything about his poor sales technique to his manager.

"I'll need a helmet, too, please."

"Right away, Mr. Page."

I can't help but smile as he rushes to his cubicle. Others linger around, a few of them whispering. It'll be exciting if someone comes up to ask for my autograph. It'll make me feel like I matter again. I sit down on my bike, getting a feel for how she feels between my legs. She's smaller and lighter than the one I have at home, but I have a feeling this one will be ridden more. I'll even teach Josie how to ride it. This will be perfect for her.

A flash gets my attention, and when I look up, I see one of the young saleswomen quickly typing on her phone as she turns away from me. My heart drops, knowing that my image is about to hit social media. I won't have to tell Josie what I'm doing because this chick just did it for me.

"Hey," I call out, stopping her dead in her tracks. "What did you say when you posted my picture?"

"I ... I didn't."

I roll my eyes and shake my head slightly. "Lying is very unbecoming and I do believe taking photos of your clients without their permission is against company policy, isn't it?"

"I'm sorry, Mr. Page. I'll remove it immediately," she says as she walks away. The damage is done. She knows it and is probably at her desk crying. I'm faced with either telling her boss or letting it go. Today is not the day that I want to ruin anyone's life, so she should be thankful. My picture is out there and there isn't shit I can do about it. When I call to talk to Noah tonight, I'll tell Josie that I had an impulse and bought a new motorcycle.

Once the paperwork is printed and everything is signed, I'm pushing my new toy out of the showroom and onto the streets of L.A. Slipping my helmet on, I turn her on, letting the bike idle while I get a feel for her. I can't wait to see what she does on the road.

It's not long until I'm weaving my way through Mulholland Blvd. After being gone for a few years, I'd have thought things would've changed, but they haven't. I slow down when I get to my grandma's street. I haven't been back here since I moved into the penthouse and I'm not sure why I am now. Shutting off the bike and removing my helmet, I look up at the big white house that I called home for a short time of my life.

The black gate and fence that protected her from intruders still stands tall. Whoever is living here has been maintaining the landscaping that she loved so much. In fact, everything looks freshly painted. My heart swells with pride for my grandparents, knowing that the home they shared is being loved.

"Can I help you?" A lady walking her dog stops next to me.

"No, just looking at the house. I used to know the previous owner."

She looks at me with confusion written all over her face. "The lady that lived here died, but her family took over her estate."

She's right, she did die ... but now I'm confused. I run my hand over my hair and think back to when my grandmother died. I told Sam to sell it or donate it, but never followed up on it.

"Do you know who owns it?"

The lady shakes her head and offers a small smile. "West something or other. The family is never here but they make sure the house is well maintained. You'd think someone lives there."

"Don't they?" I ask, even though I know the answer. The only person, other than me, who could stake a claim, is my mother and I'm not sure she even knows her mother died.

"Not for ten years or more. I've lived next to this house for fifteen years. There was a young kid one time, but haven't seen him since she passed away." The neighbor looks at the house and sighs. "I'm sure if you were interested in buying, they'd sell. The County office will have the information."

She and her dog are down the street before I'm done processing everything. There's no way I still own this house, but someone does. Someone has been taking care of this property all these years and I need to figure out who they are and why they're doing it.

When I arrive back at the club, the back alley is lined-up with cars. At best, there have been two or three back here at a time, but nowhere near a dozen or more. The benefit of having a bike is that you can park anywhere, squeezing into the smallest spots, even making your own. That's what I end up doing, right by the back door.

As soon as I'm inside, Harrison is pulling me into the green room. He looks pissed off, and that's not a good thing. It takes a lot to piss him off.

"Where the fuck have you been?"

Oh yeah, he's pissed.

"I needed to get some fresh air."

Harrison pulls off his trademark beanie and runs his hand through his short hair. "Remember when Trixie asked if Sal sent us?"

I nod, remembering well. Harrison and I had no idea who she was talking about.

"Sal is Mr. Moreno, as in Sam's father, as in majority owner of Moreno Entertainment."

I shake my head, disagreeing with him. "Nah, Sam's dad is named Anthony, but he prefers to be called Moreno. It's like he thinks he's Madonna or some shit like that."

"No," he says, with his head moving back and forth. "Salvador Anthony Moreno is his name and right now he's out in the club with a shit load of fucking reporters. Trixie hired him to do some promo work for the fundraiser and he's scheduled a press event."

"What?"

"Yeah, apparently he and Trixie go way back and she's always called him Sal. When he started his company, he started going by Anthony."

"Um ... this isn't good."

"No, it's not. We haven't done a legit interview since Sam was managing us and now that she's not here to monitor questions, I'm afraid of what shit is going to be asked."

I start to pace, thinking about what we can do. "We don't have to do it. We're not under contract to perform so we'll skip the interviews."

"You know, I thought about that as everyone was setting up." He pauses and puts his hat back on. "But we need the press. We need to be in front of the people again."

I shake my head, not willing to put myself out there. "I can't."

The door to the green room opens. Trixie steps in, looking like the Trixie of old. Her hair is jet black and her lips are painted crimson red. She looks like she's about to shatter the dreams of every wannabe musician tonight.

"I need you, Page."

"No can do, Trixie. Interviews are messy and we don't have an agent or manager to ward off fucked up questions."

Trixie walks up to me with her hands on her hips. "I gave you a shot when you needed it and now I need you. I need people to see that it's never too late to come home."

"I know that, it's why I left L.A."

"You may have left L.A., but it didn't leave you. You

still depend on the industry to provide for you. I need you, Page. You came back to help, so do it. You owe me." Her hands drop from her hips and her posture changes. She looks sad and broken. I shouldn't fall for this, but I am. She's right, I do owe her.

"Fine, but if there's a question we don't want to answer, we're saying no comment."

"I don't give a shit if you flip them off, just go sit at the table and fucking smile. Make those reporters wet themselves for all I care."

I watch Trixie leave, throwing her hands in the air and mumbling to herself. I look over at Harrison, who is stoic. "I guess we need to go out there."

"Yep," he says as he walks toward the door. I follow in step, just like usual. This was something Sam had done for us, lined us up. She always said it was important that I was the last one to enter. Even though she's gone, we're still walking the same way.

As soon as we're visible to the reporters the clicking of shutters and bright lights of bulbs are going off like crazy. I'm instantly on edge, and as I sit down next to Layla, I realize I don't want to be here. I'm also hit with the fact that for the first time in years, I miss Sam right now. When I look up, I quickly see Mr. Moreno, aka Sal, in the corner. He tips his glass to me as I fight the urge to flip him off.

**E**very fiber of my being is telling me to chase after Bianca and ask for more. Not for another apology, but for more of her story. Maybe if she can explain her life to me, I can help Liam understand, even though I'm not sure I fully grasp everything she just told me. What I do know is Liam and I, as a couple, have been robbed of a relationship with Bianca. To me, Sterling is a lost cause. Even if he showed up full of apologies, I can't see myself listening to him, let alone believing a word that comes out of his mouth.

Since Liam and I started dating, I've been the outcast —someone who would never be good enough for their son. The photographic memories Liam and I share have always included my family or Katelyn's and Mason's. The Westburys were always absent from all of them. I don't even know if his mother ever posed with him for a prom photo. My guess is she didn't, especially knowing he was going with me.

I head to work before more anger starts to set in. I can't dwell on the past or change what has happened. I can only make a change for the future, if that's what I want. I'm not sure it is though. How much effort do I put forth not knowing whether Bianca would return the gesture or not? Or whether she would be allowed to? We all know Sterling is controlling but Bianca came to my baby shower so either she's sneaking out, or he's just too old to care. Or maybe she's had enough and is standing up to him. I have to admit I find the latter harder to believe.

As soon as I enter the florist side of my business, Jenna barely pops her head up from under the counter. I give her my best 'what the hell look', causing her to shake her head.

"I'm restocking," she says, disappearing under the counter.

"I did that last night." I walk around and find the wrapping paper scattered all over the floor.

Jenna sits back on her knees and sighs. "I made the mistake of letting Eden loose for a few minutes and apparently she didn't like the way we had things."

"At least she's cute," I say to Jenna's back. Eden is adorable and has everyone wrapped around her little finger, but she's a complete terror when she's on a mission and nothing seems to be able to change her mind.

"Let me help you." I bend down and start gathering the sheets of paper we use to wrap the flowers in. "How are you doing?" I ask her, curious if I'm losing touch with reality because while I miss Liam, the pain I was feeling earlier—the heartache—has subsided and that scares me.

This is also the first time Jimmy's been gone since the shooting.

Jenna shrugs and slides her stack of paper back into the cubbyhole. It doesn't escape my notice that she's wiping away tears. I don't know if they're from Jimmy being gone, or because of Eden causing havoc. "It gets easier, right?" When she looks at me, her eyes are red and puffy. I drop my stack, adding to Eden's mess, and pull her into my arms.

"I want to tell you yes, that it does get better, but I would be lying. I think we just get used to it." Pulling back, I wipe away her tears. "It's different for each of us. I was asking myself the same thing earlier. I'm not in agony over him being gone; does that mean I love him less?"

She shakes her head. "I'm so worried, though. What if he's not ready to be all crazy up on stage?"

I return to my stack and hand it to her, waiting for her to slide the papers back in. "What does Xander say?"

Jenna shrugs again. "Jimmy says everything is fine and Xander agrees, but I can't help feeling they're not being honest with me. I've seen him get winded chasing Eden around the house! He tells me it's nothing and that he's out of shape, but how can that be if he's working out all of the time?"

"I think being on stage and chasing a toddler around are two different things. When he's on stage, the exhilaration will keep him going. Besides, you know Liam and Harrison aren't going to let anything happen to him."

"I know," she sighs, as she picks up the last stack of paper. "I think I'm looking for excuses for him to come home. I was thinking of taking a couple of days off and going out there."

Her thought gives me the same idea, but with Noah's schedule, I can't. He needs at least one parent at his games. If he weren't playing baseball right now, we'd both be in California with Liam.

"I think you should. I think Jimmy will like that, and maybe it'll put your mind at ease."

"You think?"

"I do, and you guys can find time to take Eden to Disneyland. I bet she'd love that."

Jenna wraps her arms around me in a tight hug. She knows I'd do anything for her and if that means she needs time off, she can have it. Truthfully, she does me a favor by working here.

We're still sitting on the floor when a young man steps up to the counter. We were both so lost in our conversation that we didn't hear the chime on the door.

"Sorry," I say as I scramble to my feet. "We didn't hear you come in."

"It's cool," he says. "I'd like a dozen red roses for my girlfriend."

Jenna starts to work on his arrangement while I take all of his information and process his order.

"What's the occasion?" I ask, as he signs his credit card receipt.

"No reason. I was walking by and saw the flowers in the window. I love her and think she should know that I'm thinking about her even as I'm walking down the street."

Jenna and I both swoon. "She's lucky to have you. Would you like us to deliver them?" I ask.

"Do chicks like that?"

Jenna giggles. "Is she at work?"

"Yes, she works over at the bank."

"Then yes," Jenna says, as she walks around the counter to pick out a vase. "Her co-workers will all dote on her and tell her how lucky she is. They'll be jealous. Believe me, it's a good thing."

"All right, then. How much is delivery?"

"It's on the house," I say, before Jenna can tell him the price. This young man is clearly smitten with his girl, and he reminds me of Liam. It's the least I can do for him.

"Thank you." He stays to inspect the flowers and chats with us for a few more minutes. When they're ready, Jenna tells me she's going to walk them over to the bank and asks if I don't mind manning the shop. I wave her off. She should know that I don't mind staying.

The way the café was built, I can watch the flower shop while standing at the register of the café. It was done this way because I never thought I'd need staff for both sides. The café part is booming, especially during meals. In between the peak times, we have patrons who come in who read, gossip, and even write their novels. I like to think of the café as a happy place.

Dana and David are working tonight, training Pete and Tracy, who are both older and looking to supplement their income. My plan is to promote Dana at the end of the month once she tells me if she's staying on through the summer or not.

"Hey, Josie." Dana walks by with a tub full of

dishes. When I started hiring, Mr. Powell suggested I have everyone call me Mrs. Westbury, just as we still call him Mr. Powell. He said it's a respect thing, and while I don't disagree, I find it awkward and impersonal.

"How was the lunch rush?"

She passes the bucket off to David, who nods in my direction before disappearing out back.

"Every table was full, and Tracy and Pete really knew how to handle the pressure. David said Pete is a whiz in the kitchen." Our kitchen isn't anything extraordinary since we serve mostly soups, salads, and sandwiches, but it's good to know that Pete is capable of keeping up.

"That's great," I say, glancing back into the shop to make sure I didn't miss another chime.

"So, how are you taking everything?"

"With Liam being gone?" I ask with a shrug. "It's not the first time he's been gone since we've been back together. They toured last year and are hoping to tour this summer, as well. Although, during the summer we can go ..." I trail off because Dana is looking at me like I have two heads. Her eyes are squinted as if she's in deep thought or utterly confused.

"What?" I help her along by asking instead of leaving her sitting there with a strained expression on her face, trying to decide how to phrase her next question.

"I just thought ... with the ... never mind," she says. She tries to walk away, but I reach out and grab her.

"With the what? Dana, what are you talking about?"

"The photos," she says quietly, almost ... shamefully.

"What photos?" My voice is terse. The tension is already rising.

Dana backs away with her hands up. "I really like my job here, so I'm just going to wait on those customers."

I stop her again as she tries to pass. "You won't get fired, nor will I be upset with you. Please tell me what you're talking about." I let go of her arm and she digs through her apron, pulling out her phone. After a few seconds of swiping and typing she turns her screen toward me.

I take a step back and take her phone from her. My husband and another woman are kissing. The image is grainy, but there's no mistaking where his mouth is. I push the screen up and find more of them, together in a restaurant and outside of his hotel.

"Who is this?"

"Layla Richards," she says as my blood runs cold. "According to this article, they used to be—"

"I know who she is," I say abruptly, as my stomach turns and my heart starts racing. "I need to go. Can you watch the shop until Jenna gets back? She just ran to the bank."

I don't wait for her answer as I run out the door. My car is parked down the street, in front of Xander's gym, and I pray that he isn't outside when I get there. I fight to hold back the tears as I make my way to my car.

Once inside, I bite the inside of my cheek until I'm far enough away that I can pull over. The scream is nothing like I've ever felt before, worse this time than when he left me. I grip the steering wheel, yanking it back and forth as I cry out in anger, frustration, and pain. My throat is raw and burning, and the sounds coming out of me are animalistic. I see his face and his eyes as he looks at that woman and I want to strangle him. I want to kill him for doing this to me, for doing this to Noah and our unborn child.

*There has to be an explanation.* That is what I'm telling myself as I drive home. I can't fathom the thought of Noah having to go through a divorce. I've been down this path with Liam before; I was able to move on and I can do it again, but I'm not sure about Noah.

*"What is wrong with you?"* I yell at the top of my lungs. Not at Liam, but at myself for assuming the worst. He's always said you can't trust the media, but was he just saying that so I wouldn't look or is it true? Or is this true ... that he's with another woman? This is exactly why I didn't want him to go back to Los Angeles. I can't handle this part—the Liam Page part—of his life.

When I pull into the driveway, I'm caught off guard by the sight of Bianca throwing a football around with Noah. She's still dressed as she was earlier and somehow makes tossing a ball look effortless in heels. I want to talk to her more, but now is not the right time. I pull down my visor and check my eyes. They're bloodshot and my eyelids are puffy.

*Great!*

Taking a deep breath, I open the door. I can't sit in here and avoid her, especially after everything we shared today.

"Hey, Mom," Noah says after I shut my door. I wave and pretend to look for something in my purse. The longer I stall, the better off I'll be. But I can't stand by the car forever and finally take the required steps to get to my front door.

When I look up, Bianca is watching me. She looks so much like Liam, with her dark hair and matching eyes. It makes me wonder if she got her looks from her mom or dad.

"Hello, Josie."

"Hi, Bianca. I hope Noah isn't being too hard on you."

"Oh no, he's just fine. He's teaching me how to throw a spiral."

"She's not very good yet," he chimes in. Instead of saying something snobbish, she smiles. It's the first time I've seen her smile. Her whole face lights up, making her eyes sparkle.

"Would you like to stay for dinner?" I blurt out the question before I know what I'm saying. Either Noah or Bianca let out a little gasp, I can't be sure whom, but they're obviously just as shocked as I am that I asked.

"I'd love to, Josie. Thank you."

"Come on, Grandma, you can sit next to me."

This is the first time I've heard Noah call her grandma, but she must answer to it. He has his arm out, bent at the elbow, as he escorts her into the house.

I follow them into the house and the aroma of lasagna wafts through the air, causing my stomach to turn. I press my hand against my stomach and hold my breath until the queasiness subsides. Linda is an excellent cook and insists on cooking for us, even though she doesn't need to. For half a minute I thought she'd head back to L.A. with

Liam, but she stayed. I'm glad. It's nice to have someone in the house when it's just me.

"Are you okay, Josie?" Bianca asks.

I nod. "I'm fine," I tell her, offering no valid excuse as to why my stomach is flipping upside down right now.

"Your home is beautiful."

"Thank you." We sit down with Bianca sitting by Noah as he rattles off who knows what. She intently listens and asks questions at the appropriate time. When Linda comes out, I tell her that I'm not very hungry and she offers to make me soup instead, clearly not taking "no" for an answer.

We eat with sporadic conversation. It's mostly Noah talking but I chime in every now and again. When his plate is clear, he asks to be excused, promising he'll be right back. There's an awkward silence filling the room and I know I'm the one who needs to break it.

"This really means a lot to Noah ... that you're here and that you come see him."

Bianca smiles. She sits up straight and puts her hands in her lap, ever so proper. "He's very funny and so smart. I've been enjoying my time with him."

"Does Sterling know you're here?" My tone is sharp and to the point. The last thing I want is that man beating down my door looking for his wife.

Her eyes fall to her lap and I know I've hit a nerve. "He does and doesn't approve. But I need to do this for myself. For far too long I've done things his way, and I've missed out on so many years with my grandson, not to mention my own son. I'd like to go to Noah's baseball game, if you think that'd be okay?"

I nod, letting her know that it's fine. "He'd like that," I say as I try to keep my voice from breaking.

"Do you love him?"

"Who?" I ask.

"Liam."

My head moves up and down, telling her yes. "Of course I do. Why would you ask me something like that?" Now my voice cracks and tears threaten to fall. I love him but, in this moment, I'm not sure that I trust him.

"Because when you arrived home you were crying. I know what it's like to be alone and to miss someone. Those weren't the tears you were shedding. Your tears were angry."

"How could you tell?"

"I've cried many tears, and the ones that made me look the worst were the angry ones."

I'm taken aback by what she's saying, and hate that she's observant enough to know the difference in my tears. Right now, I'd like to ask her to leave, but Noah's coming down the stairs and I don't want to hurt his feelings. He needs Bianca in his life, and as much as part of me wants to stop their relationship, I won't do that to him.

I leave them at the table and head into the kitchen with our plates. From a distance I can hear my phone ringing. I hope it's not Liam because I'm not ready to talk to him. I rush to my phone, not recognizing the number.

Stupidly, I answer. "Hello?"

"Josie Westbury?"

"Yes, who is this?"

"Roger Jones, Editor at Gossip. Can you confirm that Liam Page has filed for divorce?"

I set my phone down and rush into the bathroom, expelling the contents of my stomach into the toilet. Here I am again because of Liam. I try to hold it together because the last thing I want is for Bianca to ask questions.

When I sit back on my heels, she's handing me a towel. I can't keep the tears away any longer, nor can I keep up this stupid façade that I trust my husband.

"I'm sorry, you don't need to see this." I get up and head to the sink, rinsing my mouth and splashing water on my face. From behind me, the toilet flushes, causing another wave of tears. I don't trust Bianca, and yet I'm vulnerable.

She sets my phone down on the counter and steps through the doorway. "One thing I learned from growing up in the world you're living in is that you can't trust everything you hear or see. Call him, Josie." The door shuts, locking me in this small space with my demons.

# 22

## LIAM

"Thank you for being here today," says the short brunette who is standing at the podium next to our table. Besides the band and Layla, four other guys are sitting at the table with us. I don't have a clue as to who they are, but they must be important to Trixie since they're here and willing to help her.

"If you didn't sign in with your seat number, please let me know." She holds up a clipboard, but there are no takers. "My name is Wendy and I'll be your moderator today. To keep things orderly, please raise your hand and I'll call out your seat number."

Burke appears with glasses and pitchers of water. "What about the vodka?" I ask, but get no reply. I lean into Layla and ask her if she's ready for this. When I hear shutters clicking, I know I've made a grave mistake. "Fuck," I mutter under my breath, only to feel her hand on my knee. Thank God for tablecloths or I'd be more screwed than I already am.

"Before we start, I'd like to introduce you to the panel. First we have Adam, Lem, Chett, and Dex from Wild Nobility." Wendy, helpfully, sheds light as to who the other four musicians are before introducing Layla and then us to the waiting crowd. "Okay, now that the formalities are out of the way, let's begin," Wendy says to the delight of the audience. Hands fly up into the air and I use this opportunity to fill my water glass and drink it down before I have to answer any questions.

"Number twenty-seven," Wendy calls out.

"How do you find time to balance your personal and professional life?"

I look at Layla who is answering first. She smiles and leans into the microphone. "Being a songwriter, it's easy for me to be a mom first. I write when the lyrics are in my head, but I don't have to be in a certain location to do that. I always have my phone with me and can easily make notes on that if inspiration strikes."

I take a deep breath and pull the microphone to me. "We work nine-to-five like everyone else, but with the flexibility of taking time off when needed for our kids."

"We're not just a band, but a family. Our family comes first," Harrison adds.

"We're far too busy to have personal lives," Dex, one of the guys on the end, answers. Someone should tell them that being in love and having kids will trump being in a band any day.

"Number four."

"Do you ever give in to temptations, or find yourself battling them?"

"I got into some trouble early on in my career, but since I got those under control, I've been okay. Right now, my only temptation is men." Layla has the crowd eating out of her hand with her answers and the women laugh at her response. "It's hard to keep my hands off a good looking man."

"Since I moved out of L.A. a few years ago, I've been happy and living a great life. My only temptation is my wife."

Harrison and JD's answers are similar to mine while the guys from Wild Nobility talk about how they battle with urges every day. They might want to think about rehab.

Hands fly up in the air and Wendy says, "Number fifteen."

"This question is for Liam and Layla. Liam, you had a very close relationship with Layla when you were starting out in the business. How does it feel to work with her again after all these years?"

"Layla and I didn't work together so this will be our first time. We were just friends."

"With benefits," someone yells out.

Clearing my throat, I sit up a bit taller. "As I said, we were friends. Harrison and Layla had more of a working relationship."

This is why I don't do interviews, because people can't just ask questions about music. They have to get personal. I take a drink of my water and fiddle with my bracelet.

"Number one."

"How do you describe your perfect day?"

"The sun is shining, lyrics are flowing, and my daughter is happy," Layla answers and then I'm up next.

"My perfect day would be with my wife and son. It doesn't matter what we're doing, as long as we're together."

"I'm the same as Liam. Being with my wife and kids makes every day perfect."

"Ah, I'm happy when I'm with my little one or when my missus is walking about starkers."

"Jesus, JD," I say, causing everyone to laugh.

"Number three."

"What is the worst rumor you've heard about yourself?"

We all start to laugh because where do you even start?

"That I had died from a drug overdose on stage," Layla says. I look at her and she shrugs. I hadn't heard that one, although I really wasn't paying attention all these years.

"Um ... for me, I guess it would have to be ..." The rumor I hate the most is the one I'm constantly emailed about: Are you cheating on your wife? I never answer them, which is probably code for: I am. Thing is, I can't say that now because they'll run with it and twist my words. I do what every musician is expected to do; I lie. "Mine would be the constant rumors about my many stints in rehab. I've never been in one, nor have I ever been addicted to drugs."

"Are there any rumors about me?" Leave it to Harrison to be perfect.

"That I'm gay," JD says.

"We all know that's not true," a female voice rings out.

"Damn right, love."

At the other end of the table, Lem clears his throat. Apparently he's ready to answer. "Our biggest rumor is that we don't get along. It's not true."

I look down the table and can tell he's lying. The other two band members haven't said a thing during any of the questions, only Dex, who I'm assuming is their lead singer. He looks emo, and is probably a pill popping tweaker.

"Number eight."

My favorite number.

"My question is for Liam and Layla. Have you read Calista Jones' biography?"

My blood turns cold as I lean in. "That would be an unauthorized biography, and the answer is no."

"I'm sorry, I wasn't finished with my question," number eight says.

"That's not my problem." Number eight sighs, but doesn't sit back down.

"Layla, will you and your daughter be visiting or moving to Beaumont now that it's been revealed that Liam Page is her father?"

"Are you f—"

"Liam Page is not the father of my daughter. My daughter and her dad have a very good relationship. He's very active in her life and always has been. This is the last time I'll discuss this with anyone so I suggest each and every one of you print it clearly."

I want to applaud Layla for standing up for me and to

the reporters, but I'm so fucking pissed off I can't see straight. My recovery time is nil as the next number is called.

"Number eleven."

"What's the best part about performing and recording music?"

Yet again, Lem starts speaking before Layla can and all four of us turn to stare at him. He clearly doesn't care because he's rattling off a diatribe about his life. By the time he's finished, we've all forgotten the question.

"Number twenty-two."

"Liam, how does your wife feel about you being here rekindling old friendships while she's at home preparing for your new arrival?"

That question gets the reporters riled up and they start firing off questions right and left. It's not a secret we're adopting, but it isn't exactly public knowledge either.

"My wife is fine. Our son is playing in some very important baseball games right now, so she stayed home with him," I say, dodging the question about the new arrival.

"And the baby?"

"At the moment, my wife isn't pregnant." I leave it at that, hoping they get the hint.

I refill my water glass, wishing it was something stronger. I'm starting to get agitated and wonder if Moreno set this shit up on purpose to prove that we need someone like him. Yet again, I find myself suddenly missing Sam because if she were here, then it would be guaranteed a few of these questions wouldn't be asked.

"Number six."

"Liam, I've read the biography by Calista Jones and am wondering how it feels to have your lover's personal diaries made public?"

"Fuck this shit," I mumble under my breath. "Do you really want to know?"

All the reporters nod. *Assholes.*

"Anything you read from Sam Moreno should be taken with a grain of salt. She was mentally unstable and in need of psychiatric care. We took her and Moreno Entertainment to court for a restraining order, which Mr. Moreno is hell bent on breaking ... repeatedly. This Calista Jones wrote a book without my authorization, and if I could sue the shit out of her I would. Are you out there, Calista?"

To my surprise, a woman stands up. "I am."

"Perfect, do you have any other intrusive questions for me or are we done here?"

"I actually have one." It's Mr. Moreno who steps forward. "You just made a comment about my daughter, one that I find very offensive, to say the least. Are you honestly going to say that you weren't in love with her?"

I slam my hands down on the table and stand up. "Never have I said I was in love with Sam. I don't give a shit what she put in her diary. Even this long after her death, I'm still finding out about all of the dishonest things she's done or said. She lied about being pregnant and she kept my son away from me, or was that you? Your daughter was sick, and when she didn't get her way, she wreaked havoc on anyone in her path. If I was so in love with your daughter, I wouldn't have tattooed another woman's name across my chest for her to see every day."

I pause and rest on my hands, catching my breath before looking back at the reporters. "I don't think you understand the damage you can do to someone's life. You take your fucking pictures and make up your shitty headlines just to cause problems. You use computer programs to manipulate images into something they're not, and laugh your asses to the banks while lives and marriages are destroyed. You want to write that I'm a pig because I hugged a fucking friend who I hadn't seen in ten years, and that I'm cheating on my wife ... look in the fucking mirrors and ask yourself if you're a decent human being. I'm here to tell you, you're not.

"Do you want to know why we left L.A.? So we could raise our kids without the likes of you assholes looming around us. I'm so fucking done."

I walk away and can hear footsteps behind me. As soon as I'm in the green room the lamp closest to the door is flying across the room, shattering into a million pieces. The door shuts, and when I look behind me it's Harrison and JD.

"I'm sorry," I say, running my hands over my face. "I lost it and you'll be the ones to suffer in the end." I wouldn't be surprised if they ditch me for another band. I'm hotheaded and my temper sucks. Families should be off-limits, but they're not, and mine is going to be paying dearly because of that fact.

"You were right to get up and leave," Harrison says, as he sits down.

Sighing, I shake my head. "I shouldn't have said that shit about Sam, even if it is true."

"She brings out the worst in ya, mate."

"The thing is, she wasn't always like that. I did that to her. All she wanted to do was love me and make me this big star, but I was so fucking hung up on my mistakes and my past that I refused to let her in. When I did, it was for sex because she was easy. I knew she wanted me and I led her on repeatedly."

A knock on the door stops me from speaking. JD answers it, and Calista Jones is standing on the other side.

"Sorry, darlin', I'm pretty sure that anything you have to say is going to result in a no comment from us. Move along, now." JD tries to shut the door but her hand stops it.

"I think you should listen to what I have to say."

"All right, we're all ears. Say your peace, then be on your way," JD instructs.

"I'd like to speak privately with Liam."

"Nice try, but that ain't gonna happen, love," JD says, clearly in control of the room right now.

"Fine." She straightens her suit jacket. "Mr. Page, I've done nothing wrong. The diaries were sent to me, along with a list of people I should contact about you. Your threat to sue me has not fallen on deaf ears, but I must warn you ... if you do pursue legal action, I'll publish Sam's diaries in full and I don't think you want that."

"Are you threatening me?" I ask, as I step forward.

"No more than you are threatening me. Let's call it an impasse, shall we?"

She turns on her heels and leaves, closing the door

behind her. My mouth hangs open, and while I'm tempted to call bullshit, I know she's not bluffing. Who knows what the fuck Sam said in her diaries? One thing I know for certain is that I don't want to have to defend myself for the rest of my life. I've already had enough.

## 23

---

## JOSIE

I dial his phone repeatedly. It rings eight times before going to voicemail. He's either not near it, or just doesn't want to answer it. At least I can take comfort in knowing that he isn't declining my calls. Before I give up, I leave him a message telling him that I love him and that we need to talk as soon as possible. I know he'll be able to hear the distress in my voice, and pray that his love for me is just as strong as mine is for him so that no matter what's going on, he'll be honest with me.

Bianca and Noah are sitting in the family room when I come out. Noah's going to suspect that something is going on and I'll have to get creative with my answers to his probing questions when he asks them. The fact is, I won't know what's going on until Liam calls.

The sound of my voice echoes from the television, causing Noah to laugh. "What on earth are you watching?"

"Your DVD's," Bianca says, handing me a cup of tea. "Sit down, he'll call soon."

I sort of love that she has so much confidence in her son right now because mine is lacking. She grew up this way, with the media always in her face about things. I can't imagine what her parents' divorce was like for her, knowing how things get twisted in the media.

"Thank you." I hold up the mug, and she smiles before turning her attention back to the television. I sit down in the chair and watch Liam run across the screen. The announcer is screaming as he ticks down the yardage from this run. The kid Mr. Powell hired to film the games follows his every move until Liam enters the end zone.

"That's going to be me someday," Noah tells Bianca as he fast forwards through the other team's offensive run. "I wear number eight just like my dad."

"Why did you choose that number?" she asks him.

Noah shrugs. "I don't know. I've always liked it."

Bianca beams at Noah and turns her attention back to the TV when he presses play. I'm on screen now, cheering for the team. Secretly, I was only cheering for Liam and Mason, but no one ever needs to know that.

"You were so pretty, Mom."

"Gee thanks, Noah."

"Your mom is beautiful, Noah. You should tell her so every day." My mouth drops open at Bianca's words. She doesn't look at me as she speaks and, for that, I'm thankful. I turn my attention back to the TV and pretend the last few seconds never happened.

As soon as my phone starts ringing, I'm moving out of the room and upstairs to our bedroom. "Hello?"

"Hey, I got your message."

His words give me pause. He sounds curt and disinterested.

"Are you busy?"

"Not at the moment," he sighs, sending me into high alert.

"What's wrong?" I ask, knowing something is bothering him.

"Same ole shit, just a different day."

"Right." I close the door to our room and sit down on our bed. This room is too big for one person and feels so empty without Liam here. I'm starting to hate it.

"Um ..." I clear my throat. "Why do you want a divorce?" My voice is barely above a whisper and tears are streaming down my face as I ask the question.

He doesn't say anything, but I can hear rustling around in the background. Is he with her now?

"Li—"

"Josie, what the fuck are you talking about?"

"This guy called and asked if I could confirm that you filed for divorce."

"And what did you say?"

"What does it matter? Answer the question, Liam. Do you want a divorce?"

"Goddamn it, Jojo. Why the fuck would I want a divorce? Do you really think I'd go to some slime ball fucking reporter to tell them before I talked to you first? Is that what you think of me?"

"No, but the pictures I saw ..."

Whatever Liam was doing, he's now still. There's nothing but static air between us.

"Liam?"

"What?"

"Do you love her?"

"Are you fucking kidding me?" he yells into the phone. "How many times I have I told you never to read those shitty ass columns?"

"That doesn't discount the fact that you kissed her!" I fire back.

"*I didn't fucking kiss her!*" He's yelling something in the background that I can't understand. "For fuck's sake, I gave her a hug. She jumped into my arms when I opened the door and those sorry excuses for humans took a bunch of pictures. Those bastards did everything they could to change the images around. It was a hug."

"Why didn't you tell me?"

"I don't know. I knew I should've, but it's sort of hard to explain over the phone and I kind of counted on you not looking at the tabloids. Every excuse I have is stupid. But, Jojo, you need to listen to me ... and listen good. I love you. I am one hundred percent committed to you. I'm committed to our family. You're the only woman I think about, baby. I don't like doing this shit over the phone, Josie, and I really hate that you've been crying."

"I'm sorry."

"Good, you should be. If you can't trust me, how are we going to survive? All they're doing is testing you, trying to make you break. I promise you, if at any time I'm not happy, I'll tell you, just as I expect you to do the same for me."

"I'm so scared I'm going to lose you," I tell him through sobs.

"The only way I'm leaving is if you're telling me to."

He knows that will never happen, unless he does something stupid and I'm left with no choice. Before we hang up, he tells me that he loves me and that he plans to video chat after Noah goes to bed because he's all worked up and needs to see my boobs. I can't help but laugh.

———

I startle awake and drop my phone onto my face. I must've fallen asleep after Liam and I hung up earlier. I hit the home button to see if I've missed any calls. I missed one, but not from Liam. Aubrey called. I press her name and wait for the call to connect.

"Josie, thanks for calling me back."

"Of course."

I leave our bedroom and walk down the stairs. I'm not sure how long I was out for, but it's dark out and I can faintly hear the TV.

"I spoke with Meredith earlier, and ... Oh, Josie, there's no easy way to say this ... but she's decided to keep the baby herself."

I stop dead in my tracks and squeeze the phone even tighter. "What?"

Aubrey covers the phone, talking to whoever else is in the room. It's likely Nick, and I hope she's not sharing this news with him, although the chances are she's already told him.

"The boyfriend, he's back and wants to marry her. I had to give her all the options and encouraged her to make the right choice for the baby. I told her that a new marriage could be hard with a newborn, but she's adamant and came by the office today to withdraw her consent for adoption."

"Oh ..."

"I have others that will be suitable—"

"No, Aubrey. It's okay. Liam's not home and I ... It's okay, Aubrey. Thanks for calling." I hang up and sit on the steps. There are no tears left to shed, and after the day I've had, I'm completely numb.

Bianca appears in the bottom of the steps; she peers around the corner. I can't tell if she's gauging my reaction to her standing there or not. I try and smile, letting her know its okay to come and talk. If she's here putting in an effort, I will also. "Are you okay?"

"That was Aubrey, which means Nick is on his way over." I take a deep breath. "The baby Liam and I were adopting ... his mother has decided to keep him." I shake my head, and watch as a tear falls from her eye.

"I'm so sorry, Josie."

"Me too."

"But, hey, Noah still gets a sibling because Nick and Aubrey are having a baby."

I shrug as if it's no big deal. I'm effectively the most defective mother on the planet. Can't conceive and can't adopt.

The doorbell rings and Noah is running through the house to answer it before Bianca and I can even move.

"Nick!"

"Noah!"

They exchange high-fives, and Noah offers me one as he flies by me, heading up the stairs. I'm getting the impression that Nick has asked Noah to spend the night, and while I should balk, right now he knows I'm not going to.

Their enthusiasm makes me want to hurl. I know he means well, but his happy attitude is not welcomed in my house right now. We make eye contact when he closes the door. His mega-watt smile drops when he sees Bianca. I know what he's thinking, and he has every right to.

"Bianca, this is Nick. Nick, Bianca. I don't think you guys have officially met."

Bianca steps forward and holds out her hand. Nick does the same. The handshake is quick and very cordial.

"My grandson speaks very highly of you, and I must say that I'm very appreciative that you stepped up when my husband and I didn't. Thank you."

I think both my mouth and Nick's are matching as they hang open in shock.

"It was my pleasure. Noah's a great kid."

Noah the Great is bounding down the stairs, sounding like a herd of elephants. He kisses me on the cheek and plants one on Bianca, too, much to her surprise.

"Where are you going?" I ask with a fake attitude.

"Nick asked me to spend the night. It's cool, right?"

I nod. Even though I want to sleep with Noah in my arms tonight, he'd be better off with Nick and Aubrey.

"I'll be out in a minute," Nick tells Noah, who dashes out the door without even a second glance.

"Aubrey and I would like to take him for a few days, give you a chance to go see Liam."

I shake my head. "I won't miss his game."

"You won't have to. There's been some field damage, so the game is pushed back a week."

"You should go, Josie," Bianca pipes up. I scowl at her, letting her know it's not okay to be on Team Nick right now.

"Aubrey will even fill in at the café."

"I can't. I already told Jenna she could have some time off."

Nick comes over and stands in front of me. He cups my cheeks, just like he used to do when we dated. "Josie, it pains me to say this, but you need to go see Liam. You need to grieve with him and not bottle it up. I know you, and sadly he's the same way. Talk to him."

He kisses me on the forehead and tells Bianca it was nice to meet her. As soon as the door shuts, she's sitting on the step below me. She's been here for hours and she doesn't have a hair out of place or one wrinkle in her clothes.

"When Sterling refused to let me leave, I stopped communicating. I wasn't a good example for my son and know that he struggled with how to express himself. Please don't make the same mistakes I did. Go to California and be with him."

The thought of being in his arms as early as tomorrow is very appealing, but the thought of showing up with bad news isn't. We just had a major fight, and as much as I want to be with him, seeing him there isn't my idea of a good time. I'll have to compete with everyone for his attention and that would be a first for me. I'm not sure I could handle it.

"I'll think about it."

Bianca stands and straightens out her skirt. "Thank you for tonight, Josie. It really means a lot to me, and I know I don't deserve your hospitality."

"Bianca?" I say her name, just as she reaches the door. "Does he hit you?"

"No." She shakes her head, but her eyes are looking down at the ground.

"Did he use to?"

She takes her hand off the doorknob and clasps her hands in front her, much like she was earlier today. When she doesn't answer, I prod again. "Did he ever hit Liam?" I want to say that Liam would've told me, but I can see him keeping this locked inside.

"No. Sterling is a lot of things, but physically abusive isn't one of them. He's mean, condescending, and some will call him a bully."

"Do you love him?"

She shakes her head no. "I haven't since before Liam was born."

"So, why stay? Why not reach out to your to mom and ask her for help? Don't you think she would've helped you?" I stand and go to her. Her eyes glisten with fresh tears.

"My mother died when Liam was about three years old."

I take a step back and shake my head.

"What?" she asks.

"Your mother died sometime after Liam moved to California. She's the reason he went."

Bianca covers her mouth and lets her tears fall. When

I go to her, she puts her hand up, shaking her head. "I'm sorry, I must go."

Before I can ask her to stay, she's out the door and down my driveway, ignoring my calls to her.

"Son of a bitch," I say as I slam my door. I need a stiff drink ... or ten. I also need to tell Liam how screwed up his father is—maybe he'll know why Sterling would lie about Betty being dead.

I want to throw my phone across the room, but that would undoubtedly break it, resulting in me having to go out and buy a new one. I can't even imagine what the headline would be: "Liam Page Secures a Secret Phone For His Mistress" or something equally as asinine. Instead, I throw it onto my bed, cover it with a pillow, and beat the ever-loving shit out of it.

One would think that I'd feel better, but I don't. The agony in her voice is the only sound I can hear in the room. When Josie asked if I loved her—her being Layla—it tore my heart out. I should've never paused when she mentioned the pictures, but I couldn't find the words to tell her that it's all a lie. The only thing I could think of was, "It's not how it looks," and, in my eyes, that makes me look as guilty as fuck. Everything about that conversation went wrong. I knew something was up with all the missed calls and her disjointed voicemail. I should've answered the phone differently, but after the bullshit from the media junket, my mind was fried.

Losing my cool with my wife isn't something I'm proud of. Fighting over the phone isn't either, and it's definitely not something I like to do. But finding out my wife believes those shitty ass magazines before even speaking to me is fucking painful. Time and time again, I've shown her where it says I was in one place, when in fact I was with either her or Noah. For her to assume that I'd kiss another woman tells me that something is wrong in our marriage, I just don't know what. But we need to figure it out and fix it because I need her to support my career, just as I've supported hers. I can't do this without her.

I told her before we hung up that I'd call her after Noah is asleep so she and I can have some adult time. I miss my wife and, frankly, my hand isn't cutting it anymore. Cold showers and lotions are becoming my enemy. I need her to recharge me, to fuel me.

The whiskey taunts me, teasing me. There are too many habits here for me to fall back into and drinking heavily is one of them. The last time I intentionally set out to get drunk was the night before I left to go back to Beaumont. I was lonely and desperate, spending the majority of my nights in a stupor so I wouldn't have to remember in the morning. That all changed when I hopped on my motorcycle and checked in at the seedy motel just outside of town.

I pour two fingers of whiskey into a tumbler and bring it to my lips. My hard liquor of choice swirls in the glass, waiting to be tasted. One sip won't hurt. It'll soothe my anger and pain. It'll help me fall asleep, and maybe I'll dream something happy about my life, instead of the recurring nightmare that I've been having.

It's not a nightmare, though, at least not when it starts out. Moving the chair to face the window, I sit down, setting my glass of whiskey on my knee. I close my eyes and it only takes a couple of minutes before the scene replays all over again.

"I can't be with you anymore, Josephine."

The slap burns my skin as I hold my hand in place of where hers had just been. When I look at her, I see rage. Never in the years that I've known her, have I seen her like this. And I swear she's just grown five inches and is towering over me.

"Get your spoiled ass in my room now, Liam Westbury, before I cause a scene."

I do as she says, jumping when she slams the door behind me. Her room is decorated with pictures of her and me, Mason and Katelyn, and the four of us together. It looks like Kodak took a crap in here, and it makes me jealous that I'm not a part of her life here.

Josie wraps her arms around me, kissing the spot she slapped. "I'm sorry, baby ... it's just that I'm pregnant."

Pregnant.

Pregnant.

"Beaumont's Golden Boy Named Manager at Stop 'N Shop."

I startle awake, spilling the whiskey down the side of my pants. I remember the night I went to her dorm to ends things, but the dream I keep having doesn't end like that. She tells me she's pregnant and my life fast forwards to working in a grocery store to support my family. I would've dropped out of college and married her on the spot. I would've never been able to provide for her the way she needed me to.

I meant to get her pregnant; although she doesn't know it and I don't think I can ever tell her. It was my intention, the night I left campus and drove all night to get to her, yet I didn't know it was until I felt myself on edge and I made the decision not to pullout. I wanted her pregnant. I needed the excuse to move back to Beaumont and be with my friends.

One weak moment is all it takes and the rest of the whiskey is down my throat. There wasn't much left, at least that's what I'm telling myself as I finish off the glass. The burn feels good and instantly starts to numb my self-inflicted pain. My pity party has a reservation for one, and I've already arrived.

Pouring another two fingers, I don't waste any time letting the potent liquor coat the back of my throat. I've missed this flavor and I can tell it's missed me. I pour another, and another, until the bottle provided by the hotel is barely inches from the bottom. The more I drink, the louder her voice is.

"Do you love her?"

"Do you love her?"

"Do you love her?"

"*No!*" I roar as I throw the glass against the wall. The bottle of whiskey follows it quickly, shattering into tiny shards of glass as the rest of the booze makes its mark on the otherwise dull wall. I bend over at my waist and start to heave, barely making it to garbage can. It's been so long since I've puked up liquor and it's a good reminder as to why I shouldn't drink excessively.

After a long, hot shower, I'm in bed with my laptop, waiting for Josie to connect so we can chat. When she finally does, I'm graced with my beautiful wife, her hair loose on her shoulders and wearing one of my T-shirts.

"Hey, I've been looking for that," I tell her before she can say hi. I know she kept the shirt, but teasing her about it is fun and I like to see her smile.

She grins, pulling the collar up to her nose. "It doesn't smell like you anymore."

I adjust myself to a more comfortable position in bed, putting my arms behind my head. My chest is on full display for her, so I'm hoping she can see her name.

"Do you see my tattoo?"

"Yes."

"What's it say?" I ask her.

"Jojo."

"And who is Jojo?"

"Me," she says.

"Hmm ... does Jojo love me?"

She nods. "More than words."

"I love you, Jojo. I know I'm not home to show you, but I need you to trust me and believe me when I tell you there isn't another woman in this world that can compete with you."

"Are you sure?"

"Fuck, baby," I say as I sit up. "What can I do to prove it? I told everyone at the press junket that I love you and they'll still twist my words. They need the drama to sell their story. We don't need that shit in our lives; we have too much going for us."

"I just worry that I'm not enough. I'm not into that scene and sometimes I feel like you need someone who is."

"You are more than enough, Jojo. I don't know what I can do to show you that. You're the one I want, day in and day out, for the rest of my life. If I can't have you, I don't want anyone else."

"Please stop." She's laughing so hard, she's disappeared from the screen. I know it's cheesy to recite lyrics, especially ones that I haven't written, but getting her to laugh was my goal.

"Liam," she says in a sweet, quiet voice after she's calmed down. "When you came back I never thought we'd be where we are right now. Please have patience with me. I'm scared and feel like I don't belong in your world right now."

"I don't need anyone but you. But if you want to put on a short mini-skirt and some fuck me heels, I'll happily prove that fact to you by bending you over the couch and making you scream my name."

"Oh God."

"Yeah, you can say his, too." I pause and study the woman that I love, the person I would quit this life for if she asked me to. "Baby, can you do me a favor?"

"Sure."

"Show me your boobies. I really miss seeing them."

Josie rolls her eyes, but takes my shirt off anyway. My eyes bug out slightly because they look larger than the last time I saw them.

"Jojo, did you get a boob job while I've been gone?"

"What? No," she scoffs at me, rolling her eyes. "Why would you say that?"

"Because I know your boobs very well, and unless we're in super high-def, they look bigger."

"Be nice, Liam or I'm shutting you off."

I fall back and place my hand over my heart, causing her to laugh. I take advantage of her high spirits and ask her to touch her boobs. She rolls her eyes, but does it anyway. And when I ask her to get kinky with me, she happily puts herself on display for me, reminding me of everything that I'm missing.

---

W hen I get to *Metro* the next day, Harrison is on stage, playing for Layla and her former guitar player. This moment brings back memories, both good and bad, of the first time I ever stepped foot into this place. Once again, Layla owns the stage. It's like she hasn't even taken a break from performing by the way she's moving to her music.

JD joins me as I lean against the bar. Before yesterday, I hadn't shared much about my past with him and figured that after the spectacle I made at the interviews, he'd be full of questions. He hasn't said or asked anything, and right now I'm very grateful.

"She's good, mate."

"She can definitely perform," I say, nodding in agreement.

"Everything all right, Liam?" JD asks as he studies me carefully.

JD and I are close, but not as close as Harrison and I. I look at JD now and see how much he has grown up over the past couple of years. I guess getting married, getting shot, and having a kid—all within the matter of months—will do that to a person.

"I'm okay, JD," I tell him, sincerely.

He nods, and bounces on his feet for a few minutes. "I know about Layla."

"Not much to know," I say, wishing I could change the subject. "I was young, heartbroken, and high. I think you've been there a few times?"

"Yeah, no kidding. I just hope I don't bump into any of them when the missus is around, if you catch my drift."

"That, I do."

I don't know what the hell I'd do if Josie and Layla crossed paths, or if Josie were to ever find out any of the details of the hook-up. It's a fight that we don't need to have, ever.

As soon as the set is done, Layla jumps off stage and walks over to me. I hand her one of the bottles of water sitting on the bar, even going as far as to be a gentleman and open it for her.

"Thanks," she says, out of breath. "Shit, performing takes a lot of out of you. I think I need a year to get ready."

Glancing at my watch, I laugh. "I think you have about twenty-eight hours before the first show starts."

"Right," she says before finishing the water. "So listen, Trixie was hinting about wanting to add some more sets, so I bit the bullet and offered to do some duets with you."

If I had anything in my mouth, I'd be choking right now. I look at JD, who doesn't look happy, and then back to Layla.

"What?"

She shrugs, as if it's no big deal. I mean it's only my marriage on the line here, not hers.

"Trixie wanted to keep you on stage longer; she says you're the bigger draw, so I told her we'd do some duets. You know, spice it up a little."

"Shit," JD mutters, taking the words right out of my mouth. I'm guessing Jenna has told him about Josie's freak-out and he knows what's coming next.

"I don't know if I can do that, Layla."

Stepping closer, she places her hand on my chest. "I recall you and me moving very well against each other back in the day. All you have to do is remember that night." She turns and walks away, but doesn't get far. "Oh, and Trixie wants your shirt off when you're on stage."

I pick up a stool and cock it back, preparing to throw it but Harrison steps in my path, while JD takes it from my hands.

"Tell her no," Harrison says.

"I tried."

He shakes his head. "What is it with you and these chicks? How come they never listen to you?"

"Because they all want his dick," JD throws it out there as if it's a common occurrence—me being propositioned.

"JD, seriously? Sex sells, you know that. Trixie is playing off them damn photos." I throw my hands up in frustration. I don't mind doing duets, but not with Layla and not after the fight with Josie.

"Do you think its Trixie or Moreno making the call?" Harrison asks.

JD and I say, "Moreno," at the same time, and Harrison agrees with us.

"So, are you gonna take your shirt off then?" JD asks, and I shake my head.

"Never have and can't say that I will unless Josie is front and center and I'm singing to her."

Even when I'm home in Beaumont and performing, I don't take my shirt off. My tattoo is for her, and her alone.

**E**verything happens for a reason. You may not know the reasoning at the time, but eventually it comes to light. Two days ago, I found out that the baby Liam and I have been planning to adopt for months is no longer ours. Meredith, the mom, changed her mind. I get it, I do. A school counselor brought up adoption when I was pregnant with Noah. She was trying to encourage me to stay in school. I never planned to drop out, just live at home until I could graduate. My parents were there to help. I know not everyone is as lucky as I am, but that's where I thought I could help Meredith. I should've known, though. She never let me buy her anything.

I roll over and shut my alarm off before the offending buzzer can jar my already awake body. Sleep has eluded me since Aubrey told me the news. I thought that I'd be more upset, but the fact of the matter is I'm not, and that scares the shit out of me. I should be beside myself with grief, crying my eyes out in agony over the heartache I feel. But all I can tell myself is that this child wasn't meant to be ours. Still, I have a room full of stuff that he needs, and I plan to give it to him.

My phone rings and Liam's face appears. I slide the screen open and there he is, my husband. The one I have vowed to love, honor, and cherish, and apparently lie to. I haven't told him about the baby and Meredith. I can't, at least not over the phone. Right now I feel like we're Humpty Dumpty and one push will break us. It needs to be done face-to-face, in person, not over the computer or phone. I want to hold him when I tell him the news.

"Good morning," he says right before he brings a mug of what I'm assuming is coffee to his lips.

"Morning," I reply, as I stretch. He leans forward, trying to get a peek. Unfortunately for him, there's nothing to see. Since he made a comment about my boobs looking bigger, I've kept them hidden. I don't want to tell him that I've been standing in front of the mirror each time I go to the bathroom to see if, in fact, they are.

"What are you doing today?"

"Well, I'm going to take a shower—"

"And think of me?"

I roll my eyes. "Is that all you think about?"

Liam nods since I've caught him mid drink. "Yes, babe. Every freaking minute because I haven't been able to touch you and it's driving me nuts."

"You know this isn't the first time you've been away."

"I know. I missed you then as well, but this time it's

worse because I have downtime and you know how I hate having downtime."

"I know. Anyway, after my shower, I'm going with Katelyn to take the kids to the cemetery and then we're going to the park." I don't tell him that I'm meeting with Aubrey to fill out some paperwork. Meredith is required to pay us back for the expenses she incurred while contracted with us. The girl doesn't have any money and part of me feels we should just let it go, but the other part thinks this would be a good life lesson.

"I need to call Noah later."

"I'll have him call you when we get to the park. I'm picking him up at Nick's."

"Okay, go take your shower and think about my hands all over your body."

"I always do," I tell him as I blow him a kiss.

"Love you, babe."

"Love you, too."

The screen goes blank and the room fills with silence. I wish Noah were here, but I understand Nick's view on having him at his house for a few days. I have things to deal with that Noah just won't understand.

Crawling out of bed, my legs ache. These past few days I've been sleeping far too long, even if it's restless. Passing through my half empty closet, I remind myself to ask Liam for a date as to when he's coming home. I need him here, and if he thinks home is going to become Los Angeles, he needs to tell me so we can figure things out. It'll suck, but he'll have to travel back and forth. He did it after he found out about Noah, and he can do it again. Although, I just want him back in Beaumont with us.

Stopping in front of the mirror, I lift my shirt over my head. I angle myself to see if I can see what he's talking about. I don't want to acknowledge that I've gained weight. I haven't been to the gym in almost a month, and clearly it's starting to show. I add calling Xander to my list of things to do today.

I step into the shower built for two and blast the hot water. It burns my chilled skin, but it's a welcomed pain, reminding me that I still feel something. The more I think about the baby, the more it makes sense. Liam and I never discussed names. Neither of us brought it up. When I came across his grandfather's name I thought it would be a good name, something to carry on. But I also thought Liam would insist we were naming the baby Mason, and he never did.

*Mason* ... every day I think about him and the differences he's made, even since he's been gone. If it weren't for him, I wouldn't have Liam, and most importantly, neither would Noah.

"*Hey.*"

*Mason sits down next me on the park bench. I say hi, but never meet his eyes. I'm focused on Noah and his determination to be a big boy on the playground.*

"*Have you talked to Katelyn?*"

*I smile, knowing full well why he's here. "I have."*

"*I knocked her up good.*"

*When he starts to laugh, I follow suit. Leave it to Mason to turn something scary into something funny. We sit there, watching Noah run from the slide to the swings and back.*

"*He's missing out, Josie.*"

*Sighing, I nod. I try not to think about Liam and everything he's missing, but each time I look at my son, I see his father.*

*"You're going to be an amazing father, Mason. Just promise me you'll never leave her."*

I wipe away the tears that have fallen. He made that promise, but some higher power had different plans for him. The memories I have are starting to fade and I hate that. Mason needs to live on in our lives, and the lives of the girls, but it seems that we're talking about him less and less. Maybe that needs to change.

Once I'm dried off and dressed, with my hair braided, I'm out the door. The sun is shining, the birds are singing, and I can't help thinking today is going to be a glorious day. Nick texts to tell me he'll meet us at the cemetery, saving me a trip to his house.

When I pull into the cemetery, Katelyn and the kids are already there. I walk by her car and wave at Quinn, who is staring out the window. Katelyn asks him each time if he wants to get out, but he opts to give the girls their private time. He waves back and offers a sweet Harrison-like smile. Between him and Noah, we'll be beating the girls away with clubs.

"Aunt Josie, look." Elle points to the freshly laid flowers on Mason's grave. Each week they're here, cleaning and removing any debris. Harrison has been known to come as well, but never tells Katelyn what he says. He tells her that's between him and Mason.

"Very beautiful, Elle. Your daddy loves them, I'm sure."

Peyton sits just beyond Mason's grave, watching the

entrance. I look at Katelyn who shrugs and decide to go see how she's doing.

"What's going on?"

"Nothing. Just waiting."

"Did you visit with your dad?"

She shakes her head.

"How come?"

"Elle is too nosey."

"I see." I pull my legs to my chest to match her position. "Have you asked your mom to bring you by yourself?"

She shakes her head again.

"I think if you did, she would. Or, ask Harrison. You know he'd bring you."

Peyton shrugs. "I don't want my dad to get mad about me wanting to talk to my dad."

If anyone on the outside of our group didn't know the situation, they'd be confused. "I think both dads will understand. I know Harrison will. He loves you, Peyton. You know that."

She sighs and kicks her legs out in front of her. "I miss him and Uncle Liam. When are they coming home?"

Pulling her into my side, I kiss the top of her head. "Soon," I tell her, praying that I'm right.

After we finish up at the cemetery, we're park bound. Peyton is riding with me and as soon as she sees Noah, she's out of the car and racing toward him. Nick tells me that Aubrey will call me later to discuss some business and tells Noah that he'll see him later.

The kids run off to the playground as Katelyn and I

walk hand-in-hand to the bench. We can sit here for hours and watch them play.

"I have something to tell you."

"What is it?" she asks, without taking her eyes off the kids.

I lean my head on her shoulder, waiting for the tears to start. When they don't, I am even surer this is the right decision for me, even if I didn't make it. "Meredith is keeping the baby."

Katelyn turns in a snap, causing me to hit my head on the wooden bench.

"Ouch, shit, that hurt."

"Oh crap, Josie, are you okay?"

"Yes, and no. My head hurts, but surprisingly I'm okay with Meredith's decision." I rub my head, wondering if I have a concussion.

Katelyn grabs my free hand and holds it. The stroke of her thumb against my hand is soothing, but not doing much for the headache that I'm getting.

"I'm so sorry, Josie. I know how much you guys wanted this baby. Do you need me to do anything?"

"Help me clean out the room?" I say, sheepishly. Cleaning is never anyone's 'fun' job. "I think I'm going to give Meredith the stuff. I don't want it, and it's really for the baby, not me."

"I think that's very noble of you, Josie. You're a strong woman."

"I don't know about that. I'm not even upset. I mean, I was when Aubrey called, but I don't feel like I think I should."

"Everyone reacts differently. Doesn't make you any less of a person."

"I guess. I still haven't told Liam. I'm thinking of going out there this weekend since Noah's game has been moved. Maybe surprise him before breaking his heart."

"Hearing it from you in person will be better ... plus, your other news."

I look at her strangely. "What other news?"

"Oh come on, Josie. If I'm noticing, he has to be noticing."

I slide away from her and give her my best "what the hell" look.

"You're pregnant."

"Am not."

"Are too. I've been there before."

"So have I, in case you've forgotten. I'm not pregnant."

"Your boobs are bigger and so is your ass."

My mouth drops open, but she just shrugs. "How dare you!"

"Eh, it's the truth, and you'd tell me the same thing."

I turn back to watching the kids and count off the days since my last period. And when that doesn't work, I try to remember the last time I bought tampons at the store. Still coming up blank.

"Did you figure it out yet?"

"I don't know what you're talking about," I tell her, crossing my arms in defiance.

She leans into me, resting her chin on my shoulder. "Josie, I think you're pregnant. I'll watch Noah while you scoot over to the hospital for a test."

"What if I'm not?"

Laughing, she sits up straight. "Then Xander has a lot of work to do."

Katelyn is ducking before my hand even starts flying. I smack her good before I get up and walk away. I know she's wrong, and I refuse to get my hopes up, but now she has me wondering.

---

I've been here before, many times. There's a small bandage on my arm from where my blood has been drawn. I've peed in a cup and I've stripped down and put on a hospital gown. I've calculated my last period to the best of my ability, realizing as I was giving my information to the nurse that I am, indeed, late. Now, I wait. Everything in this room is a focal point for me. The ugly border that someone thought would be appealing. The years-old magazines that never get replaced even hold my attention. If my ass wasn't hanging out of the back of my gown, I'd rummage through the cabinets just to see what they keep in there. But I'm not moving.

I refuse to get my hopes up. I shouldn't even be here, but Katelyn's right, I have gained weight. Weight loss I could attribute to stress, but not gain.

The soft knock on the door tells me my doctor is about to come in. She smiles at me, which is no indication that I'm pregnant.

"How are you feeling, Josie?"

"Fine, nothing out of the ordinary." She notes something in my chart and asks me to lie back. I cringe when I hear the snapping of her latex gloves. I put my feet in the stir-ups and close my eyes. This is the most uncomfortable feeling ever.

My doctor makes it quick and painless, telling me I can sit up. Her back is to me, as she writes in my chart again. She turns and sits in her stool, holding my life in her hands.

"You've been trying for a long time to get pregnant, Josie."

I knew not to get my hopes up. I nod in confirmation. No words are needed.

"With that said, let me be the first to say congratulations!"

My mouth drops open and I know for sure I didn't hear her correctly. "What'd you say?"

"Congratulations, Josie, you're pregnant."

"I ...wh— Are you sure?"

"All of your lab work, your urine tests, and the check I've just completed confirms it. You have a baby growing inside of you."

I cover my mouth in shock and tell her thank you.

"Don't thank me, thank your husband."

"Oh, I plan to."

She laughs because she knows our history and has been trying to help us conceive for a while.

"When am I due?"

"Well, that's the thing, Josie. According to your records, you indicated that you're last cycle was last month, but you're measuring at about eighteen weeks."

I don't tell her that I'm not very accurate on that date.

It's like a test question you didn't study for and it catches you off-guard. I clearly failed this test.

Her words sound muffled, as if I'm underwater. "I'm sorry, what did you say?"

"You're eighteen weeks. Baby Westbury is due in November."

I put my hand up, and she pauses. "If I'm eighteen weeks, that means I've missed multiple periods and you know I've been meticulous about keeping track. How can I be this far along?"

She sets her folder down and clasps her hands. "Your body has been going through a lot of stress. Between your attempts at conceiving and the adoption process, your body has simply been functioning. It's not uncommon for women in this case to miss two periods and not give it a second thought. Once you and Liam stopped trying, your body relaxed, but you didn't. And in rare cases, the human body doesn't recognize that there's a life growing inside of it. I'm going to schedule an ultrasound for later this afternoon."

"I can't," I say, shaking my head. "Liam isn't home and I can't do that without him."

"When will he be back?"

I sigh and bite the inside of my cheek. "I don't know. He's working in L.A. right now. I need to go to him, though, and tell him. Is there a doctor out there that can do the ultrasound?"

She nods and goes back to my folder. "I'll have it set up for you." She walks out, closing the door behind her, and just like that, the brief happy moment is marred by what-ifs. The biggest what-if I'm facing is what if this pregnancy isn't viable. What if, because I was so wrapped up in conceiving, I ignored my body and have hurt my chance at having another baby?

If that's the case, Liam is going to hate me.

W
e take the morning off to go surfing. After renting a car, we drive out to Harrison's condo—the one he refers to as an apartment because someone lives above him—to hit the waves. It's guy bonding, or whatever you want to call it. We need it. In Beaumont, we're always doing shit, either together or with the family, and since we've been in L.A., we go to our separate rooms once we've finished working and don't see each other again until it's time to leave for the next thing on our agenda.

As soon as we step out, JD is running toward the water, jumping over the small, decorative picket fence. We can hear him hollering until the ocean drowns him out.

"He's like a wind-up toy," Harrison says, as he opens his condo. Tess is standing there with open arms to greet her son. It's as if she hasn't seen him in years, when in fact, it's only been a few months.

"Hey, Mom," he says, as he picks her up and twirls her around.

When he puts her down, I'm next. She comes over to me, placing her hands on my cheeks. "I hear a baby is on his way?"

"You heard right. Josie and I are adopting."

"I'm so proud of you! Your grandma would be as well."

"Thanks, Tess." I kiss her on the cheek much to her delight.

"And Jimmy is already in the water, I see."

"He needed a bath," I say, earning a nice swat across my shoulder.

"You boys go have fun, I'll have lunch ready," she tells us before she disappears down the hall.

"I don't know why we didn't stay here," I comment to Harrison, and he looks at me like I'm crazy.

"Could it be the traffic? Or the fact that we'd have to get up at the crack of dawn?"

"Oh, I have a novel idea, why doesn't Trixie use some of the money that Moreno is funneling through her club to hire people to fix it up instead of using us? Then we could rehearse here at night and surf during the day." I waggle my eyebrows at Harrison who ignores me by turning his back and heading toward his large glass wall. This is one of my favorite things about this place. The door collapses, opening wide to the outdoors.

Just outside of the wall is where Harrison keeps all of his surfboards and wetsuits, plus anything else you need for the beach. His kitchen patio is state of the art and puts my newly installed outside kitchen to shame. His condo is south enough from L.A. that it hardly rains, affording us beautiful weather all the time. This is where I'd like to live if Josie ever agreed to move here. Fat chance of that happening after this whole picture shit with Layla.

When we catch up with JD, he's body surfing with a few little kids. They're all laughing and keep asking him to say different words. Little kids are easily fascinated by his accent. As soon as he sees us, he tells them he has to go and maybe he'll see them around.

"New friends?" I ask, handing him the wetsuit.

"Hilarious. You're just jealous that I have that universal appeal to everyone, mate."

"Oh, believe me, I'm not."

We step into our wetsuits and strap our ankles. The three of us, with our boards under our arms, look out into the ocean. We've been here before—same beach, same pose—right before shit started changing for us. Actually, it's me who initiated the change and sometimes I wonder if I've steered them in the wrong direction. I know neither of them would give up Katelyn or Jenna, and the lives they're leading, but sometimes I wonder what would've happened if I hadn't gone home to say good-bye to Mason.

Where would I be right now? Dead? I don't know why death is my first option, maybe because I felt like I was dying a little each day. Then I saw Josie again for the first time in ten years and everything changed.

"Let's go," Harrison says, walking out to the water. JD and I follow, dropping onto our boards and paddling out. I'm not great on the board, but I try my hardest and it's a lot of fun. Harrison and Quinn, on the other hand, are great and put JD and me to shame.

We ride the waves until Tess hollers for us to come in for lunch. JD runs up to the house, picking Tess up and getting her all wet. She squeals in pure delight and pinches his cheeks when he puts her down.

Tess joins us for grilled chicken, corn on the cob, and salad. Apparently, Harrison told her we're not eating very healthy.

"This looks delicious, Tess. Thank you."

"You're welcome, Liam."

Small talk is made, and it's mostly about her grand-children—all five of them. Tess has always doted on Quinn, we all have, but when she met Noah, Peyton, and Elle, she immediately took them in as her own. Eden has just been the icing on the cake for her. I know she's going to be in heaven when the new baby arrives.

"Has Anthony been by?"

JD, Harrison, and I all drop our forks at the same time, but Tess keeps eating. It's like she doesn't know that she's asked about the devil himself.

"Sometimes I forget you know the same people as my grandmother," I say to Tess, who smiles softly. I look at Harrison and ask, "Do you remember that party? The one where Anthony was talking to Ness Cacco?" I'll do anything to change the subject from Anthony Moreno.

He nods. "Yvie was trying to hit on you."

"Oh my," Tess says, covering her mouth. "I swear, that girl. I'm waiting for her to tell me its okay to let people know she's engaged."

"*What?*" the three of us say at the same time, shock

and surprise evident all over our faces. Clearly Yvie has been hiding this little bit of information from all of us.

Tess turns red and covers her mouth. Harrison pulls on her hand, but she shakes her head.

"Please tell me it isn't that scumbag director?" I ask.

Another head shake.

"Xander?" Harrison asks.

Tess's eyes go wide as she stuns us into silence.

"Spill now, Mom." Harrison demands.

Her hand drops from her mouth and she starts filling us in on the details. "Xander proposed about a month ago, but Yvie has asked me to keep it quiet until she could give notice at the ballet and get moved."

"She's moving to Beaumont?" JD asks.

"Yes, by the end of the summer. She's going to teach ballet above the gym."

"So that's why Xander has been remodeling," I add, causing Tess to nod. She looks so upset that she gave away Yvie's secret, but we're all family, we won't tell anyone. "You okay, Harrison?" I kick his shin to get his attention.

"Yeah, it's just weird thinking she's old enough to get married."

"Um, you do realize that she and I are about the same age."

He looks at me with squinted eyes. "Yeah, but you're a dude and shit."

Confusing explanations brought to you by Harrison James ... and that is one of the many reasons why I love him.

After lunch, we have to say our good-byes. Tess tells

us she'll be up for one of the five shows we're going to play at *Metro* and asks us to come back and see her. Harrison promises, of course.

---

A s soon as we pull into the hotel to shower and change, I spot Moreno waiting in the lobby. We bypass him on purpose, and he knows it judging by the smirk that's on his face. We ride the elevator in silence, the only noise coming from our beating hearts. We know why he's here, but the thing is, JD and Harrison get to escape him. I don't. He'll be knocking on my door any minute now.

"I think we should go to your room." It's JD who suggests this, and if it wasn't socially unacceptable, I'd handcuff both of them to me so they had to come in.

"I agree," Harrison adds. "He's been coming after you, alone, when it's a band decision. Unless he just wants you ..."

I shake my head. "Even if that was the case, he knows I won't go anywhere without you guys."

The elevator dings and the door opens. Each step to my penthouse seems to take forever. And it seems like another eternity before the knock comes. Harrison answers the door, holding it open for Moreno to enter.

"Gentlemen," he says, as if he's welcome here. He sits in the same chair as he did last time, setting his fedora on the edge. Hospitality indicates I should offer him a drink, but after the meltdown I had the other night, I asked that all liquor be removed from my room.

"Page, can't pay your bill I see?" He motions to the empty liquor tray.

"Nah, I just have a problem with people who show up to my room, uninvited, and help themselves to my booze."

Moreno chuckles and pulls out a flask. Seriously, can't this man go one day without a drink?

"Let's talk business, boys."

"Let's talk restraining order," Harrison fires back.

Moreno waves it off as if it's nothing important. We could call the cops, but the likelihood that they'll care is slim. They're busy dealing with drug deals and dead prostitutes. Our gripe is a waste of time and Moreno knows it.

He brings his leg up, resting his ankle on his knee. "I'm going to cut to the chase. You need me. After the media frenzy the other day, you need strong representation."

"You caused that frenzy," I point out.

"Eh, it was purely to show you what you'll be dealing with if someone like me isn't around."

"This sounds like a threat, Moreno," Harrison states.

"Just stating the facts." He shrugs and stares at JD. "You're young. Make sure these guys make the right decision. If they don't, you know where to find me."

"Nah, I think I'll pass. I'm happy with my mates, ta."

"I don't understand why you want us," I say, as I sit in front of him. Leaning forward, I rest my elbows on my knees. "What can we even offer you?"

Moreno mirrors my position and chuckles. "Sex appeal, fan following, original music, instruments ... the list goes on and on. I'm not interested in that pop rock computer shit. I want real music. I've told you before; your stage presence alone makes women wet themselves. Sam was right when she signed you."

"I'm glad you think so, but I'm not sure we're interested."

He looks from me, to Harrison, and finally to JD. "I think you need to ask your friends what they think." Moreno doesn't wait for a response as he gets up and leaves.

"What do you guys think?" I don't wait, asking them right off.

"I think we have a gig to get to," Harrison states before standing up and walking out of the room, JD following him. Neither of them says anything else, leaving me to wonder if I'm the only one who feels this way. If I am, I can easily be replaced.

---

"I think Harrison is going to be beat for our show." JD is pacing backstage, glancing every now and again at Harrison as he plays for Layla. JD wasn't around when I first met Harrison. I used to watch him play for multiple bands, night after night. He awed me, which is one of the reasons I needed him with me when I signed with Sam. The other reason is because he was my friend, and I couldn't see walking this path without him.

"He'll be fine," I say, trying to calm JD down. "He's used to this." He may not be used to surfing all morning and then coming in to play multiple sets, but I don't say that to JD.

"No, he used to be. He's old now."

I crack a smile and fight off a laugh, but to no avail. I'm buckled over, holding my sides as I laugh at JD. Harrison may be older than him, but he's not old by any means.

"Stop worrying, we'll be fine."

JD shakes his head, throwing his arms up in the air.

"Hey, why don't you tweet or whatever it is you do. We could use some more people out there." I point through a small opening and show him the crowd. It's not what I thought, but better than nothing. I spot Moreno in the back corner. I'm not sure why he's here—there's no new talent playing tonight and the one band that could be interested in him is already signed. He's likely here to get under my skin, which he's very good at doing.

"I did tweet, but all the birds in L.A. know I'm married so they don't want to come see me ... us."

"That's great, JD. So, because you're off the market and they can't hook-up, they're not our fans anymore?"

He shrugs and offers me a slight 'I'm sorry' smile. I grin back, letting him know that I'm just bullshitting him.

"Are you ready for your duets?" Trixie appears next to me with a smug expression on her face. If I didn't know any better, I'd say she's trying to hook Layla and me up.

"Not interested," I tell her.

"It'll be fun, sexy. The women will go nuts and they'll buy a ticket again for tomorrow night." Trixie walks way, effectively ending our limited conversation.

"I need some liquid courage," I say to JD, who is

glued to his phone. He's probably sexting Jenna and I want to get out of here before he drops his drawers and starts taking pics of himself. I send the same shit to Josie, but from the privacy of my hotel room.

The greenroom is fully stocked with booze and food. I make myself a sandwich, eat it quickly, and follow it up with a beer and two shots. I'm going to need more if I have to get through performing with Layla. I also need to tell Josie before the pictures hit mainstream. I need to be a better husband in that regard.

Pulling out my phone, I press her name and listen to the ringing on the other end. After four rings, her phone goes to voicemail. I hang up and try again. In between each call I'm taking a shot, numbing myself for having to sing with Layla. It's not that I don't like her; it's the song choices. Each one is sexy and has me saying words I only want to say to my wife. After the third time with no answer, I leave a message.

"I'm about to go on stage. Trixie has asked for some duets with ..." I can't bring myself to say her name. "Remember wh— I love you, Jojo."

I couldn't do it. I couldn't say the words "remember what you see isn't real" because it sounds like I'm trying to cover something up and I'm not. I'm a performer, it's my job. Josie knows this and accepts it.

Tonight, Liam Page is back.

## 27

---

## JOSIE

I haven't told anyone about this pregnancy. It's out of fear that I keep the news to myself. How could I, or my body, not have known that I'm pregnant? Yes, I'm one of the lucky ones who didn't suffer from morning sickness but, as a mother, I should've known I have a child growing inside of me. The thought of not knowing and, therefore, not having cared properly for this baby sickens me. I'm afraid to go to the appointment. I'm afraid to hear the words that my pregnancy isn't viable. I don't want to see the look on Liam's face when the doctor says those words.

Closing my eyes, I mentally chide myself for thinking the worst. Everything could actually be fine and I could be overreacting. Tomorrow holds the answers, and I have to hang on to every positive thought I can until I'm told otherwise.

Liam will be overjoyed when I tell him that I'm pregnant. We've been trying for so long, while not as long as some, to me it feels like years. Knowing how he is with Eden, I'm confident Liam will excel with a newborn. I have so many thoughts of him rocking our baby to sleep or singing him, or her, a lullaby that he writes especially for them ... although I may have to censor his lyrics.

The airline attendant walks by, asking if I need anything. It's late, but drinking orange juice seems like the right thing to do. Flying First Class has its perks: more legroom and hip room, more choice on the menu, and constant service. Not to mention the fact that the bathroom is closer.

After my appointment this afternoon, I went to Nick's office. He knows I've been under stress and knows that I'm missing Liam. I had to take him up on his offer to look after Noah so that I can see Liam, even if it ends up only being for a few hours. I joked that Nick has all the benefits of a divorced dad, but without the financial obligation. Only he proved me wrong in that respect because he and Aubrey do their fair share of providing for Noah, even without being asked. Nick and I breaking up was probably the best thing to happen to either of us.

When you have time to kill, like when waiting for your flight, you tend to let your mind wander or, in my case, you take advantage of the stores in the terminal. This is what I did, and I've made a mistake with my purchase. The tell-all book about Liam sits in my lap. Something told me I needed to finish it and having left mine at home, I bought another copy. I haven't opened it yet, though. It sits in my lap, weighing me down and taunting me.

The flight attendant returns with my juice, nodding

toward the book and asks, "Are you reading that?"

How do I answer? Yes, I've read some, but not sure if I want to read anymore? Do I tell her Liam's my husband and I'm trying to fill in the missing ten years from his life because we don't talk about the time he was away?

"I've read some," I tell her.

She crouches down next to me. "I read it. I had to. I have the biggest crush on Liam Page, but I have to tell you, I find most of this book as complete garbage."

I like her. I want to tell her who I am, but she won't believe me. Living in Beaumont has kept me sheltered from the media, and they don't dare take our pictures in town. I think I've been in the press maybe three or four times and, at best, they're grainy images.

"I'm finding it a little hard to read myself."

"I'm waiting for his press release about Layla Richards' daughter. I'm sure now that the book is out, he won't be able to deny her anymore."

I gasp and cover my mouth. She shakes her head. "It's such a shame, too. I mean, he has a son as well, and now a daughter. He's such a Hollywood cliché."

I feel my skin becoming clammy as I listen to her words. "Excuse me," I say, as I stand. "I need to use the restroom." I drop the book in my seat and sidestep her. The stupid smile that's plastered all over her face makes me want to kick something. Right now I'd like to kick Liam.

Once I'm inside of the tiny stall, I slide the latch and the light comes on overhead. I wish I could shut it off because I don't want to see myself in the mirror. The ugliness of Liam's career is starting to eat away at me. Every time I turn around someone has a bomb to drop or a secret to expose, and those bombs and secrets are turning out be deadly.

I don't know how long I'm in the restroom, but a knock tells me my time is up. The flight attendant is standing there with a cup of ginger ale in her hand. I want to hate her, but she didn't do anything wrong. It's not her fault that my former boyfriend turned husband did some crap that's coming back to bite him in the ass.

If Liam and Layla have a child, I can't be mad—we weren't together. He moved on, and so did I. He didn't know about Noah. If he had, he would've come back. He would've been there for Noah, even if he couldn't be there for me.

Opening the book, I scan the table of contents for Layla's name and flip to her chapter. She has a whole freaking chapter when all I have is mentions of a woman who blackmailed him into marriage. I can only bring myself to skim the sentences until I find "daughter".

---

**In my reporting, I uncovered that Liam Page entered into a romantic relationship with Layla Richards shortly after arriving (we're talking days, people) in Los Angeles. The pair met at the famed *Metro* club after being introduced by his best friend and drummer, Harrison James.**

**I was unable to track down Layla**

**Richards, but did speak to her former husband who had this to say about Liam Page: "I hated that fucker. He knew Layla and I were married and he still chased after her. Their drug-induced affair produced a child that I wanted nothing to do with."**

**At the time of print, Layla Richards' daughter is eleven years old.**

---

I close the book and lean my head back, shutting my eyes. I don't know how much more I can take. Even if he tells me everything, I don't know if I'll be able to stay. This girl is either the same age or close to the same age as Noah. Liam left me in October and days later he was with someone else. If that doesn't tell me how he felt about me, I don't know what will.

The cabin lights come on in preparation for our arrival at LAX and the flight attendant comes by to pick up any trash. I'm tempted to put the book in there, but I'll need it for later. I need him to read the same words that I have and deny each and every one of them. He needs to tell me in his own words that this book is full of lies, that he's not the person Calista Jones is making him out to be.

This is my second time at LAX, and both times I've been beyond nervous. Finding a taxicab is easy—the driver tells me he knows the club and we'll be there in about a half hour. My mind is traveling a thousand miles a minute as we drive down the freeway. I stare out my window, trying to catch as much of the city life that I can. I hate this place for what's it's done to me.

When we arrive, there's a line of people wrapped around the block. I want to surprise Liam, but have a feeling this was a mistake. I should've called him, or at least Harrison or Jimmy, and asked to be put on the list. If Jenna were already here I wouldn't have a problem, but she decided to visit her parents for a few days before flying out here to be with Jimmy.

I pay the cab driver and step out into the nightlife of Los Angeles with my suitcase behind me.

"Now who's the cliché?" I say to myself. I look like the poster child for wayward travelers. The people in line, mostly women, glare or snarl at me. I get it, I'm older and carrying a suitcase. I look like a fruitcake. My surprise for Liam is not well thought out and I have a feeling I'll be standing outside until I can get ahold of him.

As I approach the door, I can hear him singing. I wanted to be here for his show and it looks like I'm going to miss it. There's a large man at the door with a clip-board. I know from stories Liam has told me that there will be a list of names on it. What are the chances he's put my name down? I think I have a better chance at winning the lottery tonight.

"Hi, I know this is going to sound silly—"

"End of the line is down there somewhere." He points down the block without making eye contact with me.

"Right. Look, my husband is Liam Page and I'm

trying to surprise him."

"Uh-huh, and I'm the Pope. End of the line."

"Look, let me show you." I pull out my wallet and flash my driver's license. I know he's appeasing me when he flashes his light on it.

"Your last name is Westbury."

"So is Liam's," I tell him, wondering how he doesn't know this.

"End of the line, ma'am."

My last ditch effort is to show him family photos. I hate that I have to let him see moments that we've shared together, but I have no other choice. I pull out my phone and open my photo app.

"Here, look through my phone. Liam's my husband and I'm really trying to surprise him."

To my surprise, he flips through the images, studying each one. He speaks into the radio that's hooked to his shirt as he hands my phone back me. He doesn't say anything, just continues to look at his clipboard.

"Is she cutting?" The voice belongs to a blonde with an all too small dress on. Even in her heels she's shorter than me.

"No, she thinks she's Page's wife."

"I don't think, I am," I snap back.

"Huh, he didn't say anything about a wife last night."

I see nothing but rage and wonder what a night in jail will feel like. I'm about to punch her lights out when my name is called. I turn sharply toward the door to find a short woman with jet-black hair and bright red lips. The girls in line start calling her name, Trixie, but she and I are having a stare down.

"Come with me." She turns back in the club, leaving me on my own to meander through an angry mob of women.

The second I step in, people are dancing and drinking around me. I can hear Liam on stage, but can't see him. I try to follow Trixie, but she's too short and I've lost her. It's okay, though, because I needed to be inside and now I am.

People are glaring at me as I work through the crowd, hitting them with my suitcase. This isn't ideal, but right now nothing in my life is. I'm finally in a spot where I can see and I wish I wasn't. In this moment I wish I were home, snuggled up in bed with my son and watching a movie.

My husband is hot, I agree with every woman, and man, who says it. The sex appeal grows when he's on stage. His shirt is sweaty, sticking to his body. I know from experience that the people in the front row can see the outline of his muscles and his six-pack. They can also see the faint outline of my name tattooed on his chest. It's not a small tattoo either. Jojo is spread across his chest in large letters with swirls all around it. He's proud of that tattoo. Hell, I am, too. Every woman that has been with him knows my name.

But he loses a lot of sex appeal to me when I see him on stage with a cigarette hanging from his fingers. I know he smoked for a while, years ago, but he quit when Quinn was born. At least, I thought he did. Maybe I've been blinded by love all this time and didn't realize he still smoked. If that's the case, I'm stupid.

I move closer, pushing my way through the crowd. I

want to be up front. I want him to see me. He needs to know I'm here. The jostling between bodies makes me nauseated, but I'm determined. I'm almost there when a female voice starts singing. The people around me calm down and start swaying.

The singer stands next to Liam, angling her body so his arm is pressed against her chest. He doesn't move it. Instead, he looks at her as he strums his guitar. After a few lines, he's singing, but he's not looking at the crowd, he's looking at her. I glance over at Jimmy and Harrison and they're both lost in the music.

Liam lets go of his guitar and it hangs there, slightly behind him. He's moving with her around stage, exchanging lyrics that call for love and sex. She sings about falling love, and he sings about just needing sex. When he returns to his mic stand he pulls his shirt up a little, flashing his stomach to the crowd, much to their delight. I've never seen him like this. He doesn't perform like this when he's at Ralph's or even the café. I'm not sure I like him a whole lot right now.

As soon as the song ends, the crowd parts and I'm able to work my way up front. He's never going to see me because he's too busy music fucking his stage partner so I turn my focus to Jimmy. I stand near him, calling his name every time he gets close. When he finally sees me, his eyes go wide. I grimace knowing he knows Liam has fucked up.

Jimmy moves toward the center where Liam and his musical conquest are and he nods in my general direction. Liam scans the crowd, and it's evident when he finds me. I wiggle my fingers and flip him off.

## 28

---

## LIAM

They say before you die your life flashes before your eyes. I don't know if that's true or not, and it's not my intention to find out anytime soon. What I do, however, know is true is that your life does flash before your eyes when you make eye contact with your very angry wife who is flipping you the bird. For my wife, that means business. It's a rare occasion that she'll say or do something mean spirited, but after tonight I fear that ... One, I'll be dead. Two, I'll be packing my bags, which means I'll want to be dead. Or three, she'll cut off my dick. Of those options, I'll gladly take three.

I know I wasn't doing anything wrong, but I'm sure that's not how it looked to her. She's seeing another woman on stage, touching me and singing some explicit lyrics—lyrics that I've returned in kind—and her mind has started swimming. Right now, I'm the guy who can't catch a fucking break and am about to give it all up and live a quiet life in Beaumont. Hopefully, I'll still have a wife, but in the event I don't, I'll have my boys.

I'm trying to figure out in my head why Josie's here. It's not that I don't want her here, but the last I knew Noah had a game and she needed to be there for the both of us. I signal to the stagehand to come out. When he does, I point at Josie and tell him to take her to the green room. As far as I'm concerned, our set is over. The remaining songs are duets with Layla and right now those can't happen. It's going to piss Trixie off, but I'm doing this for free. When I say I'm done, I'm done.

"I'm cutting it short," I say to Harrison and Jimmy as we walk off the stage. When Harrison looks at me questioningly, Jimmy tells him Josie is here. Harrison gets it. If Katelyn suddenly showed up, or even Jenna, we'd stop. As soon as the crowd realizes we're done, the boos start, followed by chants of, "Encore!" Normally, we'd come back out, but tonight will be different. I have a fuck load of damage control to do and I'm not exactly sober enough to do it.

I'm such a coward that I let Harrison and Jimmy walk in first. They greet Josie excitedly and she tells them the show was good, from what she saw. Why couldn't she have been here an hour ago before we went on stage? As soon as they move out of the way, I pull her into my arms and get lost in her perfume. I'm holding her tight and have my nose buried in her hair, but it doesn't escape my notice that her arms are slack at her side. This isn't good.

"I'm happy you're here."

"Are you?" she asks in a harsh tone.

I pull back and cup her cheeks, rubbing the pad of

my thumbs along her cheekbones. "Yes, I am. You have no idea." I lean down to kiss her, but I'm interrupted by the door slamming against the wall.

"What the fuck, Page? We have four more songs."

I close my eyes and take a deep, calming breath. Without breaking eye contact with Josie, I say, "Not tonight, Layla, my wife is here." I realize my mistake when Josie turns rigid in my hands and tries to step back. I shouldn't have said Layla's name. She's seen the pictures of us together and has already questioned if I'm in love with her.

I don't know what she's put together in her mind, but I have a feeling I'll be paying for it later.

"Well, are you going to introduce me?" Layla demands. Without even looking at her I know her hands are on her hips and her foot is tapping.

Reluctantly, I drop my hands from Josie's face and set one on her hip. "Layla, this is my wife, Josie."

"It's nice to finally meet you," Layla says, stepping forward and shaking Josie's hand. "I've heard so much about you."

"Funny, Liam hasn't told me a single thing about you."

Layla's face drops. She doesn't deserve to be treated harshly by Josie, but I know better than to correct her right now.

"Ah, shit," JD mutters in the background as he watches the scene unfold in front of him.

"Josie, did Katelyn happen to come with you?" Harrison asks, trying to diffuse the ticking time bomb that's about to explode.

"Sorry, Harrison. This was a spur of the moment trip, but I saw her and the kids today. Everyone is good." He nods, and pulls out his cell phone to call home, I assume. He's good like that, so is JD. Me, I sulk and take care of business before I call home because I don't want to interrupt Josie at work even though I know she'd stop what she's doing to talk to me.

I turn back to Josie, ignoring Layla. "Wanna get out of here?"

"I don't know, are you allowed to leave?"

I fight every urge I have to roll my eyes. "I'm allowed to do whatever I want."

Josie seems to be in agreement that it's time to leave. "We'll take a cab, right, since you've been drinking?"

I purse my lips and nod. Taking her hand in my mine, I grab her suitcase with my other one as we head toward the door.

"Liam, what about our set? They're waiting for us!" Layla hollers after me.

"Not tonight," I say again as I push the backdoor open and step out into the night air.

This was a mistake. I'm not prepared for the onslaught of people lined up to get into the club. It only takes one person to recognize me and scream out my name. Luckily, I'm able to grab the door before it closes and I push Josie back in, pulling the door shut behind us.

"Sorry."

"For what? It's your life, right? Isn't this what you want?"

My wife is a fucking angry firecracker right now, and she's testing me.

"I enjoy it, yes."

"But not with me?"

I squint my eyes in confusion. "What?"

She points to the door. "Why can't you show people who I am? Do you have any idea how humiliating it was to wait out front and beg the security guard to let me in? He didn't believe I was your wife because no one has ever seen us together."

"I do it to protect you and Noah."

Josie crosses her arms over her chest. "Noah's not here and we're not at home. When you have the opportunity to showcase me, you don't."

This woman infuriates me. She doesn't want to be a part of this side of my life, but wants people to see us together? I can't fucking win.

"Fine. Don't say I didn't warn you."

I grab her hand and bag and push the door open. This time they're waiting. They know we have to come out of the door and everyone is there waiting for us, both fans and paparazzi. Between the screams for my name, the hands grabbing me, and the light bulbs going off, I'm disoriented.

Josie clutches the back of my shirt with her freehand, a move she's done many times back when we were younger. I loved it then and I love it now. I keep her close, and can feel her knees bumping into her suitcase.

My name is yelled and questions are tossed out.

"Who is she?"

"What about Layla?"

"Did you file for divorce?" They're in luck tonight because I'll actually answer a question for them.

As luck would have it, there's a waiting cab that we rush to. I open the door and Josie slides in. I should follow her, but I stop to turn and face everyone instead.

"To answer your question, the woman with me tonight is my wife. As for Layla, she and I are friends. Nothing more."

I slide in and shut the door, telling the cabbie where to go. Josie is staring out the window, and when I try to pull her closer, she takes her hand away from me. *Fuck!* Leaning my head back, I close my eyes. How did something as simple as coming to play a few shows end up in such a cluster fuck? I don't know if it's Moreno or that fucking book, but things with Josie haven't been right since I mentioned coming back to L.A. I know what this town means to her; maybe I shouldn't have come back at all.

The bellhop is there to open the door when we arrive. Josie gets out while I toss some twenties at the driver. Grabbing her hand, I pull her through the lobby. People stop and look, but only long enough to see who we are before they go about their business.

Thankfully, the elevator is already at the lobby; the only problem is that it takes forever to get to my floor. When the doors open, I don't take her hand. The show's over and we're clearly fighting. Her footsteps are quick behind mine as she follows me down the hall. I open the door, holding it for her as she steps in. If this were any other time I'd have her pinned against the wall, but right now she doesn't want me to touch her. I let her look around, hoping she remembers the first time we were here—in a room similar to this one—while I put her suitcase in my room. I glance at the bed, imagining her spread out on the white comforter while I ravish her. It would mean no more lonely hand jobs. If only I could be so lucky.

Josie is looking out the window when I come back into the room. I click the stereo on and open the playlist of songs I wrote about her. I did this the last time she was here, too. Using this moment to my advantage, I step up behind her, my lips ghosting along the exposed skin on her back.

"For years I stood there and stared out the window wondering if you were down there, searching for me." Moving her hair aside, I kiss her neck. "I wrote song after song about you, hoping you'd show up at a concert, praying I'd see you in the front row. I knew if I did, I'd never let you go again."

My fingers slide under her shirt and dance along her waistband. I know she's pissed at me, but I also know she loves me.

"I'm not perfect. I never claim to be. I've made so many mistakes, but the last few years have been the best of my life. You and Noah, you're my world. I would never do anything to ruin that."

Josie turns in my hands and meets my eyes. Hers are glassy with unshed tears. "How long after you left me did you sleep with Layla?"

I step back and drop my hands. "How do you even know about that?"

"Why would you keep it from me?"

Groaning, I rub my hands over my face and groan. "Because it's my past, Josie. We both have one. In fact, yours doesn't go the fuck away and is still helping to raise our son. Speaking of Noah, where is he?"

"With Nick," she mutters.

"That's what I'm fucking talking about!"

"That's not fair."

"Yeah, well, neither is this," I say, throwing my hands out. "You want to know about my life when we weren't together, ask away, but don't get pissed at me when you don't like the answers."

Josie slides down the window to sit. I shake my head and wish I hadn't gotten rid of the booze. Leaning my head back, I look at the ceiling. I can't even believe I'm about to tell her this shit. I might as well sign my divorce papers tonight as well.

"How long?"

I take a deep breath and let it out slowly. I'm unable to look at her, so I stand next to her and stare out the window again.

"It was ... Fuck!" I roar, slamming my hand against the glass pane. "It was days, Josie. It was fucking days later. I met her at the club and we went dancing. I was in a bad place that night and she gave me some Ecstasy and I went back to her place."

I can hear her crying and want to comfort her, but I know she won't let me.

"Did you use a condom?"

"Come on, Josie."

"Answer me."

"I don't know," I answer honestly, shaking my head.

"She has a daughter who is a few months younger than Noah."

"I know. She told me the other day when she got to town—"

"She's yours?"

I laugh. "No, she's not. Layla was ... Layla was easy. She was into a lot of E and a lot of men. I'm not gonna lie, I liked her because she was so different from you, but I wasn't ready for anything then and by the time I was, she was married."

"Her husband isn't the father of her daughter."

"Jesus, how the hell do you know this? It's in that book, isn't it? Did you read that fucking book?"

I step in front of her and crouch down, pulling her chin up so she has to look at me. I search her eyes for my answer. It's there. Plain as day. "You did. You read the one thing I asked you not to."

"I had to. I had to know if you loved her!" she screams at me, pushing me away. I fall back onto my ass and she stands over me. I know who the 'her' is, and it's not Layla. "Why did Sam have such a hold on you that you couldn't come back? What did she have that I didn't?"

"Nothing."

"Then why wasn't I enough?" Tears stream down her face and I feel my eyes starting to burn.

"I wasn't enough for you." I stand so we're eye to eye. "I wouldn't have treated you right if you were here with me. I needed to grow up. I'm selfish, Josie. I wanted the whole fucking world and I couldn't have it. I wanted to be with you, Mason, and Katelyn, but I was fucking stuck. My best friend ditched out on me and I didn't want to look like a fucking loser, so I came here because my grandma offered me a different life. A life where no one had any expectations of me, and if I failed no one would give a fuck."

I avert my eyes, pinching the bridge of my nose. Inhaling deeply, I skip the part about meeting Sam and how if I hadn't, I would've come home that week. Instead, I tell her when the downfall started. "After my grandma died, I started drinking heavily. I partied every night and took women home because I could. No one cared about what I did, except for Sam, and she only cared because it wasn't with her. I was too far gone to come home and, if I had, I wouldn't have stayed."

It's a long moment in time before I'm standing in front of her again, cupping her face. Pressing my forehead against hers, I let her tears wet my hand. "Please don't let those years I was gone haunt us."

"But they are."

"How?"

Josie clutches my wrist as she closes her eyes. "Because I read that book. I broke your trust and now I'm questioning everything about our lives. There are things in Sam's journal that hurt us."

"Like what?"

"Like Mason ... he came here for you, right after you signed with your agent. He waited at her office for two days looking for you."

I drop my hand and step away.

"I didn't know." If Sam weren't dead, I'd be strangling her right now. The fact that she kept so much from me, kept me from knowing I had people who cared about me, burns me on the inside. This is just one more reason why

I can't be a part of Moreno's plan. He raised that bitch, and he's just like her.

"Would you have come home?"

I nod. "He would've kicked my ass first, before telling me you were pregnant. I would've come back for you, but I know you would've ended up hating me. I had a dream coming true and nothing was going to stop me. I would've asked you to marry me, and I would've brought you back here whether you liked it or not."

"She came to Beaumont and saw me, pregnant. She's done so much to us and can't even pay for the hurt. She lied to you, and you didn't even know it."

"Sam was a manipulator, and she was good at it," I tell her.

Josie moves to the small sofa and sits down. I sit across from her, next to the window. "I can't change the past, Josie. I can only promise you that the things I did, I'll never do again. I would never disrespect you or our marriage."

"You did it tonight, though, and you know it."

I shake my head. "I didn't. You saw an act. It's no different than a music video or a movie. I put on a good show, but you're always the one on my mind. When I was singing with Layla tonight, I was picturing you. It's how I get through my days. Hell, it's always been like that."

I crawl over to her, determined to hold her. Parting her knees, I settle in between them. "You're my life, Jojo. You're the only girl I've ever loved. I told you that I'd marry you some day; I just never specified how long it would take for that day to arrive. But, clearly, I'm good for my word. You know that."

Josie leans forward and places her lips on top of my head. I should tell her not to since I've sweated like a pig on stage, but I can't interrupt the moment.

"I have a few things to tell you."

"As long as you're not asking me for a divorce, you can tell me anything."

Her fingers trail down the side of my face, a look of apprehension on her face. Right now all I want to do is pick her up and comfort her, and then make love to her.

"Sam never sold your grandmother's house. I believe you still own it."

This should shock me, but it doesn't. I kiss the palm of her hand and smile. "I had a feeling. I went by there the other day and the neighbor said the same family still owns the house. Can I take you there tomorrow?"

"Maybe. Have you ever taken anyone else there?"

I shake my head. "Just Harrison and Yvie."

"Okay. The next thing I have to tell you, and this one is hard, so bear with me, is that Aubrey called the other night to inform us that Meredith is keeping the baby. I thought I'd be sad, but I wasn't. The more I thought about it, the more I saw it as a sign as we weren't ready to adopt."

I try not to let my pain show on face. I know how badly she wanted this baby—hell, I did, too—and for him to be ripped away from us is hard to grasp. "We can try another agency, or do that drug shit your doctor was talking about."

"No, we can't, because tomorrow I have an appointment at the hospital for an ultrasound. According to my doctor, I'm eighteen weeks pregnant!"

I f ever there is a moment that I needed to capture, this is it. Unfortunately, pulling out my cell phone to take his picture doesn't seem like the right thing to do.

This is the expression I've been waiting for. There's a gleam in his eyes that lights up his entire face. He looks shocked but elated, maybe even proud of himself. His eyes roam all over me, from my face to my stomach and back up again, even stopping to check out my boobs.

He grips my sides as a wide smile of understanding slowly appears on his face. "Say it again."

"Which part?" I ask, knowing full well what he's referring to.

"The part where you said I finally knocked you up."

"I don't think those were my exact words. I think I said something along the lines of: I'm eighteen weeks pregnant according to my doctor."

When you know someone as long as I've known Liam, you can tell when he or she thinking hard. Case in point was when I was with Katelyn at the park. She was telling me I'm pregnant, while I was simultaneously denying it and calculating in my head when my last cycle was. Katelyn knew exactly what I was doing, just as I know exactly that Liam is thinking now.

"How is this possible?"

"Well, when a man and woman have unprotected—"

He silences me with his lips, then his tongue. He deepens the kiss, pulling me to the edge of the sofa. "I know how, Jojo. I was a very willing participant. What I mean is, months ago we stopped trying and started looking into adoption. This means you were already pregnant, which also means that the last round of pregnancy tests were wrong. And don't take this the wrong way, but why aren't you puking your guts out like Jenna was?"

"I never had morning sickness with Noah. As for the tests, I'm not sure. I saw my doctor earlier today, and she said sometimes, with stress, the body doesn't send the normal indicators."

"If you didn't know you were pregnant, is the baby okay?"

One night, I caught Liam reading one of my pregnancy books. He was on the chapter about miscarriages and stillborn babies. We didn't talk about it, but I knew it had touched him profoundly.

"I don't know. In my heart, I feel like the baby is fine. The more I've thought about it, the more I feel pregnant. Katelyn even told me I was fat. This morning at the park, my best friend looked me in the eyes and told me I'm either pregnant or Xander has a lot of work to do." I laugh and cry at the same time because while I love Katelyn, she was mean today, but in a good way.

"You're not fat."

"I will be."

Liam shakes his head. "I read in one of your books that you can still work out and do yoga to stay in shape and that it's healthy for you and the baby. If you're thinking about how I'll see you—because I know you're comparing yourself to those women you saw tonight—then you have nothing to worry about. From the time I was fifteen I've thought you to be the most beautiful woman I've ever laid eyes on. The fact that you're carrying our child only intensifies that thought. Tell me what happens tomorrow."

He pushes a few pieces of fallen hair behind my ear and lets his hand fall down the front of my shirt, palming my boob in the process. He makes no bones about the groping action, just smiles like it's no big deal.

"In the morning I have to go to the hospital to have an ultrasound done. The doctor wanted to do it right away, but I couldn't do it without you."

"Thank you for waiting." He leans in and kisses me softly on the lips. It's too soon when he pulls away, leaving me longing for more.

"We have a lot more to talk about, like how you went against my wishes and read that book, as well as what happened with Meredith."

"Like how I saw you smoking on stage?"

"Touché. In my defense, I was pretty drunk because I had to perform with Layla. I didn't want to do it because I didn't know how to explain it to you. You also have a voicemail from me that probably doesn't make sense."

"It didn't, but I get it now ... sort of." I pause, giving some thought to what I'm going to say. "Liam, we need to find a happy medium. I don't want to be one of those wives who question everything that she sees or hears. It's not fair to you. I'm having trouble letting go of the past even though for most of it, I wasn't even involved. I'm afraid I'm not enough for you and that's not because of something you're doing wrong—"

"Jojo, you've got to trust me," he says, cutting me off. "You've got to accept that I'm not walking away from you or Noah, ever," he pleads with me. He's right. I need to get over whatever it is that I'm feeling. I shouldn't be insecure in my relationship with him.

"I'm sorry for making things harder." I realize it's too late to take back what I just said. His expression has changed.

"Want me to show you hard?"

I roll my eyes and bury myself in his neck. This is home for me, wherever he's at. He picks me up and carries me to his bedroom. The last time I was in his penthouse, I could only imagine what his room looked like.

He carries me straight to the en suite, setting me down on the vanity. When he steps away, he lifts his shirt, gracing me with his beautifully defined chest. My name is like a beacon screaming at me, telling me that everyone who saw him like this knew my name. When he steps toward me, my hands grab for him. His eyes close as my fingers trail over his chest. He lifts my shirt and unclasps my bra, causing me to break contact with him.

Liam pulls me until I'm standing and slowly undoes my jeans, pushing them to my ankles. He slips each boot off, setting them to the side before he helps me step out of my jeans. Lips ghost up my legs, followed by his hands, until he's back at my waist. He looks up with a wicked smirk on his face as he tugs my panties, ripping them from my body.

I gasp and he laughs. "I'll take you shopping tomorrow."

This slow method of undressing me is about to drive me insane. He blows on my core, sending waves through my body. He thinks teasing is fun but, right now, I'm finding it rather mean. I rub my thighs together to give myself some friction while hoping to spur him on, but he just watches my eyes.

I reach for him. I need to get him out of his jeans. I have to feel him pressed against my body. His erection strains against his jeans, needing to be freed. He steps back and slowly undoes each button of his jeans. Liam knows I'm eager, but is making me wait. When he bends over to untie his boots, I feel naked and alone.

His hand snakes between my legs until he's at my center, pressing his thumb to my bud. I move forward for more, but he has other ideas as he pulls away and drops his pants. I lick my lips at the sight of his cock poking out of his boxers. He chuckles and grabs himself. The smirk he had earlier is back and now I'm finding it wildly sexy. Liam knows he's hot, and he knows that I think so as well.

"Stop playing around," I say, irritated that he's teasing me.

"What do you want, Jojo?"

"You." I step to him, crashing my body into his. He catches me with a groan and instantly brings my legs up around his waist, burying his finger deep inside of me. I move ever so slightly against his hand as he fumbles to get his jeans off.

Liam pushes me against the shower wall, and with one hand still buried deep between my legs he uses his other to turn the water on. I don't care if it's too cold or hot I just want to feel him wet and slick against my body.

I hiss when the water touches my skin; it's hot and steaming up the glass door. The tiles are cool on my back and already damp. In an instant, his cock replaces his fingers. He groans at the contact, biting my shoulder.

"Fuck, I've missed you," he says as he pumps into me. I lock my ankles together, holding him place. He steps back, putting as much space between us as my legs will allow, and takes hold of the top of the shower door. I lean my head back against the tiles and push onto him, keeping with the rhythm of his hips.

"I could watch you take my dick all day." He licks his thumb and places it on my clit, rubbing vigorously until I start to shake. "It feels so good when you're about to come. I can't wait to feel you squeezing my fucking dick, Josie." His words encourage me. I tweak my nipple, pulling on the already sensitive bud to push my impending orgasm.

"Ah ... ah ... oh shit!" The throbbing between my legs is too great. I dig my hand into his shoulder and he moans, thrusting harder until he's collapsed against me. He jerks a few times, spilling into me.

Lips are pressed everywhere: my collarbone, neck, cheeks, and finally my mouth. Our tongues dance together as he holds me against him.

"You're truly the best surprise, ever."

Liam doesn't give me time to respond as he pulls us under the water. It's like a waterfall, only softer. We take turns washing each other, both going slow and using extra care when needed. After we rinse off, he gets down on his knees and shocks me when he kisses my stomach. His eyes meet mine, and if we weren't under a stream of water, I'd swear he was crying.

We dry off and walk hand in hand to bed. If this had been his other penthouse, I wouldn't be doing this. I don't think I could bring myself to lie in the same bed as one of his painkillers.

"The ultrasound will be fine," he tells me as he slides his fingers through my damp hair.

"How can you be sure?"

"I can't explain it. When you told me you were pregnant everything felt right. I wasn't worried, or freaked out. It's like this is supposed to be our moment. I missed so much with Noah and you're giving me another chance at being a dad to a newborn. I got the older kid stuff down, but I'm actually looking forward to two a.m. feedings. Besides ..."

He moves closer and presses his lips against mine, then my chin, my throat, and finally trailing his tongue around my nipple until he pulls it into his mouth.

"I told you your boobs were getting bigger. A man

notices these things about the woman he spends hours a day studying."

I laugh at his absurdity, but can't deny that he does stare at me an awful lot.

He moves to the other breast before making his way back to look me in the eyes. "You think I'm joking?"

I shake my head. "I know you're not joking. I just wonder why you're always staring at me."

Liam lies down and motions for me to roll on my side. Snuggling in behind me, he pushes his leg in between mine. He puts his arm under my head and lets his hand rest above my boob. I have the urge to rub my ass against him, but I hold back, waiting for his answer.

"Sometimes I wake up in the middle of the night and wonder how I got there. I look at you, next to me, wearing a ring that I put on your finger, and try to wrap my head around it all. I'm so fucking lucky you even let me into your life, let alone the fact that you took me back after everything that happened, so it feels like you're not real sometimes and I have to stare to burn you to memory."

Liam pushes my leg up and slides into me. "Fuck, you're still wet."

My back arches as I cry out. He kisses every available inch of skin he can reach from this position as he thrusts into me. He holds me to him, grunting with each thrust he makes.

"Yes, yes, yes," I repeat. "Don't stop, Liam. Please ..."

He growls in my ear, muttering a string of curse words as he grips my hip harder, pushing deeper into my center.

He slides between my legs. "Touch yourself," he demands, pulling my hand down to my core.

"Fuck, that's hot," he says as the moves faster, groaning with each slap of his body against mine. He pushes my knees to my chest, switching the angle.

"Harder," I beg as I take hold of his leg and help him pound into me.

He flips me over and brings his knees up, going to work. His mouth is clasped onto my breast while the other bounces free. His fingers dig into my hip as he slams me down to meet each of his thrusts.

"Fuck, I'm so deep."

"Oh God ... I'm ... oh shit!" My legs begin to shake. He quickly twists me so he's on top, letting me ride out my orgasm. He leans down and kisses me, capturing my cries as he continues to fuck me. Slowing down, he pulls my leg over his shoulder. Each thrust is met with eye contact.

"Fuck, baby," he says as he leans back on his knees. He cries out, grunting and moaning my name as he releases. I take everything he has to offer and more, greedily.

Liam collapses on top of me, spent from exhaustion. I run my fingers through his hair and hold him to my chest as he wraps himself around me.

"As I was saying, tomorrow will be fine," he says, out of breath.

I laugh, causing my boob to hit him in the face. He climbs up my body, kissing the path he's taking along the way.

"We need to sleep because tomorrow I'll be showing you off all over town." He kisses me deeply before rolling onto his side and pulling me with him. It's easy to fall asleep in his arms, but staying asleep and not worrying about what daylight will bring is another story.

**M**y leg bounces up and down while we wait for Josie's name to be called. My nervousness is tenfold. Not only are we going to confirm that she's indeed pregnant, but last night I should've spilled everything, like how I have a new motorcycle. I never felt there was a good opportunity to just blurt it out, but today I'm realizing there was. When she called me out for smoking, I could've told her then, but I didn't and that makes me an idiot.

I've been watching Josie all morning for any type of breakdown, or waiting for the shock to wear off that Meredith has decided to keep the baby. There isn't any. She said it was a sign that we weren't ready, but I don't believe that. I think the "higher ups" knew she was pregnant and just set things in motion for us. Still, I'm torn up about the baby boy we were set to adopt. I question whether he's going to have a good life or not. It scares me to think the wrong decision is being made for someone who can't speak up for himself yet.

We've been here before, getting an ultrasound, but this time it's different. I was excited the first time because it was my first experience seeing a baby on the screen. Now, I'm downright freaking out because this baby is growing inside of my wife and I put it there. There's a certain amount of pride that goes along with knowing you've knocked your wife up and I feel like I should be beating my chest with my fists like Tarzan.

Josie places her hand on my knee to stop my leg from moving up and down. It's her left hand and the diamond I put on there years ago sparkles in the rays of sun that are beaming through the window. Since I'm in the habit of spending money, I think she needs something new to remember this monumental day. A stop on Rodeo Drive is in order once we're out of here and celebrating.

I clasp my hand with hers and bring it to my lips. She looks at me and smiles before turning her gaze back to the door where the nurses come out to get the patients. A few other expectant mothers stare, but not for long. I'm the only guy in here right now and it saddens me to think these women are going to their appointments alone. I wouldn't want Josie to go by herself. Besides, I might miss something important and I'm just not okay with that possibility.

When the lady across from us lifts her magazine I stifle a laugh.

"What's so funny?"

I lean into Josie so I can whisper into her ear. "Look at the front of her magazine."

Half a minute later, Josie is covering her mouth and mumbling, "Oh my God."

"See what I was talking about?"

She nods, agreeing with me that the headlines are ridiculous, especially the one about us: "Liam Page Lets Wife Out of Hiding".

"I'm sorry I kept you in the dungeon so long."

Josie shrugs. "Eh, at least you gave me conjugal visits."

"Yeah, I'm good like that."

We both burst out laughing just as the nurse calls her name. If anything can shut me up fast, it's this appointment. I squeeze her hand, letting her know everything will be okay.

"Hi, Josie, I'm Elaine. I'll be your nurse today."

"I'm Liam." We all shake hands as we walk down the hall.

"Oh, we know who you are, Mr. Page."

"Fantastic." I run my hand through my hair and think of the worst-case scenario when the staff blabs about this appointment.

"Don't worry, all of our staff has signed non-disclosure agreements. We are all here to treat our patients not share their personal lives," Elaine reassures us as we walk down the corridor. We turn the corner and she motions for us to go into a room.

"I'm going to get your vitals and then the tech will come in and do your ultrasound." She flips through the chart page by page. "It says here we're confirming your pregnancy today?"

"Yes, to see how far along I am."

"Wonderful. I love watching everyone's expressions when they see their baby for the first time."

I like Elaine. I like that she's focused on Josie and doesn't give a shit about me, even though I'm the dad. I sit in the chair across from Josie while Elaine takes her temperature, blood pressure, and tells her to lie down. When she's done, she tells me its okay to move closer to my wife so I can see the baby.

"This is a lot different from when we did this with Meredith, huh?"

"I'm scared, Liam."

I bend down so we're eye to eye. "There's nothing to be scared of, babe. I'm right here, holding your hand the whole way."

"What if something's wrong with the baby?"

"What if everything is perfect, Jojo? What if the baby is growing nicely and doing all the things it's supposed to be and just waiting for the day he or she is supposed to come out and meet us?" I lean in and kiss her, holding my lips against hers until the door opens again.

"Hello, Josie and Liam. I'm Gus and I'll be showing you your baby today."

"Hey, Gus." I reach over Josie and shake his hand. He seems cool and hip. I like him as much as I like Elaine.

"Have you had an ultrasound before?" he asks.

"With my oldest, but it was years ago."

"Well, can't say much has changed except the images are clearer, but we still use the same cold gel," he says with a smile, trying to lighten the mood. Gus starts pressing a few buttons, and the screen comes alive.

"All right, Josie, I'm going to lift your shirt, add the

gel, and then we'll see your baby." He does as he says and the gel causes Josie to hiss.

"Cold?"

"Duh," she says, rolling her eyes.

"Okay, guys, here's your baby." Gus is pointing the screen, but I don't see anything there. I lean closer until I'm over the top of Josie's legs trying to see what Gus is pointing at. Josie is up on her elbows trying to see, too.

"Dude, throw me a bone. Where's my kid?"

Gus laughs, but I'm not finding this funny. I need this dude to show my wife that she has a baby in her belly that's coming out in a few months.

He pulls the screen closer, using a pen to trace the baby to show us the head, shoulders, two arms, a tiny torso, and a set of legs. Josie gasps when she realizes she can see the baby.

"And here's the heartbeat." Gus turns the speakers on and our baby's heartbeat surrounds us. It's the best freaking sound in the world. Leaning over, I kiss Josie hard. When I look at her, tears are streaming down her face. I wipe them away, but shed my own.

"Thank you," I whisper against her mouth. "Thank you for loving me enough to give me this opportunity."

I press my lips to the side of her belly, peppering her skin with kisses. "Hey, little baby, it's your daddy. I can't wait to meet you. You have such a huge family already. Your big brother, Noah, is going to love you and teach you how to get everything you want from Mommy and Daddy. He's going to protect you and be your best friend. There's also Quinn, Peyton, Elle, and Eden. Eden is going to love you so much. Elle is going to dress you up whether you're a boy or girl. Peyton will teach you how to throw a football. Quinn will teach you all about music. Don't even get me started on all your aunts and uncles because they're going to spoil you rotten. Your mommy and I are so happy that you're growing. I love you so much already." I wipe away the tears that have fallen before looking at the screen in time to see an arm and leg move.

"Looks like you have a soccer player in there," Gus says, as he presses more buttons on the screen.

"I can't feel anything."

"Give it a few days, Josie, you will."

"A soccer player? Gus, are you saying it's a boy?"

"Hmm, hold on ... let me see if I can get a good position." He moves the wand, pressing down on Josie's stomach to move the baby. Knowing my kid, he'll probably flip the camera off. "Sorry, guys, she moved too fast for me to get a good look, so best guess would be sixty percent chance it's a girl, forty percent boy. But you're measuring more closely to twenty weeks, so you'll have another ultrasound in about ten weeks or so."

"Can you give us another minute to see the baby and listen?" I ask, not ready for this to be over.

"Sure." Gus turns around to face the computer but keeps one hand on the wand.

"What did I tell you? Do you hear that, Josie? That's our baby that you've been taking care of for weeks now." Josie's tears match mine as we stare at the screen and listen to the heartbeat. I pull out my phone and flip the camera so it's facing us. I slide it to video and hit record.

"This is our first video journal for baby Westbury.

Here we are at your first ultrasound. You're in the background telling your mom how much you love her." Josie
laughs, but continues to cry happy tears. "We can't wait
to meet you."

---

I have the driver take us back to the hotel after the
appointment. It's my plan to take her to my grandmother's, but only after I let her kill me for buying
another motorcycle. Instead of going inside, I take her
hand in mine and walk her to parking garage. The valets
don't necessarily like the guests doing this, but its better
this way.

"Where are we going?"

"I have something to show you."

I'm trying to think of how I'm going to word this.
Truth is nothing is going to sound good no matter what
type of spin I put on it. It was an impulse purchase that I
should've discussed with her first.

We round the corner and there's a line of bikes
parked in front of us. Her grip becomes tighter, and I
squeeze back, letting her know everything is okay. When
we come to my parking number, I inhale deeply and
prepare for the worst.

"I'm sort of an idiot, but I think you know that by
now." I scratch the back of my head and look at her with
puppy dog eyes. By the expression on her face, I get the
impression she's not buying it. "So ... I kind of bought
this."

"Kind of, as in you did but are too afraid to tell me ... or kind of, as in it's a lease and can go back?"

"The first one?" I question myself because it's just easier than pissing her off.

"Uh-huh. Did you 'kind of' knock me up?"

I shake my head. "No, I did that on purpose." I try to smile, but her 'I'm going to kill you' look has me shaking in my boots.

Josie walks over to the bike, walking around it. "It's cute."

That's my cue. "You could learn to ride it. I mean, after the baby is here. I'd teach you."

She walks back over and sets her hands on her hips. "You need to learn how to communicate with me." She jabs me in my chest to emphasize her point. "I'm serious, Liam. Talk to me about everything."

"I know, you're right." Josie stands there with a satisfied look on her face as a result of my instant agreement with her.

"I know this is going to be a stupid question, but do you want to go for a ride? I bought a helmet for you. It's not like the one I have at home, this one doesn't go fast at all and we'll take all side streets." I waggle my eyebrows at her. We have a lot of fun on the Ducati that I have home, and could have some fun here.

Josie shakes her head. I get it. "I'd like to go to the house, though. Can we take a cab?" By house she means my grandmother's place. I nod and pull out my phone to call the bellhop and ask him to get us a Town Car.

I'm looking forward to getting out on the open road with

this bike, but until then, it's parked. As soon as we're back on the street, a black Town Car is waiting. I tip the bellhop and tell the driver where to go. I should've rented a car for us to get around in. I don't like it when others have to drive me around. I ask the driver to stick to the main streets because I want Josie to see as much as she can. As we drive into the Hollywood Hills, the houses get bigger, grander. A lot of people live beyond their means around here, but my grandmother didn't. Her biggest splurge was the parties she liked to host.

Josie all but hangs out the window as the driver maneuvers the hills. Every few houses she points and I tell her who lives there, or who used to. I realize that while she's here, we need to do the Hollywood tour so she can learn where the rich and famous live.

We pull up to my grandma's house and the black steel gate blocks my way. I type in the last code I remember, which is my mother's birthday, and the gate starts to move. It's fitting that the first time I've come back is with Josie. If it weren't for her, I don't think I'd be doing this right now.

As soon as the driver parks, Josie is sliding out of the back and looking around; nothing has changed. I don't know who has been taking care of the house, but I have to find out. There's only one more keypad that I can use to gain entry and that's around back. With Josie's hand in mine, we walk along the brick walkway leading to the backyard.

"Holy shit," Josie says when she sees the pool and the landscaped yard.

"Yeah, I didn't really use the pool when I was here."

"Why not?"

I shrug. "Too busy, I guess."

I flip the door open on the keypad and press in the code. The door unlocks, allowing us to enter. Taking a deep breath, I hold the door for Josie and she steps in, immediately mesmerized by the grandeur inside.

"Liam, this is ... wow!"

It's been about eleven years since I stepped foot inside this house. I never came back after she died. I told Sam to get my shit and sell it. I didn't want it. Of all the bad things that Sam did, this wasn't one of them. I'm thankful she didn't do what I asked.

Josie follows me around the house. My fingers are touching everything. One would expect layers of dust, but no, this house is spotless. I avoid the living room, instead choosing to go to what used to be my room.

I flick the light on and everything looks the same. The watch I used to wear sits on the dresser. The night before my grandmother died I had taken it off and never had a chance to put it back on the next day. I leave it there, afraid to touch it.

"This was my room." I sit down on the bed and pull open the top drawer of the nightstand. There she is, all eighteen years of her. I pull out the picture of Josie, remembering the night it was taken like it was yesterday. It was the night of homecoming. We had been crowned king and queen. Times were simpler then.

"I kept this in my bedside table and would look at you every night. You'd help me write songs, and you'd listen to my problems. The first song I played after I got signed was something I wrote for you. Right after the show, Harrison and I were told we were heading out on tour. He wanted to celebrate, so we went and got the tattoos. That's the night I got your name across my chest." I take a deep breath. I haven't told this story to anyone, ever.

"The next day, I woke up to a loud crash. When I came out of my room I found my grandmother lying on the floor. I called 9-1-1 and tried CPR, but she had a brain aneurysm and was dead before she hit the floor. One day I'm on top of the world and the next, at the bottom of the barrel."

"I'm so sorry, Liam."

I set Josie's photo back in the drawer and close it. "I had lost you and Mason because of my stupidity and then I lost my grandma. That's when I started getting numb just so I didn't have to feel the pain."

"I have something to tell you."

"What's that?"

"Your mom cornered me in the park the other day and apologized. She told me so much about her life, your grandparents, and a little bit about your dad. Later that day, when I came home, I found out about the pictures of you and Layla. She was there with Noah and I invited her to dinner. She was with us when I got the call from Aubrey about the baby. We talked a lot afterward and the best part of the night was seeing her laugh. I've never seen your mother laugh before, but that night she did. She and Noah watched your games on DVD while sharing ice cream and when it was time for her to leave, I asked her why she never took you to meet your grandma. She said that Sterling had told her she passed away when you were three."

Liam looks at me like I'm a foreign object that doesn't belong in his home. "He did that?"

I nod, biting my lower lip. "I told your mom that wasn't the case. I think you need to bring her here, show her that her childhood home still stands."

"What about you, would you consider living here?"

"In Los Angeles?" she asks.

"No, Hollywood. In this house, would you consider it? I need to be here, Josie, or the band is going to fail. I need to be in Beaumont or my family is going to grow up without me. What if we compromise? We can spend the school year in Beaumont, and the summers here. We can live here and raise the kids. Fill my grandma's house with love and laughter. I think she would've liked that. I'll still have to travel back and forth, but I'm not ready to give up my music ... unless you ask me to."

"I've learned my lesson about forcing or suggesting anything. I think what you've proposed will work. What about Harrison and Jimmy?"

"Harrison has a condo or apartment, whatever he wants to call it, south of here, but he could buy something close to us if he wanted to, so could JD and Jenna. Honestly, I think JD and Jenna are probably moving here anyway."

"What about the café?"

Liam cups my cheeks. "Hire more people. I keep telling you that. Hire more people to cover for you. It'll be worth it."

"Okay."

"Yeah?"

"Yeah, let's do this."

## 31

## JOSIE

Los Angeles was an eye-opener for Liam and me. We realized that we needed to work on our communication skills and stop worrying how the other might react when we have bad news. We hid stuff from each other that could've been very hurtful to our marriage. I still have looming questions about his past, mostly where Sam is concerned, but for the most part things between us are better than ever.

It's been almost four months since the band went to L.A. to help out Trixie. In the end, the fundraiser was successful for *Metro* and Trixie's call sheet started filling up again. I'm not saying it was all *4225 West*'s doing, but I do believe the guys helped out a lot. Of course, being front and center for their performances was the best part. Jenna and Katelyn joined me for the last show and we rocked out like groupies, except we went home with the band for the night.

It's the end of summer and life is winding down, or

about to explode, depending on which way you look at it. I'm due in about five weeks, and instead of being home and getting ready, I've spent the past week and a half sitting on bleachers while I cheer my son and his baseball team on in the Little League World Series. We have one game left—the championship—and Noah is pitching.

We're all here; Liam chartered a plane to make sure of it so we could all support Noah and Nick. Harrison, Katelyn and the kids, Jimmy, Jenna and Eden, my parents, Mr. Powell and Ms. James, Yvie, and a very pregnant Aubrey ... even Bianca is here. Xander has taken the position as team trainer and is on the bench, which is making Liam jealous.

"Why don't you use your good eye? You know, the one between your—" Liam's hand clamps down over my mouth, causing me to mumble, "ass cheeks," into his hand. When he finally removes it, I glare at him out of the corner of my eye.

"Jesus, Josie, you're going to get tossed out of the ball-park. Do you want that?"

"No," I say with a huff.

"You'd think being pregnant would calm you down, but I think it's making it worse."

I turn away from Liam and face Aubrey, who is holding her belly and laughing. As I look around at my family, everyone is laughing, except for Bianca—she's giving me the thumbs-up. Getting kicked out is the last thing I want, but I can't help it when the umpire makes a shitty call and my son is batting.

But I know if I got kicked out, it would embarrass Noah and I'm not about to do that. He's worked so hard to get where we are today. Liam's right, I need to be on my best behavior.

"It's okay, Aunt Josie! If I say it the umpire won't kick me out; I'm too cute." Peyton wraps her arm around me and sticks her tongue out at Liam, who throws his hands up in the air.

"I know, but Uncle Liam is right. I need to be good."

Peyton shrugs and wiggles her way in between Liam and me, but leans her head on my bulging belly. Liam and I have decided to wait until the baby's born to find out what we're having. He thinks it's a girl because it'll be payback for how rotten he's been and because Nick and Aubrey are having a boy. Liam says that this is his punishment. He says luck is not on his side and he'll be damned if his daughter marries an Ashford. I usually just nod and agree with him, even though I think we're having a boy.

At the end of the inning, Aubrey and I stand and stretch. Since Yvie moved to Beaumont two months ago, she's been teaching us yoga. It's helped a lot and I've been able to keep my weight gain to a minimum. Not too many expectant moms travel with their yogi, but having her on the trip has been amazing. She's making sure our blood pressure doesn't skyrocket from a combination of the heat, uncomfortable seating, and ballpark food. I may or may not have eaten my fair share of hotdogs since I've been here. I blame the stress and the fact that I'm eating for two.

Noah takes the mound. He doesn't look nervous at all, but Liam does. Liam's hunched over, resting his elbows on his knees with his ball cap turned backwards. I know it's hard for him to see Noah with Nick, but honestly, it's been good for everyone involved. Nick loves coaching and has been offered the Varsity Coach spot at the high school. He's yet to give them an answer, though; he says he needs to get through baseball first and discuss it with Noah.

Bianca, who was sitting with my mother, comes and sits next to Liam. He puts his arm around her and gives her a hug. This is another thing that's transpired out of my impromptu trip to L.A.—a relationship with Bianca.

When we returned to Beaumont, he went to her and they talked for a long time. She spends more and more time at our house now, and she and I get along pretty well. I'm still hesitant in some regard, but I'm trying. It was Bianca and my mother who cleaned out the nursery to get it ready for this baby. We gave everything we had to Meredith and her son, Daniel. Meredith cried and apologized profusely, but it was the right decision. I see her every now and again at the park, but I don't talk to her or ask to see Daniel. I've closed that chapter and moved on.

I asked Katelyn not to throw me a baby shower this time. One, I didn't want to explain to everyone where the other baby was. Two, I want to buy stuff that I like and I'm waiting until I pop this sucker out before I splurge on too much. Katelyn promised me a massive shopping trip as soon as we're back in Beaumont. It'll be a girl's weekend with the grandmas.

We're tied one-one with Japan and everyone is on edge. The grandstands are split down the middle, with us having a large cheering section.

Junior Appleton is catching, and as much as it pains me, he and Noah are good friends. Don't expect me to invite Candy over anytime soon, though. I'm still not over her trying to steal Liam from me ... twice.

I have to stand in between the batters Noah is facing and stretch. My back is starting to ache from sitting down for too long, but thankfully it's almost over. We're in the top of the fifth and we're taking the field.

"You okay?" Liam asks as he hands me a bottle of water.

I nod and keep shifting from foot to foot, pressing my hands into my lower back to relieve some of the strain. "Just stiff from sitting for so long," I tell him. When Noah strikes out the third batter, ending the inning, I sit back down, only to have fingers start kneading my back.

"Relax," my mom says as she digs her fingers into my lower back. "You're full of stress right now and there's no reason to be."

I take a long drink of my water and point to the dugout where her grandson is about to step up to the plate. "He's my stress," I tell her. "And yet he's so calm about everything."

"That's because he's just like Liam. I remember watching many games and biting my nails because I thought we were going to lose and there was Liam, cool as a cucumber."

I bump my leg with Liam's, and he smirks. "He was cocky, Mom, there's a difference."

Liam turns and winks and I blow him a kiss. When Noah's name is announced over the loud speaker, my mom stops rubbing my back so we can watch.

"Let's go, Westbury, keep your eye on the ball!" Liam yells after Noah swings and misses.

He digs his right foot into the dirt before stepping in to face the batter again. The pitch is delivered and I reach for Liam's hand, squeezing tightly, as Noah steps with his left foot and starts the bat rotation. The thwack of the ball hitting the bat ricochets loudly throughout the stadium. Our side is yelling at him to run, while the other side is yelling at their kids to drop the ball.

It's a hit down the left field base line, good for a double.

"Okay, Appleton, bring him home!" Liam shouts. Junior Appleton is a big kid for his age, but a damn fine baseball player. He works just as hard as Noah does on his game, spending extra time with Nick. The thought occurs to me that Nick is like everyone's surrogate dad. He's always willing to help the kids learn and get better. I know for a fact that when the boys won the state title he was beside himself and almost brought to tears when Liam said he'd cover the charges for the team to fly. We haven't spoken much since we've gotten here because he's been busy with team and coaching events, but I can't imagine what he's feeling right now. Knowing him the way I do, he's telling himself that this is just another baseball game.

Junior is faced with a full-count. Liam is as anxious for him as he was for Noah. Candy is on the bottom bleacher, rocking back and forth. I feel her pain.

The loud clank brings us all to standing. The outfielders are running and Noah is holding tight to second with his eyes focused on Nick. Goosebumps take over and Liam and I squeeze each other's hand. I don't know what to watch, the ball or my son. As soon as I see the ball fly over the outfielder's head, I'm screaming as loud as I can.

When Noah crosses the plate, I'm jumping up and down along with Aubrey. Two pregnant chicks shouldn't jump at the same time because it messes up your equilibrium. Liam catches me as I wobble and Harrison grabs a hold of Aubrey, but that doesn't stop us. When Junior rounds third, we become louder. Everyone is screaming. The ball is thrown and Junior slides. The whole stadium grows quiet as we wait for the umpire.

When he goes out wide, calling Junior safe, we erupt in cheers. We are up by two runs in the bottom of the sixth. If Noah can hold off the power hitters for the Japanese team, we win.

"Oh God, I have to pee." I cross my legs in an effort to hold it.

"Want me to walk with you?" my mother offers. I turn and glare at her. She must think I'm nuts if I'm leaving when my son is pitching in the LLWSC game.

"Are you crazy? I'd rather pee my pants than miss Noah pitching."

"She's not crazy, Josie. She's just offering. Face forward like a good girl and watch your son. I'm sure by all the daggers you just put in your mom's chest, she knows you're willing to pee down your leg," Liam says as if nothing is amiss.

"Don't be gross," I say to Liam, who throws his hands up in the air.

As soon as I sit down my mom is back to giving me a massage. I feel a little bad for Aubrey because I'm getting pampered, but I really like it and I don't want my mom to stop.

"Come on, Westbury." Liam is upset because Noah just walked a batter, putting a runner on first base. "It's just you and Junior out there," he says, encouraging him to work with his catcher.

The second batter strikes out swinging. It's our first out. We're just two outs away from the championship. All the moms are rocking back and forth with our hands in praying position. The younger kids are the cheerleaders, using their chants to distract the batters. Behind us, the broadcasters are talking and over the course of the ten days we've been here, they've done specials on certain kids. Noah was one of them. Noah does a lot stuff that makes me proud, but I was over the moon when he answered the question about how it feels to be Liam Page's son with: "I don't know, Marv, how does it feel to be your dad's son?"

After the interview, the broadcaster apologized to Noah and asked to do the interview over again. Noah gave him another chance and finally got to talk about himself and his passion for baseball and football. I'm sure somewhere during the television broadcast they brought up Liam's high school career and cover from *Sports Illustrated*.

The third batter hits a pop fly, which is easily caught by our third basemen. The runner has to stay at first, even though he tried to act like he was going to run. The next batter up is Japan's big hitter. He's hit a homerun in every game, except for this one. Junior calls timeout and heads to the mound, followed by Nick. You can tell they're talking strategy because Noah and Junior have their mouths covered. Nick brings the rest of the infield in briefly before heading back to the dugout.

"What's going on?" I ask Liam, who is staring intently at Noah.

He shakes his head. "Nick's just calming him down, telling him where he wants the pitches to be."

I'm so nervous that my heart is going to burst out of my chest. I close my eyes when Noah starts his pitching motion, opening just in time to see the batter start his swing. The ball is hit and we all stand, our side breathing a sigh of relief when it goes foul.

"Just you and your catcher, Westbury. Find the sweet spot."

"He can't hear you," I say to Liam.

He glares at me and nods. "Yes, he can."

"No, he can't. I asked him once. He said he tunes us out."

"No, he tunes you out because you taunt the umpires."

"Do not."

This time Liam turns and shoots me a look of exasperation. "Seriously, Josie, you're acting like you're five. Hell, Eden is more mature than you are right now."

I look down the bench at Eden, who has chocolate ice cream all over her face.

"Great, now I want ice cream."

Liam shakes his head and focuses on the game, which I should be doing. The second pitch is a ball, followed by a strike.

"He's ahead in the count," I say, poking Liam in the shoulder.

"No wonder Katelyn doesn't sit with you," he mutters as he tries to ignore me.

I can't help that I'm nervous for our son, who is pitching in the biggest game of his life right now. I want to run out there and hold him.

Noah winds up and lets go of the ball. Before I can grasp what is happening, Noah throws his glove up in the air and jumps into Junior's arms.

I stand and look at Liam. "They won! Oh my God, Liam, they won!" He gives me a quick hug before he starts celebrating. I know he wants to be out on the field with Noah and hates that it's Nick that got them this far. He's so proud, though; he doesn't say anything to Noah when he chooses to go practice with Nick instead of hanging out.

When the presentations are over, we pick up all of our stuff and head out to meet Noah. I tried telling Liam to go on ahead, but he's waiting for me, helping me down the stairs. A lot of parents are gathering at the entrance where the players will come out, each of us proud, but half of us somber because someone had to lose. Thing is, if your son or daughter makes it this far, they have nothing to hang their heads about. This is the best there is in Little League Baseball.

Noah comes running out and right into Liam's arms. I'll never get over the sight of those two together.

A warm sensation washes over me, causing me to feel lightheaded. Hands are grabbing at me, telling me to lie down, but I can't see who's talking to me. I can only see Liam and Noah.

"Josie?" I can hear my dad calling my name, but he seems so far away.

"Someone call 9-1-1."

*Yes, I think that would be a good idea.*

## 32

### LIAM

"MOM!"

Noah's bloodcurdling scream causes me to freeze. I try to hang on to him as he pushes himself out of my arms, but I'm unable to. Everything is happening in slow motion. The way Noah is falling out of my arms, the way I'm turning just in time to see my wife start to fall to the ground, the way people are looming around her, but moving at a snail's pace.

"Josie!" My words are muffled and sound robotic and it takes me what seems like an hour to get to her when she's only a few feet away.

Her father is there to help her to the ground, and someone is yelling for 9-1-1. I'm by her side, holding her hand and trying to get the words that are running through my head out of my mouth.

"*Nick!*" I scream as loud as I can. He's a doctor. He'll know what to do.

"Josie, baby, can you hear me?" Her lips move, but

there's no sound coming out of her mouth. Next to me, Noah is crying, begging his mother to wake up. I look up at the people around us, all family, all concerned.

"Where's the damn ambulance?"

"It's on its way, Liam," Jenna tells me as she holds a crying Eden in her arms. I turn my attention back to Josie and check for a pulse. She has one, but I'm not sure if it's normal.

Nick and Xander bust their way through the on-lookers and bend down next to her.

"What happened?"

"She was watching Noah and Liam and started to wobble. I caught her before she fell," Mr. Preston tells Nick, who has his penlight out and is shining it in her eyes. He's doing things I've never seen him do before. I've only seen him be a part of my son's life, not trying to save one.

"Nick, is my mom going to be okay?"

"We need to get her to the hospital so she can be looked at. Remember, buddy, I'm a doctor for kids like you." But that doesn't stop Nick from checking her over. When he places his hands on her belly, I start to panic.

"Ashford, is something wrong with the baby?"

"I can't tell, but I believe she's in labor."

"It's too early," both her mom and mine say at the same time. I glance up quickly and find them standing together, holding each other.

I've never been so relieved to hear sirens in my life. The EMT's are instructing people to get out of their way as they bring the gurney over to us.

"What happened here?" one of them asks, but is only

focusing on Josie. Her father recounts the story while they take quick vitals and place a backboard under her.

"How far along is she?"

"Um ... thirty-five weeks." Answering that question is the hardest thing I've ever done. I used to think nothing would compare to finding my grandma on the floor or watching JD go down, but this, by far, is the worst.

"What's her name?"

"Josephine Westbury," her father answers for me.

I give him a nod in appreciation, hoping he understands why I'm tongue-tied. All around me orders are being barked out and I don't understand a single one of them.

"You need to let go of her, sir."

"Wh-what?" I ask, shaking my head. "She's my wife. I can't."

"You can ride along in the truck, but you have to let go of her." When they start to lift her, I lock down. There's a force inside of me fighting. My brain is telling my limbs to move, to let them take her, but my heart is saying no, to hold on tight. I'm losing the battle and can't stop it.

Strong hands clamp down on my shoulders, pulling me away from her. I fight, but another set of arms grab a hold of me. Harrison and Xander are keeping me sandwiched in. I could take Harrison, but Xander would give me a run for my money.

"Come on, mate. You need to be calm for your missus. They'll let you go with her in the ambulance if you can keep yourself under control. You don't want that sod going with her, do you?"

Nick is running after the EMT's and I'm left standing here. JD's right. She's my wife, not Nick's.

"I'm cool," I say, and the hands drop. I take off running, needing to catch up with the ambulance. I pat Nick on the back, telling him, "I got this," and climb in. The female EMT working on Josie doesn't look up, but tells me to sit down across from her. I do, instantly taking Josie's hand in mine. When the doors slam shut, I jump.

"What's your name?"

"Liam."

"Okay, Liam. We're going to get your wife to the hospital. Everything will be okay."

The truck takes off with a lurch, causing me to wobble a little. I lean down so I can talk to my wife. "I don't know what's going on, but I need you to be strong." As I'm whispering in her ear I hear beeping. The last time I heard this, JD was in a coma. Sweat starts to pebble on my forehead and my heart starts racing.

"What's that noise?"

"Heart monitor for your wife and baby."

"Okay, that's good, right?"

"It is. I'm making sure she's stable right now and that the baby isn't in distress."

I know I have to trust her to do her job, but in the back of my mind I fear she's not doing enough. My wife is unconscious and they won't tell me why.

"We're here."

Before I have time to react, the back doors are open and Josie's gurney is being pulled out from under me. The EMT's are running Josie in and I'm left standing on the sidewalk as she disappears through two sets of doors and down a hall.

"You look lost. Can I help you?" I look down at an older lady with white hair and a grandmotherly face. For a minute, I think she looks like my grandma.

"That was my wife they just rushed in there."

She nods and places her hand on my bicep as pushes me toward the doors. "I'm Ethel. I volunteer here in my free time. It's the best thing for me in my old age. I can spend hours rocking newborns to sleep while their moms rest."

"My wife is pregnant. She passed out at our son's baseball game today."

"The staff here is wonderful. They'll take care of her. Come on, I'll show you where to go."

Ethel takes me to the emergency room, where the lady tells me they've taken her to labor and delivery.

"Well, we best get on up there." Ethel is slow and I want to run there, but I'm not sure if I'd make it. I let her show me the way because right now she's keeping me somewhat calm.

"Good afternoon, Ethel."

"Hi, Lois. This young man is looking for his wife. They just brought her in by ambulance."

Lois smiles, but it's not very reassuring. I just want to see my wife. "She's with the doctors now. Ethel can take you to the waiting room."

Ethel tugs on me to follow her and I do. When she sits down next to me, I feel like asking her if she has someplace else that she needs to be, but the truth is I don't want to be alone. I don't know how much time passes until I hear familiar voices. Noah comes sprinting toward me and I stand up and catch him as he launches himself into my arms. Everyone is frantic, except Nick, who is calmly speaking with the nurse.

"What's going on, Liam?" Mrs. Preston asks.

"I don't know," I say, shaking my head and holding Noah in my arms. I don't care how old your child is, when their mom is hurt, they're just like babies again. I set him down and pull him into my side.

"Where is she?" her father asks.

"The doctors are with her now. We have to wait until they come out." I'm useless in this situation and my hands are tied. I want to be in there with Josie, but know I'd be in the way. I'd have to touch her, hold her, and they need the space to work on her.

We cram into the waiting room, which isn't big enough to hold our family. JD, Nick, and Harrison all take spots on the floor. Jenna is holding a sleeping Eden in her arms. Peyton is sitting on Harrison's lap with Quinn sitting next to him, while Elle is sitting in JD's lap. Noah is next to me and we're sitting in between my mom and Josie's. Tess, Mr. Preston, Katelyn, Mr. Powell, and Jenna sit across from me, as Yvie and Xander lean against the wall.

Ethel appears out of nowhere with a tray full of coffee and juice for the kids. Right now I think she's the greatest lady I've met in a long time because she's taking care of my family without even being asked.

When she stops at my mom, she smiles softly. "You know, you look like this actress I used to love on the big screen."

"Is that so?" I eye my mom out of the corner of my eye and watch her. Her silver screen days have been over for so long that her movies are hard to find.

"Oh yes, she stopped acting though, and just disappeared."

"What was her name?"

I don't know if my mom is fishing or just making conversation, but either way, their chatter is keeping the mood light.

"Bianca Page. She just lit up the screen when she'd smile."

"Oh, Bianca, you must give her your autograph," Josie's mom says, chuckling. Ethel's face is priceless as she gasps. My mom blushes, but I know she likes it. She recently auditioned for a role in the fall production at the Beaumont Theater.

"My dear, what happened to you?"

My eyes are focused on the hallway, waiting for the doctor to appear, but trying to listen to my mom as well. I'm interested in her excuse as to why she stopped.

"I had a family to raise, and grandbabies." I turn just in time for her to motion to all of us sitting around. I wish it were true, but Ethel doesn't need to know that.

I'm starting to get jittery so I stand and walk out into the hall. Nurses move around, and babies cry. Looking into the waiting room, I see family—family that didn't exist years ago, aside from Tess, Harrison, Quinn, Yvie, and JD. They've been with me through everything and never questioned me when I came back.

"Mr. Westbury?"

I look to my left when my name is called. The

doctor, dressed in blue, is taking off his paper hat as he reaches me. "I'm Doctor Rolland. I've been treating your wife. There really isn't much to tell you except that she's in labor. We can stop it, but we have to do an ultrasound first. Her blood pressure is higher than normal, which could have been caused by her being in the sun so much and from what I understand she ate half the hot dogs in the park?"

I try not to laugh because this isn't funny, but if he knows this, it means Josie's awake.

"She's okay? And the baby?"

"Baby sounds good, no distress. We'll be doing an ultrasound in a few minutes. Your wife has a headache and is dehydrated, but she's awake and asking for you. You'll find her at the end of the hall. I'll be back in a few to do the ultrasound." He turns and looks at the waiting room where everyone is standing. "Just one at a time, please."

There's no question that I'm going in first. The others can fight it out. As soon as the doctor turns the corner, I call for Noah.

"Let's go see your mom," I say, as I grab his hand. There's no way I'm making him wait. He needs to see her as much as I do.

When I push the door open, her room is dark and the machines are beeping. Noah's hand tightens and I squeeze back, reassuring him, even though I'm not so sure myself until I see her lying there looking at us.

Noah let's go of my hand and rushes to his mom's side.

"You did very well today," she says as she pushes his hair out of his face.

"You scared me so much, Mom."

"I know. I'm sorry." Josie tries to pull him into a hug, but one arm is hooked up to a blood pressure machine and her other one has IV's poking out of her skin. Still, Noah finds a way to wrap his arms around her.

When he lets go, Josie's wiping tears away. Noah comes over and stands next to me and I place my hand on his shoulder. "Do you want to stay?" He nods and I motion for him to sit in the extra chair by the window.

"Hey, Jojo," I say, as I approach her bed. She smiles softly and reaches for me. "I'm going to have to ask that you never do something like this again." I kiss her dry lips and hold my forehead to hers.

"It was the hotdogs."

I nod and try not to laugh. It comes out as half laugh, half cry. "Yeah, let's go with that."

Josie takes my hand and puts it under her head, holding it there. It's uncomfortable, but I don't care. If this is what she needs, I'll take the discomfort. Noah moves his chair closer and puts his head on her legs.

"Are you in pain?"

She shakes her head. "They're going to try and stop the labor, but I'm still having contractions. I think I was in labor during the game. That's why my back hurt."

"I should've known."

Josie runs her fingers down the side of my face. "I didn't even know. There were five other women near me who have all given birth, and no one knew."

"I froze, Josie. I didn't know what was going on and

all I could think about was my grandmother and JD ... when they tried to take you, I wouldn't let them. I was afraid I'd never see you again."

"I'm never leaving you, Liam. You're stuck with me for life."

"I'll take it," I say, as I give her a kiss.

Josie and I are just looking at each other when the doctor returns to do her ultrasound. She has one hand with me, while the other holds Noah's.

"Come here, Noah," I say when the doctor starts setting up the machine. "Do you want to see your brother or sister, or would you like to go out and wait?"

"Is it cool?"

"Aside from me being your dad, it's the coolest thing ever."

He shrugs and says he'll stay. I keep him with me, though, next to Josie, so that the doctor isn't looking for an excuse to kick him out. A few nurses come in; one checks her vitals, while the other checks her IV's.

"I forgot to tell you, a little old lady recognized my mom from an old movie. I thought mom was going to get up and dance a jig. When she asked mom where she disappeared to, she said she was raising a family and motioned to everyone in the waiting room."

"I wish it were true."

"Me too," I say. "I let her have her moment though. Sometimes I think she needs it."

"She does."

"Whoa, what is that?"

Coming from the computer is the baby's heartbeat. Noah's eyes go wide as he looks at Josie and me.

"That, young man, is the heartbeat of your brother or sister and this is what he or she looks like." The doctor turns the screen to show Noah, whose face drops.

"Where's its head?"

Now I'm looking, and sure enough, my child is missing its head.

"Well, it seems that your sibling is ready to join the world."

"It's too early!" Josie screeches.

"I'll alert NICU," one of the nurses says, leaving the room. The other nurse is jotting information down in Josie's chart and the doctor is studying the computer.

"What's going on?"

He looks at Josie and smiles. "You're going to deliver. We're going to let things progress naturally for a bit and see how much you can do by yourself, but you're not leaving the hospital until your baby is born."

"But ... but ..."

He rests a reassuring hand on her leg. "You're early, but everything will be okay. We have a great team in the NICU, who will be on standby to assist your baby. Do you want to know the sex?"

We both shake our heads. We haven't even discussed names. We thought we'd figure it out after we saw the baby.

"I know you're scared. We could try and stop the labor, but the baby is engaged, so even if we stopped it today, it's likely you'll be in active labor within twenty-four hours. I suggest you rest while you can. Right now your contractions are mild, but that will change."

He exits the room, leaving us pretty much speechless. I'm trying not to panic. Josie doesn't need this.

"Can you go get Katelyn? She went early with the twins. She'll know what to do."

I kiss her gently and tell her I'll be back after Katelyn. As soon as I open the door to her room, her mother and father stand.

Noah stands next to me while I deliver the news. I tell everyone that they can fly home, that they don't need to stay, but everyone says they're not going anywhere.

"Katelyn, she needs to talk to you." Katelyn rushes down the hall and into her room, followed by Mrs. Preston. Frankly, the one-person rule is dumb and we're breaking it. I look at Mr. Preston and tell him he should go, too. That's his baby girl in there.

"I need someone to go to the hotel and see if we can extend our stay."

"I'll do it," Tess volunteers. "Do the kids want to come back to the hotel and swim?" Quinn and Elle say yes, but Peyton shakes her head. Tess reaches for Eden, who is still sleeping.

"I think I'm going to go with you, Tess," Aubrey says. I know the chairs can't be comfortable. Mr. Powell and Nick both stand, each saying for someone to call them when the news changes.

I pull Nick aside. "Thank you. Not only for trying to help Josie when I couldn't, but also for being there for Noah when I wasn't."

He extends his hand, and I shake it. "You're welcome, Liam. There isn't anything I wouldn't do for them."

I know this, and nod. I don't want to think about a

time when I need to call Nick for help, but I'm glad that he's been there for my family. I watch him walk away, knowing that he's never going anywhere and I need to accept it.

"Liam," my mom says as she comes to me, placing her hands on my forearms. "I'm going to go order us some food. You guys have to be starving."

"Thanks, Mom." I watch her walk away and think about these past few months. She spends more and more time at our house, which doesn't seem to bother Josie. They're often laughing together. I was shocked as shit when they started shopping together. Whatever happened when I was in L.A., for her and Josie, has been a great thing.

My father is another story. He refuses to acknowledge Josie as my wife, which means he doesn't acknowledge Noah and that is unacceptable in my book. He's not welcome in our home and he knows it.

I've told my mom that as soon as the baby's born, she and I will go back to L.A. and get my grandmother's estate in order. There's a trust in my mother's name that her father left her and I think it's about time she claimed it. Maybe she'll use the money to leave my father.

One could only hope.

When I was in labor with Noah, my mom was by my side. My dad, Katelyn, and Mason waited in the waiting room for the news that Noah was here. As much as I love Liam and know he'll be by my side, helping me through this delivery, I need my mom and Katelyn with me right now.

They both come rushing in, each taking a side. My mom bumps the nurse and doesn't apologize. I'm sure the nurse is used to overbearing mothers.

"Don't be mean, Mom, she's just doing her job."

"I know. I'm sorry," she says, turning her attention on me. Her fingers push through my hair, and even at this age, I find it calming to have my mom here.

"The baby is coming early. I'm scared," I tell them both through tears. "What if it's not ready?"

Katelyn grabs my hand. "I was scared, too, when the twins came early, but look at them. They're healthy. They only had to spend a couple of days in the hospital.

If the doctor didn't think the baby was ready, he'd be doing everything he could to stop things. You've got to trust him."

"She's right, Josie. You need to have faith," my mom says. These words are easier to hear, but not so easy to believe and I won't be able to until I'm holding my baby in my arms.

Katelyn gives me a kiss on my forehead and steps aside so I can see my dad.

"Hi, Daddy."

"Hey, sweetheart. You really gave me a scare."

"I know. I'm sorry."

My dad has never been an overly emotional man. I've seen him cry only a handful of times. When I told him Sterling wouldn't help me find Liam, he said it broke his heart that I was going through this by myself. He cried then, when he held Noah for the first time, and now.

"Don't cry. You're going to be a grandfather again."

"And I can't wait." He kisses my forehead and excuses himself. Once he leaves, everyone starts to come in. Pretty soon my room is full of family and friends, and the smell of delicious pasta.

"Where's everyone else?"

"Tess and Mr. Powell took the kids back to the hotel to swim and make sure we aren't booted from our rooms since we were due to check out after the game. Nick took Aubrey there, as well, because the seats in the waiting room aren't very comfortable."

"I can imagine," I say, looking at Liam. Then to everyone else, "You guys don't have to stay." From the expression on Harrison and Jimmy's faces, they want to get the hell out of dodge.

"This is where we want to be, Josie," Bianca states as she hands me a plate of plain pasta, with plain toast and some applesauce.

"All of this is okay, I checked with the nurse."

"You did?" I choke back a sob of gratitude.

"Of course. I don't want you sick when you deliver. You need strength, so eat. I know it's bland. We'll just have to go out to dinner after the baby arrives."

"Thank you, Bianca."

She smiles and looks away, not liking the attention. When she passes by Liam, he pulls her into his arms and gives her a quick hug. They're still working on building their relationship and I have no reason to believe it will ever crumble again. She's determined to do right by her son.

Liam sits next to me while we eat. With each bite he takes, I long for the heavy cream of Alfredo sauce.

"How does yours taste?"

"Great, want some?"

I shake my head and turn back to my plain noodles with my plain toast. I could really use a hot dog right now.

When the nurse comes in, she brings me a Popsicle. I think I love her. She looks around the room and smiles once she realizes who is in my room.

"You're one lucky lady."

"Thanks," I reply as I suck on the icy treat. "I don't know which one is the dad, though, so it's a bit awkward, if you know what I mean. Trust me when I say, you don't want to be in this position."

Her eyes go wide, as everyone in the room starts to laugh. My mom chastises me for saying such a thing. I shrug and continue giving my baby a massive dose of sugar.

"You can ask for their autograph if you want, but only if you give me a discount on my bill."

"Um ..."

"She's only kidding. I'm Liam," he says as he shakes her hand. I wasn't kidding, but whatever. "That's Harrison and JD." Liam points to the guys, who are stuffing their faces in the corner. They wave, but make no effort to get up. I don't blame them. Eating is my top priority, too.

"I listen to you guys all of the time."

"Thanks, we appreciate the support."

"Do you follow me on Twitter?" Jimmy asks, except it sounds like Twitt-errrr. My nurse blushes. I roll my eyes and hand her the stick from my Popsicle. It was very good, but now I'm uncomfortable because the baby is kicking my bladder and kidney. Plus, my back still hurts.

"Are you okay?" Liam asks.

"Baby is kicking a lot and my back hurts."

"Here, sit up." Liam puts his food down and tries to crawl behind me to massage my back. It's working except I feel like I have to go to the bathroom.

"Oh crap. I just peed the bed."

People laugh, and yeah, it's funny, but it's also embarrassing.

"I'll get you fresh sheets, Josie," my nurse says as she leaves the room.

"Oh God, Liam, something's wrong." I close my eyes as pain rips through my abdomen.

"Mom?" Noah's voice rings out.

"Everyone get out of the room. Mom, can you get the nurse?" Everyone except Liam files out of the room just as the nurse comes back.

"What's going on, Josie?" she asks me as she checks the printout next to my bed. "Let's see if your water broke." She lifts the blanket just as I let out a long wail.

"Well, it looks like we're having a baby right now."

"What do you mean, right now?" Liam asks, panic lacing his words.

"Oh God, Liam, it's coming out. I can feel it coming out."

He moves away so I can lie back on the bed. I grip his hand as another contraction comes. They're so strong and it feels like nails are being scraped against my skin. I start breathing heavily in between, and when my next one comes, I can't help but push.

"No, don't push yet, Josie," the nurse tells me as she's scrambling to get my bed ready.

The doctor comes in with a yellow gown on and a stupid smile on his face. I want to kick him in his smug little face for thinking this is the time to smile. Behind him are a team of other doctors and a machine that my baby will have to go in. They're busy setting up and all I want to do is cry because it's too early.

"Didn't want to wait, huh?"

"Yeah. You know, I thought what the hellllllll!" I cry

out as another contraction hits. Once it subsides, Liam is wiping my forehead with a damp cloth.

"Mr. Westbury, when I tell you to, help Josie to sit up so she can push," the doctor instructs as he places my feet in the stir-ups and sits down between my legs.

"Look at me," I say to Liam to get his attention. I know he's getting pissed that a man is about to deliver the baby, but we have no choice.

"He hates his job," I say, trying to lighten the mood even though I'm in pain.

"Here comes another one, Josie. Go ahead and bear down," the nurse says as she and Liam help me sit up.

I scream out and start panting. "I need drugs."

"It's too late," she tells me.

Turning, I glare at her, but she doesn't back away.

"It's burning!" I scream.

"Almost done, Jojo. You can do this."

"What do you know? You did this to me. I should've learned the first time I had one of your kids."

Liam doesn't balk at the fact that I just insulted him.

"I love you so much, Jojo. You're my life, you and the kids. I can't imagine what a day looks like without you in it. I'm so fucking lucky you chose me to be the father of your children. You're the most beautiful woman I've ever seen and I can't wait to meet our baby. I hope she looks just like you."

"It's a booooooooyyyyeeeeeeeeeee!" I say as I bear down again.

"Okay, the shoulders are out. Suction," he says. "Do you want to look?" he asks, looking up at Liam, who shakes his head. "One more push, Josie, and you'll have your baby in your arms."

When the next contraction hits, I grunt, pushing down as hard as I can to squeeze the little human out of me. The soft wail of a baby cry fills the room and everyone cheers.

The doctor holds the baby up for us to see.

It's a girl.

She's a girl.

We have a daughter.

"Oh my God, we have a daughter," I say through tears.

"I told you, Jojo." He kisses me. "I love you so much."

"Dad, would you like the cut the cord?"

Liam nods and takes a pair of medical scissors from the nurse, cutting where she tells him to. Then she takes my little girl and places her on my chest. Liam is right by my side before I can even blink.

"Liam, look at her. She looks just like Noah did when he was born." She's tiny, but long and can fit in my arm. Her hair is dark, with a little nose and perfect lips.

"She's beautiful, Josie. God, she's so beautiful. Thank you." He kisses me again before kissing her. His tears fall onto my hand as he gazes upon our daughter. "Look at how tiny she is. I could carry her like a football."

I laugh and kiss him. "We have to give her a name."

"Yeah we do," he murmurs as he runs his finger over her dark hair.

"Hey, baby girl, can you open your eyes for Mommy and Daddy?" I run my finger along her cheek, back and forth until she opens her eyes quickly before shutting them again. They're dark, but will likely change.

"Aside from calling her Noah Junior, I'm stumbling for names. Mason?" Liam asks. I shake my head.

"What about Betty?" I ask, just as Liam blurts out, "What about Page, with an i?"

"I like Paige," I say.

"I like Betty, too."

"Betty Paige Westbury? And we'll call her Paige?"

"And not Mason?"

I shake my head.

"Hi, Paige," he says. Her mouth opens in agreement.

"Sorry to interrupt, but we need to take her and get her vitals. Then we'll be taking her upstairs for observation."

I reluctantly let her go and tell Liam to go with her. I don't want her alone.

"Before you take her, we need to introduce her to our family. They're waiting."

The nurse nods and carries Paige over to the station they've set up. Once she's weighed, measured, cleaned, and has had her Apgar test done, she's bundled up and placed in Liam's arms. He sits down next to me and pulls out his phone.

"Smile, Mommy." I don't; I lean in and kiss Paige's head instead. This is how I want her first photo to be.

Once my delivery doctor leaves, the nurse opens the door to let everyone in. My mom walks in first and covers her mouth as tears start flowing.

"Oh my, it's a girl. She's so tiny."

"Very tiny. She weighs five pounds, six ounces, and is

nineteen inches long. I bet she'll be tall like her mom," Liam says as he looks at me. I never thought he could look at me any differently until now. To see the love in his eyes when he looks at me is breathtaking. Leaning in, I kiss him in front of our family and friends.

Once everyone is in, Liam turns Paige to face them. Noah sits beside me, begging to hold her. It's funny how his tune has changed now that she's here. At first, he didn't want a sibling, or maybe it was just another boy he didn't want.

"Everyone, the Westburys are overjoyed to introduce you to Betty Paige Westbury. We'll be calling her Paige."

I look to Bianca for a reaction and get what I was expecting. Tears are falling and she's mouthing 'thank you'. All I can do is smile. Smile at my family and friends. If it weren't for them, I wouldn't be where I am today.

**M**y mouth is parched and my throat hurts. My hands seem heavy when I try to move them. As I open my eyes, I squint even though the lights aren't very bright. My tongue darts out to wet my lips, but they're still dry and feel chapped.

"Here." I turn to the sound of the voice. It's Harrison.

"Where am I?"

"You're in the hospital, mate." It's good to know that JD is here as well. I wonder where everyone else is.

Harrison brings a straw to my lips and I suck greedily, taking all that I can to wet my mouth and soothe my throat.

"What am I doing here?"

"There was an accident," Harrison says as he puts the plastic cup back on the track. He's sporting a beard and I'm not sure I like it. I slowly move my head to look at JD and find that he has one, too.

"What happened?"

"An eighteen-wheeler lost control and hit the bus. You were sitting up front, talking to the driver when it happened. You were thrown to the back of the bus, breaking your back. You've been in a medically induced coma for six months."

"What? What about ..." I can't imagine what Josie must be going through, and for me to be hurt in the same type of accident as Mason; her mind must be going crazy. Why isn't she here? Where are my kids? The last thing I remember is Paige being born.

"You need to calm down. You don't want to accelerate your heart rate," Harrison says.

"What town are we in?"

"Some rinky dink place called Beaumont."

Harrison doesn't smile when he says it, but I know he's happy. I'm happy. I smile at him, but his expression doesn't change.

"You love it here, don't lie."

"No, I don't. The sooner we get back to Los Angeles, the better."

"What are you talking about? Where's Josie? Where are Noah and Paige?"

"Who the hell are Josie and whoever else you said?"

I look from Harrison to JD, who shrugs. "I gotta get out of here and find my wife. Where are Katelyn and the kids? Jenna and Eden?"

They shake their heads and push me down on the bed. I start to hyperventilate, needing air.

"Maybe the accident did damage to his brain."

"Liam, calm down. Sam is right down the hall getting coffee. She'll be here in a minute."

*"I don't want Sam," I cry out. "I want my wife."*

*"Sam is your wife."*

I wake with a startle. Someone is sleeping next to me and there's a crying baby somewhere in the house. I turn away from the person and look out the window; I'm in Los Angeles. Tears prick my eyes. I just had the best and worst dream of my life and now I'm back to square one, except I don't remember marrying Sam or having a child with her.

I want to cry. My dream was so vivid, so clear. My life was good. I made my amends with people and started living again. The cries get louder, stirring a sleeping Sam next to me. Something tells me I'm the one who should get up, but I don't want to. I want to go back to sleep and remember Beaumont, Josie, and the children we had.

"Liam, Paige is crying."

"Wh-what?" I roll over at the sound of the voice I remember so clearly. Even through the darkness I can see her bright blue eyes shining up at me.

"Are you real?"

"Yes, and so is our daughter. Go get her, please."

"I fucking love you so much." I kiss her on the lips, trying to savor the moment, but my princess is down the hall needing her daddy so I must go to her.

"Hi, princess," I say when I approach her crib. Her blue eyes, wet with tears, look up at me and she pouts her tiny mouth. She lets out a quiet wail, telling me that she needs me. I hope that someday she realizes how much I need her.

"Did you have a nightmare?" I ask as I lie her down on her changing table. I hand her a little rattle to keep her occupied while I change her diaper. "Daddy did, and it was bad. I dreamt that it was me who was in an accident and not your Uncle Mason, and when I woke up in my dream, I didn't have you, Mommy, or Noah. When you started crying, I woke up again, but I was confused about being here so I thought I was only dreaming about having you." I pick her up and kiss her rosy cheek, holding her to me. She snuggles into my neck and tries to seek out the milk wagon. I make sure to put her pacifier in to keep her quiet for the walk to the kitchen. By the time we get there, she's sound asleep.

The white lights from the Christmas tree sparkle against the darkness of the room. I stand in the large picture window that overlooks Hollywood. The city lights illuminate the valley, making it look alive. Paige is barely four months old and being plagued by an earache. Her first airplane ride didn't go as planned. Nick calls it an ear barotrauma. I heard the word trauma and freaked out on him until he called it an ache. An ache I can deal with.

We are in Hollywood for a few reasons. We decided to spend Christmas here, and Yvie and Xander are getting married on Christmas night at Harrison's pad. I've taken to calling it a pad because he yells at me each time I say condo. Earlier in the fall he was able to buy the upstairs "apartment" and convert his into a two-story, giving him and Katelyn more room with the kids.

Everyone is here with us, except for Nick and Aubrey. They flew to Africa to see Aubrey's parents, who are on a Mission, and introduce them to their son, Mack. He's a cute baby with blond hair and blue eyes, just like

Aubrey. Josie says he's going to be a looker when he's older and I tell her as long as he's looking away from Paige, I'll be happy. Nick thinks I'm joking, but I'm not.

After Paige was born, and we brought her home, life became crazy. The guys, with the help of Jenna, Katelyn, and the grandmas, all busted our asses to get Paige's room ready. We put up a fresh coat of paint, new curtains, and those clingy things for the walls to make her room into a castle. Not to mention all of the new furniture that didn't come assembled, even though I tried to bribe them. Harrison, JD, and I spent twelve straight hours screwing in nuts and bolts while the girls shopped. Truthfully, it was the longest day of my life—not because I was putting a crib together, but because I was away from Josie and Paige for the day.

I've come to realize I'm the over obsessive dad. If you have a cold, don't come over. If you haven't washed your hands, don't touch my daughter. If you smell, haven't showered, or your clothes are dirty, stay far away. Those are the things that concern me the most. I'm working on watching my language around her as well, but that seems to be the hardest part of all.

Paige wiggles in my arms, letting out a faint cry. I pat her bottom to lull her back to sleep. I'm the midnight feeder, the one who gets up with her if she wakes up at night, and the one who takes the late shift when the kids are sick. This is my time with them, especially with Paige. When Noah's sick, he lies on the couch and I sit next to him, but I'm there to help when needed. It's actually my favorite time with them, the one-on-one. It's at night when I can clear my thoughts, and when I'm holding

Paige in my arms, the lyrics flow. She's my inspiration, my reason for being.

After she was born, I took a hard look at my life. Josie and I sat down and hammered out a plan ... for now, the music stays and Josie is happy with that. Before Paige was born we said we'd spend summers in Los Angeles, but now that JD and Jenna have moved here permanently, I have a feeling her stance might change.

Josie's hesitation is her parents, but since they're retiring they're willing to travel. My hesitation is Noah. He's going to excel at Beaumont High and part of me would like to see him do it in my number. I'd like to see his name next to mine in the record books. Ultimately, I'm letting him make the decision. If he wants to stay, we'll stay and make everything work. I wouldn't be the only musician in the world to have two houses.

After the first of the year, my mother is moving into her former home. I own it, and will continue to until her divorce from my father is final. Apparently, my mom could live with the mistreatment and emotional abuse, but would not live with adultery. I don't blame her. The money she was left by her father is in my name as well, something my father will never be able to touch.

I have no qualms about setting my mother up. We've made amends, and she's been a rock for Josie and me. It pains me that my father destroyed such a beautiful light. I have no doubt my mom would've reached the highest peak of stardom, although if it weren't for meeting Sterling, I wouldn't be here today.

Shortly after Paige was born, I sat down with Josie and asked why the name Betty. She finally confessed that during our issues earlier in the year, she had gone to the attic and found a box full of stuff that had belonged to my grandparents, a box I didn't know about. I spent an hour going through the contents, learning about whom my grandfather was and how much he loved not only my grandmother, but my mother as well. And I forgave Josie on the spot because if she hadn't done that, she wouldn't have felt connected to my grandma enough to name our daughter after her.

The band has a new manager and record deal with Capitol Records. We'll be back in the studio once the holidays are over and looking to go on tour by the end of next year. Josie and the kids plan to join me once football is over, but only until baseball season starts for Noah. His sports life is important to me.

Our manager is just like Sam, but nicer and missing the evil bone. The wives balked at first, but once they got to know Mira, they brought her into their fold. I do think, however, that it's a case of "keep your friends close, but your enemies closer".

The light behind me comes on and I turn and see Noah eyeing the tree. Smiling, I look down at the presents pouring out from underneath it.

"Santa came," he says. Over the past few months, he's changed. He's grown a few inches and has started keeping his hair short like me.

"He did."

"Do you think any of those are for me?"

I shrug and rub my hand on Paige's back. "I don't think Paige can open any yet so I'm willing to bet most are for you."

"Awesome. I'm going to go wake everyone up."

I look at my watch and realize Paige and I have been up for five hours, just staring out the window, reflecting on life. It was the fastest five hours of my life.

As soon as Josie enters the room, she comes over to kiss Paige, even offering one up for me.

"Merry Christmas," I murmur against her lips.

"Merry Christmas."

Paige takes this opportunity to wake up, and as soon as she sees Josie, it's a full on whimper. She doesn't need Dad anymore because the milk wagon is in town. I hand her over to Josie with a kiss on her forehead.

"I'll make you some tea."

In the kitchen, I start coffee and hot water for tea, and I plate up the pastries we ordered for breakfast. I carry those into the living room first, and am greeted by Mrs. Preston who is getting the coffee and tea trays ready.

"Merry Christmas, Liam."

"Merry Christmas." I kiss her on the cheek and even though I've known her half of my life, I can't bring myself to call her by her first name. The same goes for Mr. Powell.

I follow her back into the living room with the drinks and see that everyone is awake. I put on my Santa hat, as is tradition, and take my position next to the tree, grabbing the first present.

"To Grandma Bianca, from Noah."

My mother beams when I hand her the present and wastes no time tearing into the box that he wrapped for her. Her eyes tear up the moment she lifts the lid, pulling out the same picture book that I got on my first Christmas with Noah.

"My mom helped, but I thought you'd like to have some pictures of me when I was a baby so they could go next to Paige's."

I don't believe there's a dry eye in the house when she pulls Noah into her arms and tells him that she loves him.

"To Josie, from Santa."

I hand her the Tiffany blue box and sit back and watch. More tears are flowing when she pulls out two new bands for her wedding ring: one with Noah's birthstone and the other with Paige's. She slips them on her finger and holds her hand out for everyone to see.

"Thank you, Liam." She leans forward, asking for a kiss that I'm all too happy to give to her.

"To Grandma and Grandpa, from Noah and Paige."

I hand them a box and give my mom the same one. The grandparents tear into the box and all three squeal with delight when they pull out their all-expenses-paid trip to Bora Bora.

"You guys shouldn't have," Mr. Preston exclaims.

"I know. My piggy bank is empty now, Grandpa." Noah has everyone laughing with his joke.

"You guys will have fun, you all deserve it," I say.

The next present I pull out is for me, from my family. I shake the box first, earning an eye roll from Josie. I know I'm hard to shop for, so I know anything they can find me will be the best gift ever. I unwrap the box and lift the lid. Inside is a black box with my name engraved.

"We thought you could use one like your grandfather."

I run my hand over the top, feeling the smooth wood. "Wow, thank you. I love it."

"Open it," Noah says and I do. Inside are two pictures. The first one is of Mason and me in our football gear, and the second is of Josie and me with the kids about a month ago. It was our attempt at a family photo with a newborn.

"I don't know what to say. I'm sort of speechless."

"Well, that doesn't happen often," Josie remarks, as she shifts Paige to burp. I mouth 'thank you' to her because I know this was her idea. I set my box aside and compose myself. It's been an emotional day, all starting with the nightmare I had.

"Well, I guess that's it. We should probably shower and head over to Harrison's."

Noah throws a pillow at me and pretends to pout. I hand him his first gift and he rips into the paper, letting it fly everywhere.

"Sweet, a new glove! Thanks!"

And that is how the morning continues with Noah opening everything under the tree aside from a few other gifts we bought each other. Paige, of course, had her fair share of presents as well.

---

There are two-dozen white chairs decorated with pink tulle facing the trellis, which is facing the ocean. Flowers hang from the top, creating a cascading arrangement, and candles are lit. It is Noah's job to make sure the candles don't blow out. Why Yvie wanted to get married on the beach, on Christmas, is beyond me, but here I am, escorting people to their seats.

The ceremony is simple, but from what Noah has told me, the reception will be "off the hook". As long as everyone is having fun, I'm down for anything. When I've seated the last guest, I rush into the house and make sure Xander is ready.

Xander and Yvie surprised us all. He had gone to see her for Valentine's Day and said he knew then that he wanted to spend the rest of his life with her. He just didn't know how to make it work. Yvie was having the same thoughts, but had taken the steps to end her tenure on Broadway. During one of his visits, they were at the top of the Empire State building and he got down on bended knee, and asked her to marry him. She said yes and quickly asked if he'd renovate the second floor of the gym for a dance studio. He came back to Beaumont and started on it immediately, only for Yvie to be offered a job in Los Angeles. After a long discussion, they decided to move to California, but keep the gym open in Beaumont until the right buyer comes along. This is partly the reason why JD and Jenna have moved out here, to be close to Xander.

"You good?" I ask him. He nods and straightens his bowtie. It's my job to make sure I get him out of the house without seeing Yvie.

"All right, the coast is clear," I tell him and JD, who is his best man as well as Lindsay, Yvie's friend from New York, who is her maid of honor. Harrison has the duty of walking his sister down the aisle. I swear he cried when she asked him. Peyton and Elle are the flower girls, and

Quinn is responsible for the rings. The poor kid has been sitting in the corner for over an hour, afraid to move because he thinks he'll lose them.

Once I have the guys in place, I run back in and tell Tess that we can start. The Justice of the Peace is under the trellis, waiting. I sit down at JD's keyboard and start playing the song I learned for the wedding. This was my gift to Yvie. I thought this would be better than some recording playing on an iPod.

Lindsay comes out first, and according to Josie, she's wearing a light pink chiffon (whatever that is), off the shoulder dress. Apparently, just calling clothes by their name isn't okay. Me, I'm in a black tux made by Armani —that is something I do know.

Once Lindsay is in her spot, the twins walk out and start dropping rose petals for their aunt. They wave at me when they walk by and I notice that their dresses match Lindsay's. As soon as they get to the front, it's my cue to play the "Wedding March".

When Harrison and Yvie step out, I get choked up. She's been like a sister to me and I couldn't be happier to see her finally settling down with an amazing guy. I let the music trail off when they reach Xander, who stands there patiently waiting for his bride. I know what that's like. It's pure torture. I quietly take my seat next to Josie and kiss her on the cheek. Paige is sleeping in her arms and wearing a dress similar to Lindsay, Peyton, and Elle.

"Who gives this woman to be with this man?"

"Her family does," Harrison answers, and I want to

stand up and say 'damn right', but I bite my tongue. I'll do that later.

Harrison kisses Yvie on the cheek and shakes Xander's hand before taking a spot between his mom and Katelyn. I pat him on the shoulder and remind him he has two daughters, he better get used to it.

"We are gathered here today to witness the union of Yvie James and Alexander Knight. The meaning of true love is different for each of us. We can find it in a friend, a lover, and if you're one of the lucky ones, your soul mate. It's what you do with that love that carves a path for your future. Yvie and Xander have taken their love for each other and shared it with the rest of you today."

His words give me pause. I hadn't realized that the love I have for Josie has been carving our path, but it makes sense.

Yvie and Xander exchange their vows, and Quinn delivers the rings like a champ. Once they kiss, I'm out of my seat and back at the piano to play their song as they come back down the aisle. When Yvie gets to me, she presses her lips against my cheek. "Thank you, Liam."

I continue to play until all of the guests are out of the area. The reception is at the marina, not far from here, and most people are on their way there by the time I get the piano put away.

"Are you ready?" Josie asks me as I take Paige from her.

"Yes, let's go party," I say, holding my daughter's arm up in the air and waving it around gently. Josie rolls her eyes, but she loves me so it's okay.

The reception is huge, with all of their college and

work colleagues. I can see why they kept the ceremony to just family; the beach isn't big enough to accommodate everyone. It's a slight exaggeration, but we'd probably need three hundred chairs.

Dinner is served, champagne is flowing and I'm not drinking. It's not some new lease in life, but out of respect for my wife and the fact that she's breast-feeding and didn't pump beforehand. However, being that I'm Liam Page, I can still have a good time.

"Uncle Liam, we're ready." Elle comes over and tugs on my jacket. Just like at my wedding, the kids have put together a musical number for Yvie and Xander. Harrison and I are helping them get set up and making sure everything is tuned properly.

"Okay, Elle, do you remember your lines?"

"Yep, I know them."

"Noah, are you good?" He gives me thumbs-up.

"Quinn?"

"I'm good, Uncle Liam."

That leaves Peyton, but Harrison is taking care of her.

"This is for our Aunt Yvie and Uncle Xander," Elle says into the microphone. Once the music starts people begin moving in their seat. As soon as Elle sings the first verse to Elton John's "Tiny Dancer," Yvie and Xander are up dancing. Once they start, everyone joins in. I want to dance with Josie, but I need to be available for the kids in case something goes wrong.

The whole room is cheering loudly for the kids as they finish the song. They all bow and run off stage. One song a night is all they're good for.

"That was awesome," I say to Noah when he gets off stage.

"Thanks. I really like playing."

"Me too," I tell him.

The DJ starts in with his music and Noah asks Josie to dance. I take Paige from her who is wide awake and watching everything around the room.

"Someday, this will be you," I tell her, earning a punch to the face from her flying hand. She starts to whine, so I stand and move back and forth with her for a bit until I decide that if I'm going to dance, I'm dancing with my daughter on the floor so everyone can see her.

Paige and I move out on the dance floor and stand next to Noah and Josie. Paige and I move to the music and she coos when she sees her mother and brother doing the same. There's no shortage of love in this family, that's for sure.

When "Purple Rain" comes on, Josie and I freeze. I pull her to me with my freehand and tell Noah to join us. This may not be the appropriate family song, but it's a song that has deep meaning for Josie and me.

We sway to the music and I steal kiss or two from my wife, who has her chin resting on my shoulder. Our son has his arm around his mother and I hold our daughter in my arm. I don't know about anyone else, but I'm certain this is what my kind of forever looks like.

## ACKNOWLEDGMENTS

I never imagined this day – one where I'd write The End on a family of characters that I love dearly. These characters have shaped my life in ways I could only imagine and it's hard letting go. Thankfully, they'll live and always be a part of not only my life, but yours as well.

The Beaumont Series started with a picture and a ninety-minute email session with my best friend, confidant and beta extraordinaire, Yvette. I was writing another story and growing frustrated with it. Yvette suggested I take a break and write a story for NANO. Later that day, I saw this picture of a random guy and Liam was born. I came to her with a story of a guy who has returned to his hometown to make amends. What brought him back? Was the first question she ever asked about this story. His best friend died, was my answer. The title was: Returning Home.

For days I wrote, from sun up to sun down, ignoring everything and everyone around me, except Yvette. We brainstormed everything from names, is there a kid involved, and who do we see as Liam Page. During that time, the title changed to: Standing in Front of You. Once I was finished, I didn't know what to do and ended up giving the manuscript to Jillian Dodd. Without her and Yvette, Forever My Girl would have never existed because I'm not sure I would've published it. This was in September of 2012.

From the moment I released Forever My Girl my life hasn't slowed down. This is the little book that could and did, from hitting the USA Today Best Sellers List to selling my movie rights, each and every day this book makes me proud.

Fast forward to today. My Kind of Forever wasn't supposed to happen. I never intended to go back to the beginning and bring it full force, but the love fans have for this series, it made sense.

I'd like to thank the following people because without them, The Beaumont Series would not have happen:

Yvette Rebello
Jillian Dodd
Sarah Hansen
Holly Donaldson
Fallon Clark
Cari Renee
Eric Heatherly
Jenn Sy
Stefne Miller
Carey Heywood
Traci Blackwood

LP Dover
Georgette Geras
Tammy Bertino
Emily Plice
Holly Malgieri
Amy Broom
Tammy Williams
Audrey Kay
Veronica LaRoche
Kelli Knechtly
The Beaumont Daily

Of course my inspiration:
Stephen Amell – Liam Page
David Beckham & Ryan Stevenson – Harrison James
Brandyn Farrell – Jimmy "JD" Davis

To every Blogger who has read, posted and talked about
the series, I thank you!

A lot of have asked what happens next – well as I've said
before, and I'll say it again... the gang will be back when
the kids have their own stories to tell.

## ABOUT HEIDI MCLAUGHLIN

Heidi McLaughlin is a New York Times, Wall Street Journal, and USA Today Bestselling author of The Beaumont Series, The Boys of Summer, and The Archers.

Originally, from the Pacific Northwest, she now lives in picturesque Vermont, with her husband, two daughters, and their three dogs.

In 2012, Heidi turned her passion for reading into a full-fledged literary career, writing over twenty novels, including the acclaimed Forever My Girl.

When writing isn't occupying her time, you can find her sitting courtside at either of her daughters' basketball games.

Heidi's first novel, Forever My Girl, has been adapted into a motion picture with LD Entertainment and Roadside Attractions, starring Alex Roe and Jessica Rothe, and opened in theaters on January 19, 2018.

*Don't miss more books by Heidi McLaughlin! Sign up for her newsletter, or join the fun in her fan group!*

*Connect with Heidi!*
www.heidimclaughlin.com

Read on for a sneak peek at No Limit by L.P. Dover, a steamy romantic suspense standalone.

# JASON

"You found me."

If there was ever a moment when I needed to keep my wits about me, it was now. But how could I do that when I wanted nothing more than to snap the man's neck in front of me; to make him bleed like he did the families he murdered.

"Did you think I wouldn't?" I spat through clenched teeth. His file flashed through my mind, the pictures of the carnage he left behind . . . those children. My blood boiled.

He was poised, ready to fight to the death by the look in his eyes. "I guess it was only a matter of time."

His name was Michael Bruxton, a computer analyst with skills matching my own. But he had a sick hobby that cost the lives of three families over the past two weeks. I spent day and night searching for him, and now I found the bastard.

We circled each other in the rundown, abandoned

warehouse he'd holed up in while on the run. On the floor were tokens he stole from his victims. The baby doll with a bright pink dress caught my attention first. My whole body shook with rage. "How could you do it, you sick fuck?"

His eyes sparkled. "It's like putting paint to canvas." He looked down at the things he collected and smiled. "Their pleas for help were music to my ears."

Flashes of the children laying in their own blood, their lives taken from them at such a young age plagued my mind. They were innocent, along with their parents who only wanted to protect them. A man like him deserved to die a slow, painful death . . . and I was going to make sure that happened.

Lunging for him, we went down to the dirty floor, his head slamming against the concrete. He tried to punch me and missed. I couldn't hear anything other than the blood rushing through my veins. Pinning him with my weight, I punched him over and over, the feel of his bones crunching beneath my fist. I didn't know the families who were killed, but I fought for them, bringing their murderer to justice.

The sick fuck spit to clear his throat, blood dribbling down his cheek, and laughed. "I love it when they fight back." He pushed his arousal into me and groaned.

Jesus Christ. Grabbing his neck, I squeezed and snuffed his next words out. "You get off on pain you perverted son of a bitch?" I picked up a brick from nearby and raised it high. "Let's see how you like this." As hard as I could, I slammed it down on his face. "You said screams were music to your ears," I yelled into the silence. "Where are the screams now, you bitch?" I slammed the brick back down on his mutilated face over and over again, trying to unsee the pictures of the flayed bodies he'd left behind.

Throwing the brick across the floor, I got up and surveyed the scene, breathing hard. "Now you can't hurt anyone ever again."

"Got anything new comin' up?" Blake asked, leaning against the doorframe.

Strapping on my holster, I shook my head. After everything that happened with Bruxton, I needed a break. "I hope not. You?"

Jaw tight, he trudged into my office, gray eyes full of turmoil. "Actually, I'm headin' out for good. I just wanted to say goodbye."

"What the hell are you talking about? Are you skipping town or quitting the team?"

Blake Evans and the rest of the guys on our team were the best undercover agents in the country. We'd already lost a couple people, including my sister who decided to move away to California to settle down. We couldn't afford to lose another skilled agent.

A small smile splayed across his face as he sat down.

"I'm still going to be a part of the team. This is my life. I'll just be living it somewhere else."

"Where to?"

"Wyoming. My grandfather passed away and left me his ranch. I figured I'd go since nothing's really keeping me here. I'm single, and we're always traveling with the job. I'm never in Charlotte that much anyway."

"No shit. I think this is the first week in months I've been able to sit back and relax." I stared at him and chuckled. "Blake Evans turned cowboy. I never would've thought it."

He got to his feet. "Me neither, but it'll sure be interesting. How about we get one last drink together at Second Street before I go?"

"Sounds good, bro. I was just about to head out." We got halfway to the door when my cell phone rang. I looked down at my phone and walked back to my desk. "It's the Chief of Police from Vegas." So much for the break I wanted. Leaning against my desk, I answered the call. "Ryan Griffin, to what do I owe the pleasure?"

"No pleasure in this call, son. Are you still at the station?"

"I was just getting ready to leave. What do you need?"

Sounding tired, he sighed. "I sent you some files. Take a look at them for me."

Blake took a seat while I sat back down behind my computer. It didn't take long for it to boot back up and when it did, I found the files. "All right, I have the files opened up." The first one was a woman who was found dead two months prior, followed by two other murder victims and one who was missing. "What the fuck is this?"

"Whoever this fucker is, he's cutting them, strangling them, and then leaving them on the side of the road."

I waved Blake over. "Take a look at this," I whispered, holding the phone away. While he sat down, I moved back. "Did it all start two months ago with this first woman, or have you had similar cases?"

"Nope, all new. We've had eyewitnesses give us descriptions of the people these women were last seen with—all high rollers of Sin City. No one wants to talk. All we're getting are dead ends. I need someone on the inside who doesn't look like a cop. My people can't get close enough."

Blake moved out of the way and I glanced at the pictures one last time before closing them out. "I'll be there soon," I said, hanging up.

"That's some really nasty shit going on out there," Blake stated.

Anger boiled in my veins. The pictures of those women were going to forever be ingrained in my mind. "Yes, it is, and I'm going to make sure I find the fucker responsible."

NO LIMIT

# JASON

Three Months Later

"Going out again?" Ryan grumbled through the phone.

"That's the plan. I can't exactly do much sitting on my ass."

"One would think that's what you've been doing since you haven't figured out shit. Please tell me you have something . . . anything other than the thousands you've won."

Clenching my teeth, I took a deep breath. "I've given you more than what you were able to come up with on your own. For three months now, I've kicked ass at each casino and learned every single game. I have a name out there, but nothing's going to make these guys seek me out. I'm nothing to them."

Unfortunately, two more girls had shown up dead. Both were professional escorts from the same agency, which happened to be run by Ronnie Chatfield, a female pimp. I had yet to speak to her, but was determined to seek her out. The woman was invisible. On her website, it said the ranch was temporarily closed for business, yet more of their girls were disappearing.

The women were beautiful, some fuller than others, and way more expensive than the drugged out prostitutes you'd see on the street. These women were for the elite. Other than that, I did know what my suspects looked like, what their names were, where they worked, who their families were . . . basically, it was tracking them that was a complete bitch.

"But at least you're enjoying the money in the meantime, right?" he scoffed.

"Kiss my fucking ass. I'm here to help you out. I don't have to be here. If anyone wants to get this case solved quickly, it's me. I'm ready to get the hell away from this place."

Ryan huffed and the line grew silent. I had made a shit ton of money, but that was because I was good at the games. To get in with the high rollers, I had no choice but to learn. As a reward, the casinos offered me free rooms and other amenities. I was living like a king. There was no denying I enjoyed it, but my full focus was on the case, nothing else.

"Look, I hate to be a dick, but the FBI is breathing down my neck. If you don't figure something out soon, they're going to intervene."

I snorted. "I'd like to see them get as far as I have."

"Either way, they will show up. I just want you to be

prepared. I've worked with some of those douchebags before."

"As long as they stay out of my way, I'm fine."

"I can already tell you now . . . they won't."

Keep Reading No Limit Now

CPSIA information can be obtained
at www.ICGtesting.com
Printed in the USA
LVHW011731180219
607899LV00003B/742/P